PENGUIN

What the Wife Knew

Lia Middleton is a barrister who specialises in crime and prison law. You can find her on X @liamiddleton and on Instagram @liamiddletonauthor. She is the author of *When They Find Her*, *Your Word or Mine* and *The Confession Room*.

What the Wife Knew

LIA MIDDLETON

PENGUIN BOOKS

PENGUIN BOOKS

UK | USA | Canada | Ireland | Australia
India | New Zealand | South Africa

Penguin Books is part of the Penguin Random House group of companies
whose addresses can be found at global.penguinrandomhouse.com

Penguin Random House UK,
One Embassy Gardens, 8 Viaduct Gardens, London SW11 7BW

penguin.co.uk

Penguin
Random House
UK

First published 2025

001

Set in 12.5/14.75pt Garamond MT Std
Typeset by Six Red Marbles UK, Thetford, Norfolk
Printed and bound in Great Britain by Clays Ltd, Elcograf S.p.A.

The authorized representative in the EEA is Penguin Random House Ireland,
Morrison Chambers, 32 Nassau Street, Dublin D02 YH68

A CIP catalogue record for this book is available from the British Library

ISBN: 978-1-405-95456-3

Penguin Random House is committed to a sustainable future
for our business, our readers and our planet. This book is made from
Forest Stewardship Council® certified paper.

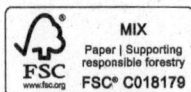

MIX
Paper | Supporting
responsible forestry
FSC
www.fsc.org   FSC® C018179

For Kate Burke –
My partner-in-crime these past five years.
Thank you for everything.

Prologue

Francis Joseph blinks numbly as the jurors file back into the courtroom, their footsteps marking the thin line upon which his fate is balanced. They have made their decision. And in just a few minutes, he will know the path that lies ahead. Guilty or not guilty? Freedom? Or the rest of his life behind bars.

Now it is time, he can't even look at them. He has spent the past four weeks scanning their faces, assessing their features for any change in expression, no matter how small. But knowing that they are aware of his fate before he is, he just can't face them. These could be his final moments of life as a free man. Better to live them in ignorance than to notice something that reveals the horrifying truth earlier than necessary.

'Will the foreman please stand?' says the clerk in her loud, clear voice. Frank closes his eyes. And instead of taking in the noises of the courtroom, the tension hanging in the almost-silence before the clerk speaks again, he forces himself to imagine how it would feel to be out. For the foreman to say 'not guilty'. To be released from this court, not to return to prison. To go home.

It shimmers into life in his mind, the house he used

to call home rising up to greet him at the end of the stone path.

He opens the gate, his hands trembling, and then the gravel crunches beneath his feet. One hand is curled into a tight fist, the other gripping the single rucksack of possessions that have made up his life since the night it all went so terribly wrong. He slowly climbs the small set of steps which lead to the front door. The key feels hot between his sweating fingers, even in the biting cold. He slides the key into the lock and –

He is home.

After all this time.

All those days hoping, praying, that it will be over soon. That they will let him go.

That twelve strangers will set him free.

He blinks rapidly, his eyes stinging. It feels like something he has already lived, but it hasn't happened. He might never get to go back.

'Have you reached a verdict upon which you or a majority of you are all agreed?' the clerk says.

Frank shuts his eyes again, tipping his chin so that his face is partially obscured from the obsessively keen eyes in the public gallery. And as he closes them, he is back there, inside his home. The hallway stretching before him, leading to his office, the formal reception room, a snug, the downstairs loo, and then the open kitchen and living area beyond. He is so close to all of this being nothing but a memory. Something to pain him as he lives the rest of his life, or at least the best of the rest of his life, in prison. If they convict him, he won't be out for at least thirty years, that's what he's been told. He'll be in his sixties or seventies by then. The world will be completely changed. But his world is completely changed no matter what they choose. Even if he is acquitted, he'll still be returning to his home alone. There will be nobody there celebrating his freedom with him. No one to open a bottle of champagne, or cry happy, burning tears of relief. His parents are six feet under. Any friends he has managed to sustain over the years disappeared when he was arrested, and Linda –

Linda is gone.

She's never coming back.

And before he can stop it, in the brief second before his eyes fly open, like the grip of a hand letting go at the feel of a burn, he is back there, in his mind.

In the kitchen.

His eyes fly open and he rubs them, blinking rapidly. He won't cry. Not now. Time inside will do that to you – you can't show weakness, not ever. Tears will only lead to trouble. To feelings that he simply can't face.

The foreman clears his throat. 'We have.'

The clerk nods. 'For the offence of murder, how do you find the defendant?'

The foreman opens his mouth to speak and –

Then it is over. The verdict is spoken.

What will happen to Francis Joseph is decided.

This changes everything.

The Husband

The Husband

I

A gentle wind blows across the Thames and pushes my hair into my eyes. I brush it back, knowing that the second I let it go, it will fall back down my forehead, obstructing my gaze. But every strand out of place is worth it for this daily walk. Even on days when it's cold, or the sun is blazing so that I am sweating through my three-piece suit. Up the Embankment, along the river, then cutting up Middle Temple Lane to chambers. It's like a hidden world in the centre of London. Nestled behind the Strand, a maze of cobbled streets opening into beautiful manicured gardens, the glorious dome of Temple Church, the stained-glass windows of Inner Temple Hall. It's a place that even some seasoned Londoners aren't aware of. A secret oasis. But while on the surface it's a haven of peace, beyond its facade it is bursting with busy minds, poring over case after case, hour after hour. Tireless ambition runs through Temple. And while I'm exhausted after being up all night preparing for a trial which didn't go ahead, the Bar does not stop. It does not relent. I need to pick up papers for tomorrow and Charlie, my clerk, said he has a big case for me. *The biggest case of your life.*

I cut across the courtyard, with Middle Temple

Hall on my left, and head down a short set of stairs, catching my favourite view back across the gardens and beyond to the river. The city in the distance. The skyline seeming so out of sorts with the world I am now in, which seems to have paused for a number of centuries. But as the sun makes its slow descent down to dip below the horizon, I veer right, heading down a narrow alley which opens out into a small square, and then turn towards chambers, relishing the sight of my name on the board outside.

Just over six months ago, it was much further down the list, appearing in the order that fellow members of chambers were called to the Bar. But now, I am tenth from the top, and two new letters appear after it.

Harry Mason-Hall KC.

The youngest criminal barrister to ever be awarded the honour of becoming King's Counsel. And it is an honour. But bloody hell, I've worked hard. The endless will it took to even get myself to the table. The dream of the Bar had felt like a distant star for so long – shining and beautiful but simply too out of reach. It wasn't for someone like me. It was for the others – the boys and girls at the private school who used to walk on the other side of the road, away from the rest of us, whose parents went to Oxbridge and had friends in law and politics. I was like an alien in a new world, surrounded by people who had grown up with privilege which to me felt uncomfortable. Posh accents and even posher country estates. Friends who were living in apartments in South West London that their parents had bought for them, not having to worry about student loans or barely making enough money during training to be able to eat. I would linger in chambers at the end of the day, checking the kitchen for any food that might be thrown away, glancing into conference rooms to see if any sandwiches or biscuits had been left over. Something to get me through until the next day. When the work did start to materialize at last, there were years and years of grafting, pandering to solicitors and keeping defendants – who would of course find themselves charged with a crime once again – on side. Countless hours, when I could have been with my wife, spending time with our new daughter, building our family, instead of bent over a desk trying to take in all the details of the trial ahead, all the weak points to penetrate the prosecution's case, all the arguments that could possibly be made for my client. Standing up in court, and defending them as if I am defending myself. As if it is my future, my life on the line. And then finally – the recognition that we all dream of, even the barristers who pretend that they have no interest in it. We have all coveted the title, the red bag, the silk robes. The admiring and envious looks of our colleagues. Six months have passed and I'm still not over it. I'm still waiting to feel like a KC. And still waiting to be treated like one.

The transition . . . it can take time.

'Evening, Harry,' says a voice as the door opens.

'Evening, Oscar,' I respond, nodding my head politely at Oscar Strachan. He is a tall waif of a man. Extremely skilled. Extremely polite. Extremely fucking annoying.

'Good day?'

'A great day. Well, as good as any in front of the bench I've had.'

'Who was the judge?'

'Woodward.'

He laughs, a hearty acknowledgement, but it is silent, his head rocking back over-dramatically. 'He wasn't too hard on you today, then?'

'Well, the defendant pleaded guilty before the jury were sworn in. So after the brutality of the trial in front of him last week, it all evened out. Karma, some would say. Although the fees from the trial would have been nice –'

'Good for you,' he interrupts, avoiding my rant about money and countless hours of work that are now lost. 'And don't worry too much about the real KC work still not coming to you yet. It will soon enough, I'm sure . . .'

'Oh, I'm not worried.' I reach for the door and throw him a casual wave. 'See you soon, Oscar.'

'Enjoy your evening.'

I pause, watching as he strides away towards the alley that cuts away and up to the Strand.

Prick.

He loves to do that. Masking condescension with false concern. *Don't worry too much about the real KC work still not coming to you yet.* It is always a worry for all junior barristers who take silk. You're too senior now for the bread and butter of the criminal bar – the thefts, the domestic violence, the assaults. The cases that are largely dull and repetitive but that feed you daily, keeping your practice alive and well. But the big, juicy cases – the complex murders, the terrorism cases, the gang trials – they are too senior for a new KC. Especially the Bar's youngest KC. Those kinds of cases only come along every so often. Yet no one can live on a trial every so often. Before I was a KC, I'd have a murder trial multiple times a year. I became known for them. But now . . . Now they slip past me, falling downwards or flying upwards to those more junior or senior. Like I am stuck in some kind of legal purgatory.

For some, this in-between time isn't a concern. Stick it out and eventually the cases will come. But I'm not like those people. I have a family to provide for. I'm not from money. The worry eats away at me every day.

But Charlie said that there was something big. Something that I would love. What were his precise words? . . . *Something you deserve.*

This is it. This will be the case – the one that shows that I've been made KC for a reason. I am good enough. And I can do it. The case that will make everything I've sacrificed, everything my family has sacrificed, worth it. It can't all be for nothing. For a career that simply plateaus, never reaching the pinnacle. Or even worse, a career that simply disappears altogether.

I stride through the door and it closes gently behind me. The waft of old wood and leather hits me as I make my way through the entrance hall and towards reception. Some chambers have decided to modernize, stripping their interiors of the trimmings of the traditional Bar and becoming sleek. All glass, all metal. But not One Court Lane. Never us. We are the Bar as it was. As it will always be. The receptionist sits behind a large mahogany desk, the black and white chequered tiles dull and worn after years of footsteps rushing through the various rooms and halls. The stairs curl upwards from behind her, leading to a maze of rooms. Most of the rooms are minuscule, occupied by two or three barristers who share the space, their desks crammed together, files piled and stacked all around them, wherever there is an empty – and sometimes not so empty – space. But some of the rooms are larger, with beautiful bay windows which overlook the river. These aren't shared. These are for the KCs. I moved into one last week. It feels strange after so many years of sharing. It's quiet. Almost too quiet. But it's not like I'll spend much time there – when I'm not at court, I prefer to work from home, unless it's so late and I have so much to do that it's easier to work and then sleep in chambers. But Piera doesn't like it when I do that. *Come home, Harry,* she whispers. *Chambers is not your home.* She always found it much easier than I do to separate work from life. But she misses it. I know she does. And I know that's why she now wants me home more often than she ever did when she was practising too. But it's simply part of the job. It consumes everything.

'Evening, Georgia,' I say to the receptionist as I move past her desk towards the clerks' room at the back of the building.

'Good evening, Sir,' she says with a wide smile.

The noise in the clerks' room hits me as I swing through the double doors. It's the end of the day, so solicitors' firms and the CPS are calling, attempting to get cases covered before the clerks leave for the day. There are always late returns, other trials over-running, cases brought forward – and somebody needs to do them. And the clerks, sitting in clerks' rooms in the heart of chambers all throughout Temple and across the country, are the ones who have to schedule our time. But figuring out who has the time and the experience and the capacity is like moving pieces about a chessboard. One wrong move and justice can simply fall apart.

'– I know you need someone, Davy, but what do you want me to do? Pull a KC out of my arse? They're all busy.'

Charlie, the senior clerk who handles all of the KCs' schedules and cases, holds a finger up towards me, winking briefly as he makes a hand gesture, his fingers mimicking a mouth gabbing relentlessly. And then another – not so polite – gesture. *Wanker*, he mouths. I smile and lean against his desk.

9

'If you really want Eadie, I can get him for you, but you remember his fee, right? If you're willing to pay that for a six-week trial then I can get him . . . Yes. Yes – but he'll need two juniors. Yes, two! He won't do it with just one; he hasn't done a trial with just one junior for over a decade – All right. Speak soon.'

He slams the phone down and then swings towards me, crossing one leg over the other with a flourish. 'Evening, Sir.'

'What have you got for me?'

'Oh, is that all the niceties I get today? No *how was your day, Charlie?* or *fancy a drink, Charlie?* Just straight in there with "What have you got for me?"'

'Well, you did say –'

'What happened with your trial?'

I smirk, reaching down into my bag to retrieve the paper file, and place it down firmly on the desk. Charlie's eyebrows raise in approval as he takes in my scrawl on the cover page.

G. Guilty.

'No trial?'

'Changed his tune last minute.'

He nods, taking the file and placing it in the tray beside him. He turns back to his screen, a mischievous smile playing around his lips.

'Charlie, don't play funny buggers now . . .' I sigh, internally rolling my eyes at myself. The me of twenty years ago would have wanted to smash someone's face in for saying 'funny buggers'. Posh twat. 'What have you got for me? Please tell me this is finally the case that will cement my reputation as a KC.'

He pushes himself away from his desk and swings around to face the wall of cubby holes where barristers' new cases are placed. I could have retrieved the file myself, but Charlie loves a dramatic flourish. And it does me no harm to pander to his nature. Don't bite the hand that feeds you and all that.

He clutches the papers to his chest and swings back around to face me. They are thick, and bound with a pink ribbon. A defence case. My favourite. In the early days of my career I used to pray for a white ribbon, especially when defence work paid a pittance and I was struggling to keep myself afloat, but now, I hardly ever work for the Crown. And Charlie has learned to stop sending them my way if he can help it. Don't bite the hand works the other way around too. It's a strange relationship between Counsel and Clerk, not always clear who holds the power. Who keeps who in employ. But it works between the two of us. Let's just hope what he has for me really is as good as he has led me to believe. I'm ready to prove myself. I need to prove myself.

'What is it?'

He leans towards me and I can already tell he is about to speak in a low voice, as though what he is about to say is a big secret, not for the ears of the junior clerks – who are all too busy on their phones, worrying about their own barristers, to give two flying fucks what case I'm working on next.

'It's a murder,' he says in a whisper, just like I thought.

A murder. Finally. But I can't reveal my hand so soon. Best to underplay it.

I cross my arms. 'Is that all?'

'Is that . . . is that all? It's your first sniff of a murder since becoming a KC! And this isn't your run-of-the-mill, *it wasn't me Guv, you've got the wrong person Guv, it was in self-defence Guv*, type of murder.'

'It isn't?'

He shakes his head. 'Nah, it's not.' His mouth stretches into a wry smile. The back of my neck tingles, the hairs standing on end.

'What is it, then?'

'Well . . . it'll be a hell of a defence to run. Hell of a defence to win. And you'll need to win it.'

'We all lose trials, Charlie. It's justice. It's how it works, we can't win them all.'

He points a stern finger at me. 'You can lose in a year's time when you've proven that you can run a trial like a silk. That you can win like a silk. If you lose this trial, you might as well go back to being a junior. You'll get more work –'

'I understand the stakes.' I sigh, leaning my neck from one side to the other until it clicks, then fix Charlie with a mocking gaze. 'It'll be the first time I've been shocked by a defence in a long time. So, come on . . . Surprise me.'

'Let's see if you can guess, then. If it's so difficult to surprise you. Defendant is a man in his late thirties.

Married to his wife for ten years. Known each other since . . . wait for it . . . university where they studied law. According to the prosecution, he comes home to find her with a packed suitcase and realizes she's going to leave him. Crown say he murdered her by slitting her throat. Now . . .' He stretches out his legs in front of him, clasping his hands behind his head. 'Guess. Guess what defence he gave in interview.'

I press my lips together and roll my eyes. 'Well, it's obvious. She was leaving him for someone else. So, he's saying it was the other man.'

He lifts his chin mockingly. 'Not even close.'

'She tried to attack him so he had to defend himself.'

'Nope.'

I sigh, crossing my arms. 'Loss of control –'

'Your guesses are getting worse –'

'He wasn't even there –'

'Ah . . . you're on the right track but still not quite.'

I pause, stubbornness urging me to keep on guessing. But curiosity prevails. 'Just tell me now, Charlie, or I'll open the file and just find out myself.'

He unclasps his hands from behind his head and grips the armrests of his chair, pushing himself to standing. He's about six inches smaller than me, but what he is missing in stature he makes up for in bravado. He meets my eye, a keen look in his own, and presses the file into my chest.

'He says she did it herself.'

A rush of energy runs through me, like electricity,

my hairs standing on end. I grip the file, my fingertips tingling. 'Now that *is* interesting.'

'And surprising. Correct?'

I tilt my head slightly to one side. 'I'll give you that this time, Charlie. I've never run anything like this. It'll be –'

'Challenging?'

'Indeed. And interesting. Thrilling.'

'It'll be one for the books. And one to show that you can do the KC work. You can take Old Bailey murder trial after Old Bailey murder trial. No bother. If you successfully defend this, you won't have to worry about getting KC work again. I'll be batting them away with a stick.'

I smile, unable to stop myself, but my stomach turns. It seems too good. 'What's the catch? I feel like there's a catch.'

A brief grimace flashes across Charlie's face.

'Charlie . . .'

'It starts next week.'

I breathe in sharply, my heart quickening.

Next week. No. That isn't possible. A trial like this will take weeks to prepare. Meeting the defendant, advising, preparing the case, the speeches, the legal arguments . . . The prosecution will have been mounting their case against him for months.

'*Next week?* Jesus Christ, Charlie, how has this happened?'

'Listen, Prior was meant to be leading, but for some

reason he and the defendant fell out and he returned the brief.'

'So he's a tricky client. Have his solicitors asked him about new representation?'

He raises his eyebrows. 'He asked for you.'

My brow furrows. Defendants don't usually ask for specific barristers. 'Really?'

'Yes, he asked for you. Apparently he still knows a lot of people from when he studied law – he does something unrelated now but he knows people. And he wanted you.'

'What about the junior? There must be a junior on this?'

'He packed it in too. And the defendant is insisting on no junior. He just wants you.'

My hand lifts to my forehead, my mind racing. 'Was this not in the news? I've never heard of the case.'

'It had a small amount of local coverage but nothing in the nationals. There's nothing high profile about it. Legally, yes, it will get coverage, but the public don't care. At least not yet. If someone covers the trial it could take hold. Or maybe not. They can't care about every murder, can they now?'

My chest tightens. It can't be done. Not in a week. It's too much. The chance of failure is almost absolute.

But if I win? If he is acquitted . . . it could change everything.

I sigh. 'All right . . . Hand it over.'

He smiles and lets go of the file.

I pull the top of the first page down, revealing the top half of the defendant's details as the paper curves over the pink ribbon which is wrapped horizontally around the pages, binding them together.

Francis Joseph.

2

The smell of curry hits me as my key turns in the lock and our front door slowly creaks open. She's got takeaway – my favourite. She must have had a hard day with the baby. She had sworn off takeaways during the week. Every night, after she puts Rose down to sleep, she cooks, and we eat together. No matter what case I have on, no matter how busy I am, we eat together. Sometimes it's the only time we spend together. There are evenings when all I can focus on is what needs to get done, what else I should be doing with that time. But then I see her face, her smile, and how much it means to her, and I'm overcome with guilt. Since when was anything more important than her?

'Piera?' I call out, setting my bag down on the console table in the hall.

'I'm in the living room,' she says. I take off my suit jacket and waistcoat and hang them on the bannister, then pull off my shoes, my back aching as I bend down. That's one thing they don't warn you of when you're training for the Bar – the occupational hazard of being on your feet all day. Your back is fucking knackered by forty.

When I step into the living room, she smiles at me, and my stomach flips. Even after all these years, after a long day, or a hard case, she is just the remedy. Even with milk stains down her top, her face pale with exhaustion, she is the most beautiful woman I have ever seen. Curled up into the corner of the sofa, her hair piled on top of her head in a messy bun, loose strands falling down her face. A large glass of red wine in one hand. She stopped breastfeeding Rose at six months. She found it more difficult than she expected to let go of that bond.

'Ms Roman, you are a sight to behold.'

'Oh, shh, you old flatterer,' she says, her voice croaky and warm. That smile stretching across her face.

I remember the first time I saw her. It was my first day of pupillage – the training year for barristers, the final hurdle in becoming a fully qualified advocate. The other pupils looked incredibly young, fresh out of law school. After my years as a paralegal, I was nearly twenty-eight and already running behind. I was so focused, so ready to begin my career with no distractions. But then, there she was. Standing on the other side of the room, talking to her supervisor. Her long hair tumbling down her back. For a moment she scanned the room and her gaze fell on mine. And there it was. That smile.

I cross the room and flop down on the sofa beside her, lowering myself on to my side to place my head in her lap. 'Enough of the old, please,' I say, groaning as a pain twinges in my lower vertebrae and I turn over to look up at her.

'I'm not sure young people moan as they manoeuvre themselves –'

'Excuse me, Piera, but I think you'll find –'

'I know, I know – I'm only seven years younger than you – you remind me all the time.'

'Well, you call me old all the time.'

'Because seven years is basically a decade. A lifetime.'

I laugh, and her dark eyes sparkle as she beams down at me. I gesture, a small waggle of my fingers, and she leans forward, kissing me gently on the lips.

'Where's Rose?'

'Upstairs sleeping. You can go in and see her –'

'I will.' I always go to Rose when I get home. Sometimes she's still awake and my heart soars at the sight of her chubby, smiley face. But more often than not she is sleeping and I place a kiss on her forehead, watching quietly as her snuffly breaths lift her chest up and down, her arms splayed either side of her.

I look up at Piera as she lifts the glass to her lips, gulping loudly. But then I properly take in her face – the mascara and eyeliner smudged on her lower lashes, the flush of her cheeks.

I sit up. 'Have you been crying?' My hand reaches forward to cup her jaw, my thumb gently stroking beneath her eyes.

She lifts her hand to cover her eyes and sniffs loudly before lowering her fingers, her eyes bloodshot.

'It was a long day with Rose, that's all. I just got . . . overwhelmed.'

'What was she doing? Not sleeping again?'

She nods, then sighs. 'I don't know what's happened – she used to nap so well. I thought it would get easier as she gets closer to turning one but . . . it's getting harder again.'

'It's just a phase. She'll get back to normal, and when you go back to work, you'll have a break and be able to focus on yourself –'

'I can't even imagine going back right now.'

I pause, watching her face closely, her lowered eyes, her mouth turned downwards. I frown. 'Really? But you love prosecuting. You said you were desperate to get back.' For the first six months, she mentioned it almost every day. *I love* her, she would say, her face flushed with maternal guilt, *but I can't wait to go back.* She missed it. Before we had Rose, being a barrister was Piera's entire life. It filled her up, gave her satisfaction in a way that nothing else could. When she went on maternity leave she only wanted to take three months off, but I convinced her to take a year. She was reluctant at first, insisting that three months was enough, that a year would set her career back by a decade. I took six weeks off to be with her and the baby and we lived off savings, and slowly she came around to the idea of more time away from it all. I didn't want her to miss out on everything motherhood could bring her, but sometimes I wonder if it has made her resent me.

20

'I know, but . . .' Her eyes fill with tears. 'I can't imagine leaving her. When I think about leaving her I feel so guilty. And . . .'

'What is it?'

'I've been out of it for so long now. There will be other barristers who have come in and taken my place –'

'That isn't true,' I say, reaching for her hand, my thumb stroking her knuckles slowly. 'You're brilliant –'

'We're all replaceable, Harry.' She raises her eyebrows, lifting her chin towards me. 'Maybe not those of us who are so special we get made silk, but the rest of us . . . we're replaceable.'

I allow the sting of her words to settle into my skin. She doesn't mean it, I know she doesn't. It's been a hard time for her, torn between her relative newness as a mother, her love for Rose, and the ever-present tug of her desire to return to the Bar.

'Well, we don't need to worry about it now,' I say, squeezing her hand. 'We still have a couple of months. And your chambers will support you. And I'll support whatever you want to do, you know that.'

She bites her lip, lowering her eyes, but then offers me a small smile. 'Thank you.' She pushes herself off the back of the sofa, straightening her spine, and sighs loudly, as though expelling all the bad feeling inside. 'Right – shall we eat? It's warming in the oven.'

'Uh . . . yes, please. I'm starving.'

We move to the table and I place her plate in front of her, her favourite butter chicken sending steam up to her face, but she doesn't touch it.

'Piera?'

'Hmm?'

'Are you sure you're okay?'

She shakes her head and smiles again, picking up her naan. 'Yes, I'm sure. Sorry.' She scoops some of her curry and lifts it to her mouth, blowing on it gently. 'So how was your day? Trial go okay?'

I fork some Madras into my mouth, sucking in air as the scorching sauce hits my tongue. 'He pleaded at the last minute. So we did sentencing and that's that.'

'Oh really?'

'Yeah, and wait until you hear what's next.' I raise my eyebrows at her teasingly.

She sits up, her spine straightening, her eyes flashing with interest. 'What is next?'

I mirror her, setting my shoulders back, my chin lifted as I prepare to tell her the big news. Pride flutters in my chest. 'A trial that starts next week. Charlie offered it to me when I went to chambers to pick up my papers. He'd been teasing me with it all day, insisting that he had a trial for me which would be the next step in my career.'

'And what is it?'

My face breaks into a smile, at odds with the words that are perched on the edge of my tongue, ready to be muttered. 'A murder.'

Her mouth drops open, her eyes wide. 'But you said it's next week. How –'

'Apparently the defendant fell out with Prior and he stepped down.'

'God, that's tight –'

I close my eyes briefly, a rush of anxiety washing over me. 'I know. To be honest, I'm kind of freaking out about it. A week isn't long enough.'

'It's not long, that's for sure –'

My eyes fly open and I take in her face. I can't read her expression but there is doubt there, just under the surface. 'You think I should have turned it down?' My breath catches in my throat. I need Piera's support. I need her to believe that I can do this. To believe in me.

She lowers her chin, meeting my gaze with an unfailing steadiness. 'If anyone can do this, you can.'

I let go of my breath in a heavy exhale. I can do this. It'll be hard: apparently difficult client, late nights, long hours, no sleep. But it'll be worth it.

She sips her wine, then cradles her glass in her hand. 'So tell me. What's special about it?'

'Victim is the defendant's wife. Her throat was slit – in the kitchen. They were at home on their own and he doesn't have an alibi –'

'What's his defence?'

I lean towards her. 'He says she did it to herself.'

Her eyes narrow, flashing with disbelief. 'His defence is that she killed herself?'

23

'Yes. I was reading through the pages on the way home. Apparently, he says that he had packed a bag for her to take to her sister's house, he got home, she had tried to overdose but it didn't work, so she did it. He was there, and she did it to herself.'

'How long had they been together?'

'It didn't say in the papers I've read so far, but married for ten years. And they met at university.' I take a sip of wine, my eyes widening as I suddenly remember. 'He was actually at Oxford at around the same time as you.'

Her head tilts to the side. 'Really?'

'God, I wonder if you crossed paths – Francis Joseph?'

She narrows her eyes, her head shaking slowly. 'I don't recognize the name. But I met so many people at uni, most of which I can't remember,' she laughs. 'What college?'

'God, I didn't even think about the college . . . That's what you get for going to your local university and not –' I pause, forcing the very posh accent that I've learnt to mimic during my time at the Bar, '– aiming for Oxbridge. You forget about colleges –'

'Oh shh, stop making fun of me –'

'You know I love your posh voice,' I laugh. 'I'll ask about his college when I meet him for a conference.'

'When are you going?'

'Tomorrow.'

A cry echoes through the baby monitor which sits on the side table. Rose is awake.

'I'll go,' I say, standing quickly. 'Unless you want to?'

'No, no,' she says, tearing off more bread. 'You go.'

'I'll be back in two minutes, let me just settle her.'

I rush out of the living room and up the stairs, slowing myself outside Rose's room. I press my ear to the door. It's quiet. I push the door open slowly and tiptoe inside.

There she is, curled up in one corner of the cot, a muslin tucked close to her body, her eyes closed. She must have cried out in her sleep. Sometimes she does that. We used to always barge in as soon as we heard her cry, and half the time we would wake her up ourselves by accident. Now we tread with caution.

I reach down and stroke her hair – what was once fair, soft tufts now growing darker and longer. 'I love you, Rose,' I whisper, then retreat slowly until I am back in the hallway and pull the door closed until it clicks.

I return to the kitchen and sit back at the table. Piera is pouring herself another glass of wine, and she points at it in a question.

'No, I'm good for now,' I say, and she places the bottle back on the table. 'So . . . hell of a case, right?'

She nods. 'What a defence. What's your gut say? Think he did it?'

'I mean, it's an outlandish defence, definitely, but surely it isn't one you just pluck out of thin air. *What if* he's innocent? What if it really was her?'

She grimaces. 'But to slit your own throat?'

'People have done far worse when their mind turns against them.'

She nods. 'Well . . . either way, it doesn't really make a difference, does it? If he's guilty, it's very unlikely he'll ever tell you, and it's your duty to represent him. And if he's innocent . . . If he's innocent, then he needs the best defence he can get. You can do this.'

You can do this. The words we have always uttered to each other, like a mantra. Our way of connecting, showing that no matter what, we believe in each other absolutely. She said it to me for the first time as I was getting ready for our advocacy tests during pupillage. I whispered it to her as she was brushing her hair the day of her first trial. She said it firmly, meeting my eye as she stood behind me in front of the mirror the afternoon I was interviewing for silk. And I repeated it over and over, her hand clasping mine, as she gave birth to Rose. *You can do this.* Our belief in each other is the foundation of our relationship. Without it, we are nothing.

'Thank you,' I say. 'I love you.'

'I love you too.' I lean across the table and kiss the side of her head, then scoop some more curry into my mouth, which has now cooled enough that I don't further burn my tongue. 'Hmmm. This is bloody delicious.'

She smiles and nods, and we continue to eat, and I talk about the case, how important my first murder trial as a KC will be for my career, thinking out loud about how I might run the case and how best to prepare in

26

such a short timeframe. Piera has always been my best sounding board. She's a brilliant barrister.

But she stays silent, staring forward into the blank space in front of her eyes, her mind somewhere else completely.

3

I turn the key and the engine stops, the car falling still and silent. For a moment, I remain in the driver's seat, my hands still gripping the steering wheel. I have done this for so long now – this is always my first step: read the file and meet the defendant. I have met countless offenders, been to countless prisons and heard countless histories and defences, but today my body feels different. As though it needs to ready itself. I glance up and meet my reflection in the rear-view mirror. My eyes harden – *get it together, man*. This is no different than any other case.

Except it's a seemingly impossible defence. But if I win this case, it will be a landmark defence. It will be reported on, it will be relied on in future cases. It will mean that everything will have been worth it. But if we lose . . . if he is found guilty – I'll be just another barrister who didn't do enough. A junior barrister who became a KC and couldn't quite cut it.

I let out a deep breath and then open the door, slamming it behind me and clicking the key to lock it. The headlights flash twice, lighting up the kerb. I move forward, glancing back once to make sure it's locked before striding on, the trees looming over the pavement sending shadows dancing around my feet. I focus on them, watching as the dark shifts into light, each moment changing. Life shifting constantly beneath us.

I yawn, lifting my gaze, and Wormwood Scrubs rises up before me like a relic of a long-forgotten past. I was up most of the night reading through all the evidence, making notes, anticipating the prosecution's arguments. Exhaustion is vibrating through me with every step. I trudge towards the prison, passing a group of boys on their bikes and an old lady crossing the road towards her house. It has always unnerved me how this prison was seemingly dumped in the middle of an ordinary neighbourhood, surrounded by terraced and semi-detached houses, a busy dual carriageway just a stone's throw away. But of course, the opposite is true. The prison was built in Victorian times and then London as we know it rose up from the ground around it.

I pause, taking in the symmetrical towers which line the entrance to the building. From this view, with the early sun pouring on to the red brick and white stone from the east, it is almost beautiful. But inside, it is quite different. Inside, the wings of the prison are lined with cell after cell, and within each cell lives a number of grown men, each of them biding their time, living day by day, waiting for some uncertain future. Inside, each wing is surveilled by an imposing watch-tower. An ever-seeing eye. Inside, the narrow corridors are claustrophobic, offering only melancholy to even the happiest of souls.

And today, inside, in the dim light and humidity of an interview room, I will meet Francis Joseph. The man behind the file.

Francis, but goes by Frank. Studied law at Oxford. Left the legal profession to work for a fintech company in the City. Relatively high-flying from what I have gathered. Married to Linda for ten years. No children.

I push through a door to the left of the large set of wooden double doors that allow vans and prisoners inside the main wall. Inside the room it is low-ceilinged and dark, the carpet dull and grey.

'All right, Tony?' I nod to the man behind the security desk.

'I'm great, Harry,' he says, nodding eagerly before biting into a sausage roll, steam rising from the inside of the paper bag. 'How are you?'

'I'm good, I'm good . . .' I pull my wallet out of my bag and extract my driving licence then push it through the hatch in his glass window – even though he knows me by name and has admitted me to the prison countless times over the last decade. 'I'm here to see Francis Joseph. We have a conference.'

'Ah yes, dear Frankie . . . He'll be ready for you.'

I scoff. 'Frankie? I've never known you to give the prisoners nicknames, Tony.'

'Yeah, but he's different to what we normally get in here . . . You'll see when you meet him.'

He returns my licence and I slide it back into my wallet, making sure to stow it safely in my bag. You can never be too sure, even with prisoners who aren't 'the normal type'. When I was a new barrister, naive and optimistic about the world and the people in it, my own client nicked fifty quid out of my wallet. It was my only money for the month. I learnt quickly not to trust any of them. Not even the ones you save from prison. Especially not them.

'Okay, you're good to go, Harry. Eli will take you to the room.'

'Cheers, Tony. See you later.'

I turn to the young man standing by the gate that leads through to the security room and then onwards to the central courtyard of the prison. He looks no more than twenty-two. Twenty-three at a push. What does he make of this world? Has it hardened him already?

'Thanks, Eli,' I say with a nod.

'Of course, Sir.'

'Oh no need for Sir. Just Harry is fine.'

He grins. 'All right, cheers, Sir . . . I mean, Harry.'

I laugh and follow him through the gate, into the grey room where I pass my belongings through an X-ray scanner and my body through a metal detector. And then onwards, my lungs expanding as we emerge from the claustrophobia of the entrance rooms and out into the courtyard. The prison surrounds us, the windows packed tightly into the red brick, cell after cell, the towers on each of the corners. And beyond the walls, guarding the outside world from inside, is not one but two fences. Inside, is gate after gate. Eli leads me through three before reaching the wing where the rooms for prisoners to meet lawyers are located. In the newer prisons they're near the front entrance so that external people do not have to pass through the prison – but Wormwood is old, impractical. And the conference rooms feel the same. Brick and concrete, enclosed. I have found myself only feet away from people I suspect or know have committed atrocities. I sometimes sit so close that I can see the pores in their skin, a drip of sweat on their upper lip. The delicate red lines in the whites of their eyes. So human. Yet so inhuman. It used to unnerve me. And sometimes it still does, I suppose. I have just learnt to disguise it. Never show them your fear, a senior barrister once told me when I was starting out. They're like dogs . . . they can smell it. And they will use it for their own benefit, one way or the other.

Eli stops outside a door, heavy and metal. Locked.

'Here's your room, Sir – Harry.'

'Sir Harry really does have a ring to it.'

Eli lets out a small chuckle. 'Sorry –'

'Please don't apologize. Thanks for escorting me.'

'He's inside. Before I let you in, do you know where the alarm is?'

'Yes, I do.' I can see it now, in my mind's eye – the round button fixed to the wall, close to the door. 'I've not needed one in years, so hopefully today will be no different.'

'Great.'

He slots his key into the lock and twists, allowing the door to swing open. 'Frank, your brief is here.'

Eli steps aside and there he is. He is sitting on the other side of the table, back straight, his arms resting in front of him, something clutched in his hand. He meets my eye and stands. He is tall, even taller than me – he must be six foot four at least – and his dirty blonde hair is flecked with grey.

'Good morning, Francis, I'm Harry Mason-Hall, your counsel for the upcoming trial.'

I hold out my hand and he reaches for it, his grip strong, his eye contact not failing. And in his other hand is a string of prayer beads, black and silver. Interesting. He is wearing a suit. Most prisoners I meet come in their prison clothes, a tracksuit, sliders. But this man is in a suit. Court dress. He wanted to make an impression.

'I'm Francis Joseph,' he says, his voice low and gravelly. 'It's a pleasure to meet you. Thank you so much for taking this case.'

Eli coughs and I glance his way. 'All good?' he asks with a raise of his brow.

'Thanks, Eli.'

He steps out of the room, pulling the door closed. And that's it. For the next hour, maybe more, I am locked in a room with a man accused of killing his wife. And together we will go through his case. Through his defence. What happened that night. How. Why. Their relationship, their history, her state of mind.

'Please, take a seat.' I gesture and he sits down,

34

slowly, as though he is the one appraising me, and not the other way around.

I place my bag on the chair next to me and retrieve the file of papers, now marked with sticky tabs and scrawled with my notes. I set it down on the table in front of me, and his eyes move away from me and on to the evidence. He'll have seen it all himself, but now it is in the hands of his defence. He'll be waiting to see how I can wield it to protect him, rather than defeat him.

I sit down opposite him and pull out a brand-new Counsel's notebook, the blue cover pristine and unbent. But I do not open it. Not yet. Instead, I clasp my hands together on top of it, and lean towards him. Before the questions must come the rapport.

'Mr Joseph –'

'Please,' he interrupts, 'call me Frank.'

I nod. 'Frank. I know we're here to discuss what has happened to you and your defence. But before we begin, please accept my sincere condolences on the loss of your wife.'

He pauses, his brow lowering over his eyes. 'Thank you . . . you're the first person to say that.'

'I find that disappointing. And I really do mean it. The shock must be impossible to process, especially given what has happened since.'

'Yes . . . it's . . . it's been a nightmare.'

'Have you had many visitors? Family? Friends?'

His eyes drop to his lap, his face pale. 'No . . . I have

very little family. My parents are dead and I have no siblings. And our friends . . . Well, our friends abandoned ship when I was arrested.'

'I'm sorry to hear that. People often don't know how to manage or process a loved one being wrapped up in something like this.' I pause but he remains silent, still staring downwards. 'And in here? Have they been treating you all right? Do you have everything you need? I see you have prayer beads – are you able to go to chapel or –'

'The prayer beads are just more of a comfort. They were Linda's so I like to keep them with me. It helps me feel close to her.'

I nod slowly, my stomach plummeting with empathy as Piera's face appears in my mind's eye. What would I keep on me at all times to remind myself of her?

'Was she religious?' I ask, forcing myself to focus on Frank and Linda, not Piera.

'They were a relic of her childhood – she isn't really religious any more.' He pauses, his eyes watering as he realizes what he has said. 'She wasn't, I mean. She wasn't really religious any more.'

'It's okay, Frank –'

'But yes,' he interrupts, coughing purposefully. 'They've been fine. Good, actually. It's just . . . the other prisoners.'

'They haven't done anything to you?'

'No, it's just . . . I'm not like them. I'm not meant to be here.'

'And I'll do everything I can to get you out.' I nod firmly.

He offers a small smile. 'I'm sure you will. That previous barrister . . . I'm sure he's a good advocate, but we just didn't see eye to eye.'

I sit back in my chair. 'Would you mind telling me what happened?'

'We had been preparing for the trial for months with the junior and then Prior came along and advised me that no jury would ever believe my defence, and that I should plead guilty to manslaughter.'

I force my face to remain neutral. I've known Prior for years – the criminal Bar is an ever-shrinking world – he would never say anything so extreme. But there's no point in arguing with Frank on why Prior had to step down. This is my case to run now. And we can run this defence. There's no other choice.

'And so he stepped down and you have ended up with me.' I smile broadly, shrugging my shoulders sarcastically.

He nods earnestly. 'I had heard of your reputation. So I was pleased you took the case.'

I inhale deeply, then set my clasped hands on the table in front of me.

'Well, I'm keen to hear everything from your side. I've read the file, of course, but it isn't the same as hearing it directly from you. So, if we could start from the beginning. When did you and your wife meet?'

He presses his lips together, pushing his hair back behind his ears. 'We met at university.'

'I actually think you were at university at the same time as my wife.'

'Really?' he says, his eyebrows lifting with interest. 'What's her name?'

'Piera.'

He shakes his head. 'I knew so many people at uni, but I reckon I'd remember that name.'

'Which college did you go to?'

'Brasenose.'

'Ah, she was at Magdalen. She studied law too.'

'Oh really? Does she practise or did she escape to the City like me?' He smirks and I mirror his smile.

'She's a barrister.'

'And do you have children?'

'A daughter.' Frank raises his eyebrows, a tinge of sadness crossing his eyes. For a moment there is silence, the air in the close space almost crackling. 'Were you and your wife at the same college?' I ask.

He nods, his eyes glazing over, as though lost in a memory.

'And were you in a relationship straightaway?'

'No, we were friends at first. For the first year or so. But then later it turned into a relationship.'

'And you've been married ten years, is that correct?'

'Yes. Well, ten and a half. Our anniversary is in November. Was . . . Jesus –' He lifts his hand to cover his face, drawing in a trembling breath.

'Frank, are you okay?'

'I . . . I just –'

'Take your time.'

He lowers his hand. His eyes are bloodshot, and glazed with tears. He licks his lips. 'I just . . . I keep talking about her in the present tense. As though she's still here.'

'That's absolutely normal. It takes a long time to truly accept that we've lost someone.'

He nods then lifts his head, settling his hands back on to the table. 'I'm okay,' he sniffs. 'I'm ready.'

'Now before you take me through what happened, I want to set out some legal background. I don't want to seem like I'm talking down to you as I know you're legally trained –'

'I only studied it at university and then I moved on to business, so you can take it as read that I've forgotten it all.'

I nod. 'I know this is your life, your feelings, your loss, and it's very easy to become overwhelmed by the detail of what happened, which can end up overcomplicating the case. When in reality the law makes things quite simple. You have been charged with murder. And to defend yourself against a conviction for murder, there are only a number of options. One – you didn't do it, it wasn't you. Two – it was you but it was an accident. Three – it was self-defence. Those are the absolute defences, the ones that will get you acquitted completely. But then there are others, the partial defences which will make you guilty of manslaughter rather than murder. Number one – you did it but you didn't intend to kill or seriously harm. Two – you suffered a loss of control. Three – diminished responsibility, i.e., you did it but you're not fully responsible because of your mental state at the time.'

I pause, watching him carefully, but he simply blinks back at me. Waiting. Based on his police interview, I had pegged him for a talker, an interruptor, one who would jump in with his story. He hardly gave the police time to ask their questions; he answered fully and with detail; he jumped in even when they were attempting to slow him down. But now, he is listening.

'Some of these defences aren't available to you. It would be very difficult to argue that your wife received the injuries that caused her death by accident.' I avoid being explicit about the injuries – saying 'slit her throat' to a man clearly in distress at the loss of his wife won't do him or me any favours. Language here is key. 'And there is no evidence that you have suffered from a psychotic breakdown which would allow you to argue diminished responsibility.'

I pause again. But he remains silent. Nothing. He is simply watching me through his red eyes.

'Now, I understand that from what you said in your police interviews, your defence is number one of the absolute defences. You didn't do it. It wasn't you, it was actually her. What I need from you now is a clear understanding between us that if there is a defence available to you, I will run it. No matter what that defence is. No matter if it's different to the one you told the police in interview. Countless defendants panic in interview, saying the first idea that comes into their mind because it sounds more believable than the truth. But if something different happened – if, say, for example, you were defending yourself against your wife – then it's best you tell me the truth now, so that we can argue the truth.'

'What I said in my police interview,' he mutters, no louder than a whisper, 'is the truth.'

I nod, making a note in my book – *no change of defence from interviews*. This is what I expected. You don't give as full a defence, as outrageous a defence, as he did in interview and then change your story. Nobody would believe a word you say.

'It wasn't me,' he continues. 'It was . . . it was her.'

I grip my pen, the nib pressing into the page, leaving a small pool of ink bleeding into the paper. 'Of course, I've read it in the file and watched your interview, but it helps to hear directly from you. Face to face. Tell me what happened that day.'

He blinks rapidly, as though his mind is buffering. And he shifts in his seat, his hands clenching in his lap. I've seen this response before – as though the person's psyche is desperately attempting to prevent them from returning to that time, to protect them. But then, after only a few moments, his body falls still and he meets my eye again.

'I had been into work that day for a meeting. It was the first time in a long time. You see, until that day I had tried to spend as much time as possible at home with Linda. And when I couldn't be there, I made sure her mum or her sister were there to keep her company. I didn't want to leave her alone.'

'Why?'

His eyes narrow, as though I'm asking him a stupid question. But even obvious questions require answers.

'Because she hadn't been well. For a number of months she'd spiralled; she had fallen into a depression so deep that I didn't know how to pull her out.'

'Had she been depressed before?'

'Yes, a number of times. But it began when we were at university.'

'Were you friends at this stage, or in a relationship?'

'Just friends. It was during our first year. I was with someone else at the time.'

'What happened to cause that depression?'

He pauses, taking a second to press down on his knuckles until they crack.

'A boy in our year passed away. Richard. Linda had become close to him . . . she was devastated.'

'And did this depression continue?'

'On and off throughout our relationship, but never so bad that she couldn't handle it. Never so bad that I was afraid for her to be on her own. Until shortly before she died.'

'Is there something that had happened to trigger this spiral? Or did it come out of nowhere?'

He swallows loudly, glancing briefly up at the ceiling.

'We'd been together nearly fifteen years. Married for ten. Linda desperately wanted to be a mother. She felt like it was what she was meant to do with her life. I wasn't in a rush but I wanted it – for her. But we struggled. And then . . .' He sniffs, the rapid blinking beginning once more.

'Take your time.'

'About a year before she died, she found out she was pregnant. I don't think I've ever seen her so happy. She was elated. She started planning everything, looking at nursery furniture online, searching for clothes, making a list of names. But at the twenty-week scan they told us that the baby had stopped developing. There was no heartbeat.'

'I'm so sorry.'

'She was devastated. In her mind, that life that she had imagined was gone. And I couldn't do anything to convince her that we could try again, that next time it would be okay. She just kept on saying, "That was meant to be my baby. That was my baby." The loss was insurmountable. But I hoped that once the grief passed, the sadness would shift and she would go back to herself. But sadness and depression are very different things. There was no getting her back to herself. Not without serious medical help.'

'And did you seek it?' I don't recall seeing any record of that in the evidence. But we still haven't had full disclosure –

'Yes, I did.' He nods aggressively. 'I took her to our

GP but they brushed it off. Said that the antidepressants she was on would do the trick and it would just take time. I went again on my own – twice, I think – but they said that she wasn't a case for referral to a mental health ward.'

'Is that what you thought she needed?'

'Yes. If I had believed I could take care of her myself, I would never have tried to get her referred. They're hellish places. But she was scaring me. I'd find her muttering to herself in the room that would have been the nursery. She'd already decorated it. And then in the kitchen, staring at the knives. I felt like I had to be there twenty-four seven to make sure she didn't hurt herself. It wasn't sustainable – I had a job, I needed to keep our life going. I couldn't become a full-time carer. So I thought a referral was best.'

'It sounds like she met all the criteria for a referral – why didn't they make one?'

He sighs, frustration seeping out of him. 'Because in front of the doctors she seemed better. More coherent. And when I tried to bring up my fears of her hurting herself, she brushed them off, acting as though I was overreacting. In front of them it was as though she was fine. "Am I not allowed to be sad?" That's what she said. And then all of a sudden I was the terrible husband making out his grieving wife was going crazy.'

'So what happened on the day that she died? You said that you had to go to work?'

44

'Yes, I . . . I'd tried to explain at work without painting a terrifying picture of Linda. I told them that she was struggling, that she needed me around. But there was one deal I'd been working on for almost a year, and a big meeting was coming up with the clients. The director said that if I couldn't attend, he'd put someone else on it. I'd lose all the work I had done, all the commission I would make. And we needed it. With her not working, we needed the money. I called her mum, but she was away, and her sister had something at her son's school. So . . . I went. I thought that when I got back I could take her to her sister's for a few days and she would feel better. I even packed a bag for her. I thought, it's only a few hours, she'll be okay for just a few hours. I told her that if she needed anything at all to call me. And I asked the next-door neighbour to check in on her. I told them that she hadn't been feeling very well and could they please just pop in. And I left.'

'The bag . . . the police photographed it.'

'Yes, that's right.'

'And the prosecution's case is that it was actually Linda who packed that bag. She was trying to leave while you were out.'

'That simply isn't true. I packed the bag. I was going to take her to her sister's house.'

I glance at my file, at the blue sticky tab marking the first witness's evidence. 'Your neighbour. That's Mrs Geraldine Grey – is that right?'

'Yes, that's right.'

45

'And she went into the house and said that Linda was sleeping.'

'Yes, she sent me a message, saying she had checked on her and she was fine, just fast asleep.'

'How much later did you get home?'

'About an hour after Geraldine messaged.'

'And what happened then?'

He inhales deeply, as though preparing himself. 'I let myself into the house. It was quiet. Too quiet. I assumed she was still asleep but something just didn't feel right. Something was wrong, but I just couldn't put my finger on it. I called out her name but she didn't respond. So I rushed upstairs and . . .' His voice trails away, his eyes widening.

'Where was she?'

'She was in bed. Her back was to the door, which I thought was strange – she has always slept on her right side, not her left. I went around to her side of the bed and that's when I saw the pills.'

'Where were the pills?'

'They were open on the floor next to the bed. If Geraldine only put her head into the bedroom and saw her sleeping with her back to her, she wouldn't have gone any further. So she didn't see them. But they were there. On the floor. So many. And a mixture.'

'A mixture of what?'

'Her sleeping tablets and her antidepressants. But then also my painkillers. Codeine.'

'Did she have free access to these pills?'

'No, I locked them away in the kitchen. I gave her what she needed when she needed and that was it. But there was a spare key that I kept in my office.'

'What did you do when you found her?'

'I started shaking her. Over and over again, trying to get her to wake up. But she was limp. So I picked up her upper body and leaned her over the side of the bed, and forced my fingers down her throat. It's all I could think to do. I didn't know how long an ambulance would take and my phone was downstairs in my briefcase –'

'And what happened?'

'She was sick. It came up everywhere.'

'How was she? Was she conscious?'

'As soon as she was sick, her eyes opened. And she fought against me, but once it started I guess her body realized what was happening, and then she couldn't stop it. When it eventually subsided, she looked at me in . . .'

'She looked at you in . . . ?'

'In a way I've never seen before. Like she despised me. Like I'd ruined everything. She was deathly white, her eyes round like saucers, but filled with just . . . hatred.'

'She was angry that you'd saved her.'

He nods slowly, his mouth downturned, his fingers tugging at the cuffs of his jacket. This is not the man who was here when I first entered the room: quietly confident, stoic. This man is haunted. As though ghosts are dancing about us in this very room.

'Frank – are you okay to go on?' I reach towards him, placing my hand on his side of the table. 'We can take a break.'

'Could I just get some water?'

'Yes, of course. I should have asked for some earlier – they normally leave some in here.'

I turn slightly in my seat and reach backwards to rap my fist twice on the locked door.

The lock clicks and the door pushes slightly open – there isn't enough space for it to open fully. Eli peers in.

'Ready to go?'

'No, no – we'll be some time yet,' I say. 'Could you please bring us a jug of water and two glasses. There's usually some here.'

'Yeah, sure. I'll be two minutes.' He pulls the door shut and the sound of it locking automatically is loud and sharp, like gunshot in the silence.

I turn back to Frank. 'Are you sure you want to go on?'

'Yes,' he whispers. 'I need to just get it out now. I want you to hear it from me, you said it was important.'

'Okay, well, let's wait for your water to arrive. There's no rush. Just take your time.'

The lock clangs once more and Eli appears again, sliding his way through the narrow gap in the door to set down a plastic jug and two plastic glasses. No matter what I believe, no matter what Frank's story is, he's been charged with murdering his wife. As far as the prison are concerned, this is a highly dangerous man.

'I'll leave you to it,' Eli says, stepping out of the room once more. 'Just knock again when you're done.'

'Thanks, Eli.'

The door slams shut. Frank has already poured water into his glass and is gulping from it thirstily.

'Sorry,' he says, stopping himself, a drop of water falling from his lips and on to the leg of his suit. 'I should have poured you a glass too.'

'It's absolutely fine –'

'I was just so thirsty.'

'Please don't worry.' I reach forward and grip the handle of the jug, filling my glass. I take a small sip. It's room temperature.

Frank sets down the glass, his breathing heavy. 'Shall I keep going?'

'If you're ready, yes.'

'I . . .' His eyes widen, dancing from side to side. 'I can't remember where I'd got to . . .'

'You said that she looked at you in a way you'd never seen before.'

'Yes . . . She was angry that I didn't let her die. She wanted me to just let her slip away. She must have thought that by the time I got home it would be too late.'

'Frank, the police took photographs of a gun in your safe. And the paperwork to go with it. They haven't removed the gun as it wasn't used, but the prosecution will ask about it. Can I ask why you had a gun in the house in the first place?'

He sighs. 'When we lived in our first home together in South London, we were broken into. Linda was awake and they held her at knife point while they robbed the downstairs.' He shakes his head, glancing down at the prayer beads which he twirls between his fingers. 'Ever since then, I had a gun. I got the licence for it. I stored it safely. I never used it. Not once. But it just made us feel safer. It helped Linda feel safe.'

I nod at him in understanding as I scrawl down the facts. 'The prosecution will try to use the availability of a gun in the house to demonstrate that there were far easier ways for Linda to kill herself if she wanted to. Why do you think she didn't use the gun?'

He swallows, his mouth trembling. 'Don't you think I haven't thought about that? Don't you think I haven't almost wished that she could have chosen that way instead of the way it happened?'

'I know. They will push this narrative, though.'

'We've had that gun for years and she knew where it was and how to access it, but she never touched it. She probably thought that overdosing was the easier way to go.'

'And once you saved her from the overdose?'

'She had gone into the kitchen. She knew I would stop her from getting the gun out of the safe.'

I nod, noting down his answers.

'Okay . . . So what did you do after she was sick?'

He blinks, reorienting himself in the events. 'I told her that I was going to call an ambulance and got up from the bed. But she started crying, saying no, saying she didn't want to go to hospital, that it would be the worst place for her and if I really loved her, I would just leave it. But I said I had to. She needed help.' He turns his face up to the ceiling, his eyes closing. 'That's when she came for me.'

'Came for you?'

'She came stumbling down the stairs. It was like she couldn't control her movements. The drugs . . . whatever was left of the drugs was still in her system. But she was shrieking. Her arms flying everywhere. And she smacked the phone out of my hand.'

'What did you do?'

'I tried to reason with her. I tried to explain that she needed help that I wasn't able to give. Not now I knew that if I ever left, even just for an hour, she'd try to kill herself.'

'What was she doing?'

'She was on the floor, rocking. Clutching her knees to her chest. And this noise coming from her . . . like a wail. A keening. I'd only heard that noise once before. When the doctor told us that we'd lost the baby.'

'And then?'

'I kept on trying to talk, thinking that once I calmed her down, I could convince her to let me call an ambulance or at least take her to the hospital. And eventually she fell quiet. But once she stopped rocking and opened her eyes, it was there again.'

'What was there?'

'That look. Like she hated me.'

'What did she do?'

'She stood up and raced to the kitchen. I . . . I followed her and . . .' His voice cracks, his eyes filling with tears which spill over and stream down his cheeks.

'Frank? We can stop now –'

'No, I need to tell you everything. I need to.'

'Okay. Just take your time.'

He takes a shuddering breath, then wipes his face roughly with the back of his hand and gives a resolute nod.

'She was in the kitchen, her back to me. But I knew what was in front of her. I knew what she was thinking. The knife block. I told her not to do anything stupid. To come with me and I would keep her safe. But she said that there wasn't any such thing as safe for her. Not any more. She said she couldn't see her way out of the darkness. She didn't know which way was up. And that I couldn't help her. And then . . . She said that if I had really wanted to help her, I would have just let her go. Because now it would be worse. That's when she turned around. And she had the knife in her hands.'

'What did you do?'

'I rushed forward straightaway, trying to wrestle it away from her. I think I hurt her – the police say I hurt her – but I was just trying to get the knife away from her. She was lashing out, kicking and screaming. The police took photos of my injuries, too. But then she held it out at me, told me to get back, that she didn't want to cause me any harm. I tried to stay calm but I begged her, I begged her not to do anything, to stay with me, that I needed her.'

I clear my throat, the tension in the air palpable. 'What did she do?'

'She just looked at me, the hatred gone, and just for a moment it was as though my Linda was there. The woman I have always known and loved. But then she whispered, "I'm sorry . . ." And she did it.'

'Did you call the emergency services?'

'Yes, I called and asked for the police.'

'Why the police and not an ambulance?'

His eyes harden. 'What are you implying?'

I clear my throat, directly meeting his eye. 'The prosecution will question why you asked for the police and not an ambulance. They will suggest that this shows that you were trying to give your defence as quickly as possible, rather than get care for your wife –'

He shakes his head, slowly at first and then faster. 'No, that's insane,' he says, his voice panicked. 'I just asked for help. I don't even think I thought about it, I just thought they would all come –'

'It's okay. We just need to cover everything the prosecution will press you on, okay?'

He takes a shaky breath and nods. I steady myself, preparing to ask another question he isn't going to like.

'Did you call the emergency services straightaway?'

'What do you mean?'

I pause, tilting my head to the side. My neck clicks. 'There's about forty to forty-five minutes between you getting home, which is recorded on your doorbell camera, to calling for help. Did you call straightaway?'

'Yes, of course! I was trying to help her, I was trying to stop the bleeding and my phone was out in the hall. I had to leave her to go and get it. I rushed straight back to her and called. I tried to save her, I did everything I could!'

He falls silent and hangs his head. 'I could have saved her. I *should* have saved her.'

I lean forward, resting my hand on his side of the table again – as close a gesture to touching him as is sensible. 'Frank, you can't blame yourself. It seems as though she had set her mind to it. Nothing you could have done would have stopped her. She could have waited for you to fall asleep and done it then. She tried to do it while you were away, to protect you. But to do it that way – she was desperate. So nothing you could have done would have stopped that.'

He lifts his head, his face flushed with emotion, his eyes tinged with something else. Gratefulness.

'I just wish I could have helped her.'

'I know. And I know that nothing I say can prevent you from feeling that guilt. You need to take all the time you have now to mourn her, and grieve. Let yourself feel it, or it will eat you alive. Any emotion you feel towards her, towards what happened, sadness, rage, anger at her – anything. Let yourself feel it.'

He nods. 'Thank you,' he whispers.

'No thank yous necessary. And you have my word

that I will do everything in my power to defend you. To ensure that the jury see you as I see you – a man devastated at the loss of his wife.'

'So . . .' He narrows his gaze, enquiring. 'You believe me?'

I lift my hand to my mouth and cough, hiding it, then take a sip of water. I have never troubled myself with deciding whether I accept what my clients are telling me. Unless they admit that they are guilty, my belief in whether they are guilty or innocent is simply not relevant. My duty is to defend them as fiercely as I would defend myself. That is all. But for the first time in a long while, looking at Francis Joseph, something stirs inside me, deep inside my stomach and pulsating in my mind, steady as a heartbeat.

Belief.

'Yes.' I nod. 'I believe you.'

4

I sit down at my desk, the papers and folders spread out, the video on my screen frozen in front of me. The body-worn camera footage from the day Linda died. I've spent the past four days since meeting Frank reading through all the statements, watching the police interviews multiple times, scouring through phone data and forensic analysis, and researching legal arguments. But I haven't seen the videos of the crime scene or looked at the images the police took of Linda. I wanted to take in everything I could about the case – cold, hard facts and data – before seeing anything that might sway my emotions. But now it is time.

I tap the space bar and it begins to play.

The outside of a front door appears, the number 10 in the centre of the door dulled in the low light. The door jolts open. And Frank appears.

Face ashen, eyes wide and brimming with horror, his white shirt soaked in blood, his hands stained too.

'Please, help me!' he cries.

'Frank Joseph?' a disembodied voice says – the wearer of the camera.

'Yes, yes . . .' Frank backs away, turning quickly and

heading down a darkened corridor and into the back of the house.

The officer moves quickly through the house, the sound of other people's footsteps thudding behind him. The hallway and stairs come into sight, brief glances at other rooms as he passes them. A quick flash of a holdall.

'She's in here –'

The footage, just for a moment, turns to a blank screen of glaring white as the camera adjusts from the dark of the hallway to the full overhead lights of the large open-plan living space at the back of the house. But then the camera focuses again.

I freeze. I have seen many violent images over the years, but it never gets easier. There is always a brief moment, just a split second, before my years of practice take over and switch off my emotions. My eyes sting at the sound of Frank's distress.

There, in the centre of the kitchen, her feet partially obscured by the island, is Linda. Her head is lolling to one side, her arms splayed beside her, her complexion almost white against the pool of red surrounding her. Blood . . . so much blood.

The video finishes again and I pause it once more, letting out a heavy sigh. I glance down at the photos that are now spread across my desk, trying to detach the bloody images from a real person who lived and breathed and loved. But my head is ringing, my eyes stinging as I take in the close-up of her hands, her wedding band dark with blood, her skin pale and lifeless.

'How are you doing?'

I jump at the sound of Piera's voice. Swinging around, she is standing just behind me, a steaming mug of coffee cradled in her hands – I hadn't even heard the door open, I was so consumed by the images of Linda. I look up at her, about to respond, but she is staring down at the pictures, her eyes wide.

'You walked in at the worst time,' I say, turning them over quickly as she sets down the mug. 'You don't need to look at those –'

She offers me a small smile and places a hand on my shoulder. 'I've seen pictures like that my whole career, remember?'

I reach up to my shoulder and grip her hand, turning my head to place a kiss on her knuckles. 'I know, but it's different when you're not the one working on it.'

Her eyes move to my laptop, the paused footage still visible. 'So you finally watched it, then?'

I nod. 'Yes.'

'And how is it? How does he come across?'

'Devastated . . .' I sigh. 'Desperate.'

She swallows, glancing away from the screen and back down at my face. She squeezes my shoulder. 'Well, I'll let you get on with it. Let me know if you need anything else –'

'Okay, thank you. I'll stop for dinner, I promise.'

She smiles and steps out of the room, closing the door behind her.

I turn back to my desk and flick back through my notebook, page after page after page of scrawled writing, analysing the evidence, highlighting where it goes for Frank's defence, where it could go against him, and question after question after question. The bundles of evidence are stacked in boxes around me, tabbed and highlighted. And I haven't even started on my opening speech.

I look down at page one of my notes – the running order of evidence.

- *Prosecution opening speech*
- *Senior Investigating Officer Oliver Noakes – 999 call and body-worn footage*
- *Geraldine Grey – neighbour who checked on Linda*
- *Eve Thompson – Linda's sister*
- *Police who attended scene*
- *Paramedics*
- *Dr Ethan Long – Linda's GP*
- *Coroner*
- *Experts – psychologist and psychiatrist*
- *Any others?*
- *Defence opening*
- *Frank*

I sigh heavily. This is the most complicated defence I have ever run. But in some ways it is the most simple.

Only Frank and Linda were there. The Crown say he

killed her – he was jealous and abusive. He says she was suicidal and did it herself whilst he tried to save her. All it will come down to is the jury and their answer to one question and one question alone.

Are they sure he is guilty?

Or could there be a chance – no matter how small – that they believe him?

That's all it takes.

My robe settles on my shoulders, the new silk sliding off on one side like always. I sigh, tugging it up my arm until it stays put. Reaching for my wig box, embellished with my initials in gilded calligraphy, I open the clasp and grasp the coarse horsehair. Glancing up at the mirror before me, I place the wig on my head, untucking the strands at the back which have a strange habit of falling down the back of my collar, making the hairs on my neck stand on end. I inhale deeply and meet my own gaze. And there it is – the look I didn't want to see in my eyes. Fear.

There is nothing to be afraid of. This is a trial like any other.

But that isn't true.

It's my first murder trial as a King's Counsel. People will be watching. Waiting for me to take a mis-step. Ready to relegate me back to a KC who only does the work of a junior – a KC who isn't good enough to successfully run a defence like this one. This trial matters.

'Good luck with your trial,' a voice says as a hand claps me on the shoulder.

My eyes snap away from my face to the person standing just behind me.

'Oh thanks, Jon,' I say with a wide smile. 'Probably won't get much further than the prosecution opening today –'

'Well, I'm stuck arguing a legal issue, so I'd rather your day than mine.'

'Enjoy that.'

'And you,' he says with a wry salute before heading out of the robing room doors to the courtrooms beyond.

I look back at myself and nod my head firmly.

I can do this. I've worked and trained so hard. It's just like any other case . . . If any other case could change my life.

The door of the cell clangs open and I step inside. Frank is sitting on the elevated bench that runs the short length of the room, looking like a small boy with his knees tucked up towards his chest, even though he is dressed in another impeccably cut suit, his tie perfectly straight, a matching pocket square peeking out.

This is the part of the job Piera says she no longer misses. Going down to the cells is like descending into hell, she used to say. And it is, or it can be. Abuse, assault, dirty protests, the smell sticking to the back of your throat and making you gag, clients who turn against you, who want nothing more than to make you the enemy instead of their ally. But it has to be done.

'Good morning, Frank.'

He stands quickly, smoothing down his trousers, his hands nervously reaching to straighten his tie, before extending down towards me.

'Good morning, Harry.'

'Please sit —'

'Why do they put these benches up here? As if it isn't denigrating enough being in a court cell, they make you sit up on a bench.'

'I think it's a saving space thing —'

'It's fucking idiotic, that's what it is.'

I smother a smirk, forcing my face to remain passive as he shakes his head and scuffs his expensive shoe on the floor. I sit down, my knees rising up towards my chest, just like his.

'It is fucking idiotic, you're right.'

He flashes a smile in my direction but it disappears quickly. He sits, his head hanging.

'How are you feeling, Frank?'

'I . . .' He sighs. 'I don't know . . . I've been feeling fine. I've been counting down the days to the trial, because once it's over and I get acquitted I can get back to my life. I've spent ten months on remand, waiting for the trial like a fucking kid waiting for Christmas. I've been waiting to finally be able to tell the truth. To prove to everyone that I'm innocent. But now it's here and . . .'

'It doesn't feel like Christmas.'

He nods. 'No. It does not.'

I hold in a sigh. I mustn't let Frank know how terrified I feel too. How the nerves are eating away at me. I thought that once I was a KC a trial like this would come easily, but the pressure is unbearable. I want them to find him innocent, I want them to believe him like I do. I don't want to let him down. Or myself and my family.

'We're just going to take each day as it comes,' I say reassuringly. 'Today will be relatively straightforward and then you'll have the weekend before witnesses begin giving their evidence on Monday. Most of this morning will be taken up with swearing in a jury and any legal issues. Possibly the whole of today. Potentially the prosecution will begin opening their case. That won't be the easiest thing for you to sit through, but you know what's coming. You know what they're going to say about you. So try to just let it wash over you. And do not – under any circumstance – react. Any negative reaction towards the prosecution will only look bad on you. Even facial expressions. I know you're a grown man, but emotions can take over. No rolling eyes. No heavy sighing at things they say about you. Feel your emotions about what happened to your wife, sure, but no outward reaction to what they say about you, please. The jury *will be* watching. And it never goes in your favour.'

'Okay.'

I peer forward but he is still staring unblinking at the ground. 'At the end of the prosecution's opening speech, they'll have laid their position on the table. And it's going to seem as though the defence is impossible. But remember, they have to get the evidence out. And we'll be there taking their case apart, piece by piece. It's not over until we've put your case forward too. So many defendants feel defeated at the end of the prosecution case. But stay positive. It's for them to prove.'

He finally looks up at me, his eyes glazed over. 'I know the truth,' he mutters.

'And they will too.' I nod. 'One day at a time.'

He sniffs, swiping a finger across both his eyes. 'Thank you, Harry.'

'Do you have any questions for me?'

He shakes his head. 'No. I'm ready.'

'Okay.' I stand, stepping down from the bench and heading towards the locked door which I bang on with my fist. 'As you know, I'll be at the front bench, and the dock is towards the back, but I'll be able to see you if you need to speak to me.'

The door judders open.

'See you in there,' I say, glancing back at him. He is still sitting, watching after me wistfully. What must it be like to watch me step out into a world he hasn't seen in the best part of a year? To watch everyone going about their lives with total freedom, knowing you might just be locked away for the rest of yours? As a guilty man that must be hard enough, but as an innocent one?

'See you in there,' he repeats back at me in a low voice.

The door shuts and his face – split in a divided expression of hopeful and woeful – disappears.

One knock, followed quickly by two more, reverberate around the courtroom. The signal that the judge is about to enter.

The clerk steps through the door and holds it open. 'Court rise,' she calls out.

I stand, my eyes drawn to the ceiling as I take in the space. So familiar and yet so imposing. I've been here a handful of times in my career, but I'll never be able to get used to it, never be able to find normality in its wood-clad walls, or the benches which sit perpendicular to the judge rather than facing him. Or the dock for the offender, sitting impenetrably in the centre of the space. I crane my neck to look over my shoulder, up to the public gallery which is suspended above me. From this angle it's difficult to see the faces of the people sitting in the benches, but I can tell it's full. You can feel it in the air; the atmosphere is vibrating, like electricity. This isn't just any courtroom – it's Court One of the Old Bailey. This room has seen the most infamous of people pass through it on their way to justice. Ian Huntley and Maxine Carr. Peter Sutcliffe. The Krays. Formidable creatures who have written their stories into the darkest pages of history.

But Francis isn't going to join them. He doesn't belong there. Not with those monsters.

I won't let it happen. He is just a man. A man mourning the death of his wife and having to defend himself all the while.

The judge enters, bowing his head towards us. I inhale deeply, my fingers tingling. Judge Hawthorne. I've appeared before him a number of times, and each time has been more difficult and more intimidating. The first time, I was blindly naive, so pleased to be appearing at the Old Bailey that I hadn't prepared myself for what was to come. But now I am all too familiar. What is to come is a judge who is direct, impatient. Unforgiving. Make a mistake in front of him, and he won't forget it.

'Good morning,' he says in his trademark low mutter, so low that if his bench wasn't lined with microphones, we'd barely hear him.

'Good morning, My Lord,' the prosecutor and I respond together. We glance sideways at each other, and her eyes dart from my face down to my feet and back up again as she assesses me.

Laura Golding KC has been a King's Counsel for nearly fifteen years. She works for both the Crown and the defence, but she is famous for one particular kind of case: stories of abused women. I've been against her only once in a case of wounding with intent. Husband and wife. My defendant did not fare well. She's going to nail Francis to the ground.

I shake my head, freeing my fingers from the fist they have clenched into, and flex them quickly, repeatedly. I can't afford to be thinking like that already. I deserve to be here, just as much as Golding. I'm just as good. I can do this.

'Are we ready to empanel the jury?' Hawthorne mutters.

'Yes, My Lord,' we both respond again.

Hawthorne sighs slowly, his breath rattling through the speakers. 'Then bring Mr Joseph in, Madam Clerk – we don't want to waste half the morning just waiting for the defendant.'

'Yes, My Lord,' she says. 'He was on his way up from the cells.'

'Well, call down and see where he is –'

A door at the back of the courtroom creaks open, and a room full of energy and life falls still. From above me, the sound of people shifting to lean forward in the public gallery. Low whispers as people take him in.

I meet his eye, and he raises his eyebrows as he sees me, his face briefly flashing with relief. He is flanked by two guards who lead him towards the dock. They open the gate and he steps upwards, one, two, three, four, five steps, until he is level with the judge, the two of them lifted above the rest of us, like players on a Shakespearean stage.

'Good morning, Mr Joseph,' Hawthorne calls out as the rest of the courtroom take their seats.

'Good morning, My Lord,' Frank responds. *Good man*. He remembered to call him My Lord and not Your Honour. Most defendants forget in the pressure of the moment. I've seen all sorts: Sir, Mr, Your Majesty.

'Mr Joseph, we are now going to move to empanel the jury who will try you. A group of potential jurors will come into this room and from that group we will randomly call twelve members who will sit on this trial. Once the jurors have been called, I will speak to them, and then the prosecution, Ms Golding, will open the case. Do you understand?'

'Yes, My Lord.'

Hawthorne nods, then clears his throat. 'Very well.'

The clerk turns swiftly and heads down to a door on the right of the judge's bench, the heavy wood closing with a thud behind her. I swallow, my mouth dry. Soon we will know who is going to decide Frank's fate – which twelve people will make that life-altering decision.

I turn my head up and to the right, to the dock. But Frank isn't looking at me, or at the judge. His head is tilted upwards and he is staring into the full public gallery, his fingers fiddling with his prayer beads, his brow sewn together in a frown. I had warned him how many people would be coming to watch. He had scoffed. *Are you not entertained?* he had said in a feigned bellow. But maybe he still hadn't realized. Maybe he didn't comprehend how it would feel to know that the worst and most important days of his life were going to be observed by strangers and tourists, as though it was some passing piece of culture. But suddenly, his face softens. For just a moment, the worry seems to dissipate. He drops his head and finally spots me looking at him. His frown returns but he lifts the corner of his mouth in half-hearted recognition.

'You okay?' I mouth.

He nods but breaks away and stares down at the ground.

I glance down at my papers which are balanced pre-cariously on the thin piece of wood that sits in front of Counsel's bench – a narrow row of seats that the prosecutor and I have to share, she closest to the judge, me closest to the dock, our teams of juniors, police and solicitors behind us.

I'm ready.

The door reopens and the clerk strides in, followed by a group of approximately thirty people. Their faces change as they step inside the room, their chins instinctively lifting at the sheer scale of the space, their eyes widening as they dart about, anticipation fleeting across their features.

I scan them carefully. An even balance of men and women would be good. A greater proportion of women would be better. You'd think the opposite would be true, but something we all learn at the Bar after years of practice – no one is harsher in judge-ment on a woman, than other women. Men are more likely to convict a man of crimes against a woman. Every time the jury enter, our minds weigh up the balance. The prosecution will be hoping for more men. It's just what we do.

It's so depressing, Piera said the first time she lost a rape prosecution, a jury of nine women acquitting the defendant.

Depressing, yes. But true.

They settle in a group opposite, standing huddled together in front of the jury's bench where twelve of them will soon take their seats. The judge leans forward, a kind expression transforming his features. He never looks our way with that face. But the jury are special. The jury need to be handled with care.

'Good morning,' Hawthorne says, his voice no longer a low growl, but full and warm.

'Good morning,' a few of them echo back, like schoolchildren addressing a headmaster.

'May I first give my sincere thanks for your attendance. Whether this is your first day waiting to be assigned a trial, or close to your last, just your being here is of the utmost importance to society. Without your contribution, the justice system could not function. And without the justice system, society would collapse. So, please know that what you are doing here is truly important.'

He clears his throat, his eyes calmly appraising them. Most are completely still, but a few shift nervously from foot to foot.

'Given that you are in Court One of the Old Bailey, you may have an understanding that this case is very serious indeed. Given the nature of this case and the potential length of the trial, my clerk is to read out a short summary of the offence the defendant has been charged with, and also the names of the defendant and the victim. Once this summary has been read out, my clerk will begin to draw names. If your name is drawn and there is any reason why you believe you are not fit to be a member of this jury, either through a connection to a person involved, an element of the case that may be too difficult for you, or because of the length of time involved, please alert my clerk and approach the bench to speak to me. I will then determine whether I am content to release you or if you are still bound by your civic duty to this court.' He slides his eyes towards his clerk and lifts his chin towards her. 'Thank you, Madam Clerk.'

She clears her throat and I fix my eyes on the jury. It can be easy to predict which way people may lean before hearing any of the evidence. If they're horrified by the summary, the chances of them being moved by a defendant are low to impossible. Let's see what kind of group we're going to get.

'The indictment that is to be tried in this courtroom before twelve of you is for the charge of murder under common law with the alternative of manslaughter. The persons involved in this case are the defendant, Francis Joseph of Islington, London, and the victim Linda

Joseph, Francis Joseph's wife. It is alleged by the Crown that Mr Joseph murdered Linda Joseph by slitting her throat with a serrated kitchen knife.'

I scan them quickly. Some of them are still and stoic, refusing to react at all, their faces forcibly passive. But a woman towards the back of the group, leaning on the wood panelling which fronts the jury's bench, is looking directly at Francis, her eyes already showing that she does not believe that *this man*, with his smart suit, carefully styled hair and handsome features, could ever slit his wife's throat. We want her. And a man at the front, who has been rocking back and forth in agitation, is now staring at the ground, his eyes round and childlike, his cheeks puffed outwards as though he can't stomach another detail. Now that is a man we do not need on the jury. He looks a bit pale, as though he might faint at any moment. Hopefully he'll claim the case is too much for him, that he won't be able to cope with the detail, and he'll be released.

My attention flits briefly to the dock. Frank is once again staring up at the public gallery, still preoccupied with what the masses will think, but he looks forward once again, avoiding the jurors to his right, before hanging his head.

'This case has been listed for six weeks,' the clerk continues, 'although we must highlight that depending on the evidence and any issues arising in trial, this could be longer, although it may also be shorter.'

'Six weeks?' someone whispers, aghast, from the

75

centre of the group. Mutters pass between them. A long trial is always intimidating. How will they miss so much work? How will they take in so much information? How is their life meant to simply stand still for the next month and a half? But after a few days, a week at most, it pulls them in. It's always the same. Reluctance turns to fascination. And fascination eventually consumes them. This trial will be their life. They will keep it like a secret, looking at their family and friends with all-knowing smiles, slowly becoming drunk on the power they have found placed in their hands.

The clerk shifts, turning her body entirely towards them, then unclasps her hands from behind her back and reveals a stack of cards, a name of a potential juror set out on each one. She pauses, turning her gaze away from them to look at Hawthorne.

He leans forward on to the bench, lowering his spectacles.

'Very well,' he says. 'Let's begin.'

I breathe in deeply, my chest rising, the moment suspended in time while the clerk lowers her glasses to focus on the first name.

'Alison Aldridge,' she calls out.

A woman half-raises her hand, waving the fingers nervously as she steps forward. The clerk directs her to the second row of seats and she awkwardly side-steps along the narrow gap between the two rows until she reaches the far seat.

There she is, the first juror. Eleven more to go.

'Paul Hanawawe,' the clerk calls again.

Number two.

A young man, no older than twenty-five, a notebook pressed to his chest, steps forward. 'Uh . . . Thank you,' he says to the clerk with a small nod then shakes his head, confused at his giving of thanks.

'Oscar Norbury.'

A tall, thin man, his glasses resting on top of his head, sighs loudly with a roll of his eyes, then steps a few paces towards her. 'Really?' he says, his teeth clenched.

'Sir, I would ask that you –'

'I really can't afford to be here for six weeks –'

'Mr Norbury,' the judge's voice rings out, his authority echoing up to the ceiling. 'Approach the bench, if you have a case to make for being excused.'

Oscar Norbury sighs once again as he walks towards the judge, the sound being picked up by the microphones and coming out through the speakers. His cheeks flush.

'Your Honour, I –'

'My Lord.'

'Sorry?' He frowns, confused.

'In this court judges are referred to as My Lord or Lady, not Your Honour.'

Norbury shakes his head. 'Um . . . okay. Judge, I just simply cannot afford to be away from work for six weeks.'

'What do you do, Mr Norbury?'

'I am a managing sales director for a tech company.'

'A large one?'

Norbury lifts his chin arrogantly. 'One of the biggest.'

'And is it fair to say, Mr Norbury, that being such a tech giant, your employer will not simply collapse because of your absence?'

'Well, yes, but –'

'You are not excused. Please take seat number three.'

I press my lips together, burying a laugh. Hawthorne knows how to handle a jury. With kid gloves on one hand, and with a steel grip from the other. Otherwise it can descend into disarray. They have to know who is in charge. Like a parent and child: respect breeds respect. Let just one walk all over you, and the others will follow. Show them you are not to be messed with, and the rest will fall into line.

Norbury has taken his seat and the clerk clears her throat once more. 'Theo Angelou.'

My jaw clenches as the man in the front row – the one who looked nauseous as the summary was read – raises his hand with trepidation, his face still a ghostly grey. He doesn't say a word, but instead makes his way across to the bench, his eyes fixed to the floor.

He is not good news.

The names keep being called and I tally them in my mind as they take their seats. Four men to two women. Three women. Four women. Five men to four women. Five men to five women. Five men to six women.

And finally, the last name. Will it be an equal split? Or will it be a female majority?

'Sylvia Mendez.'

The woman at the back who had stared at Frank with disbelieving discernment, nods, almost triumph-antly. 'That's me,' she says, her voice loud and firm. She glances across at him again, her face kind. Just like I predicted – she simply can't believe that *that man* would do something so awful. Another man, yes. But not him.

She takes her place.

Five men. Seven women.

It could have been more – but a majority is a major-ity. That's the first hurdle over. This is a jury we can work with.

But the feeling of triumph doesn't last long. I can already feel it fizzling away as two more jury members are called – temporary recruits who will listen to the prosecution opening just in case other jurors have to step down – and Golding readies her papers next to me, dragging the lectern towards her, turning to face the jury head on rather than angling towards the judge. Greeting them with a sad and rehearsed smile. This may be a jury that surprises me. They may go against all the patterns that have been established over countless years of psychology and criminology. This may be a female-heavy jury who decide that Frank is the villain. They may see his put-together appearance and envision a narcissist. Or the men in the jury may turn against

Linda, deciding that Frank is one of them – a good guy. They may go against the norms of the hive mind. As much as I have learnt my lessons over the years, there is one universal truth to jury trials which can never be overridden: a group of human beings can act in an infinite number of unexpected ways.

'Ms Golding?' Hawthorne says, nodding at her. 'Is the Crown ready to begin?'

'Yes, My Lord.'

'And there are no legal issues to resolve that weren't brought to my attention prior to the jury being called?'

'No, My Lord.' She glances my way out of the corner of her eye, a steely, questioning gaze.

'Mr Mason-Hall?'

I half-stand. 'No, My Lord.'

He sits back in his chair, shifting his weight slightly before falling still. 'Ms Golding . . .' He gestures at her. The floor is now hers.

'Thank you, My Lord. Honourable members of the jury, I appear before you as the representative for the Crown. My Honourable friend Mr Mason-Hall appears before you on behalf of the defendant in this case, Francis Joseph. Whilst the judge is the arbiter of law, and both Mr Mason-Hall and I appear as advocates, we are not the most important members of this case. There is nobody more important to a criminal trial than the twelve members of the jury. Once the evidence in the case has been put before you, it will be for you to assess it, analyse it and apply it to the law, and then decide whether you find Francis Joseph guilty or not guilty. And the charge against him is the most serious offence that can be committed by any member of society.' She pauses for chilling effect, the room so silent, even the quiet hums in the air. 'Murder.'

The jury are leaning forward in their seats. She already has them in the palm of her hand.

'Over the next six or so weeks, the Crown will set out evidence before you that will prove beyond reasonable doubt that Francis Joseph murdered his wife Linda. And he did so in a brutal and violent manner. In a way that can only be described as cold, calculated and utterly reprehensible.'

She leans forward, her forearms pressing into the lectern, her fingers gripping the edge. Her expression is open, and when she continues, her voice is low, as though she is sharing a secret with friends. 'You may look at Mr Joseph and see a man who appears as though he has his life together. A man who could never commit an act of this nature. He had a fantastic career, a beautiful home, a wife whom he met at university. As you can see, even from prison, he is dressed impeccably, not a strand of hair out of place.'

My eyes dart over to Frank – his eyes are lowered, his mouth downturned. But in his lap, beyond the gaze of the jury, his fists are clenched around his prayer beads. Frank is not a fool. He knows where this is going. His mind must be whirring, his defences rising with every word she mock-whispers towards them. In just the opening few minutes of the case, she is going to attack the very thing that will lead to a jury deciding that he potentially could have done this: his character.

'You may look at those details and see a good man, a man who would never lose control or commit violence in this way. But I ask you, as you hear the evidence against him, to not let appearances, or presumptions of how violence comes to be, fool you. Not every murder happens in a wild lashing of limbs and soaring of rage. Some murders are quiet. Measured. Thought through. That is the kind of man Francis Joseph is. A man who would appear in court accused of the murder of his wife looking as sure of himself as you or I. A man who would realize his wife is going to leave him, and coolly and calmly slit her throat with a knife from the kitchen. A man who would defend himself by claiming that, not only did he not do it, but that Linda did it to herself.'

She allows the court to descend into silence once more. The jury blink at her, their mouths gawping as their wide eyes dart across to Frank. The most shocking part of the case dropped into their laps – Frank's defence.

I inhale through my nose. *She's good.* Handing them his defence this early on in her opening, directly after placing him in their estimation as a manipulative, cold-blooded wife-killer is . . . is a genius move. From the very beginning they will see any attempt to paint him as the loving husband who was simply trying to help his suicidal wife, as further manipulation.

This case is all colours of grey. But she is painting it in black and white.

She is showing him in one light and one light only.

Monster.

6

The house is quiet when I push my way through the front door, only the low sound of voices coming from the television. My heart sinks. Rose must have gone to sleep already. I was hoping I hadn't missed her.

'Piera?'

I close the door behind me and move into the living room. Piera is curled up on the sofa, a blanket tucked over her lap, her phone pressed to her ear.

'Yep, that's fine,' she says, smiling at me and rolling her eyes. *Rachel!*, she mouths.

I smile back at her and remove my coat, tossing it on the arm of the sofa before flopping down beside her. Rachel has been Piera's best friend since their pupillage. But she can be . . . demanding.

'Okay, okay . . . I'll see you tomorrow,' Piera says. 'Bye.'

She ends the call and places her phone down next to her before turning to me. 'Hi,' she says, leaning towards me and pressing a quick kiss on to my lips.

'Hi,' I say. 'Is Rachel all right?'

She clears her throat. 'You know Rachel.'

'And you? Everything okay?'

'Yes, all good here. How was the case –'

'You first – how's Rose? Am I too late?'

She lifts a hand to my cheek, her thumb tracing my jaw. 'I'm sorry. She fell asleep about twenty minutes ago. I tried to keep her up for you, but you know what she's like if she gets overtired and I just had to put her down –'

'No, it's fine –'

'Or she'll be miserable tomorrow. I'm sorry.'

'Really, it's okay. My fault for being late. Court finished and I needed to get some stuff from chambers. I'm sorry.'

'It's the first day of the biggest trial of your life. Please don't be sorry.'

She removes the blanket from her lap and turns towards me, her knees touching my thighs. I shift closer. It still surprises me how urgent my desire is to be close to her. Even after all these years. I smile.

'What?' she asks with a wonky smile. 'Why are you looking at me like that?'

'No reason. I just love you.'

'I love you too . . . Anyway. How was today? I've been waiting all day to hear.'

I sigh. 'How was today . . . It was . . . it was an opening.'

'What does that mean?'

'It means that Golding is not allowing any nuance into the prosecution case at all. Within five minutes of opening, she had painted Frank as some kind of narcissistic, sociopathic control freak who killed Linda without thinking twice.'

'What happened?'

'Okay . . . So, there's nothing about it happening in a fit of rage, on impulse, when he discovered she was going to leave him and flew off the handle. She's placing the case as if he's controlling, calm, and planned it meticulously. And that his defence is just another manipulation.'

'But what would be his motive?'

'Control,' I mutter. 'She was too much trouble and he wanted rid.'

'Really?'

'Yes, and she's using everything about him to back that point up. His suit, his hair, for God's sake! But I can't tell him to dress differently now, because then that will look like a manipulation too.'

Piera chews on her lip, her forehead furrowed. 'You can win them back. You're brilliant.'

'I hope I can be brilliant enough.'

'You can. I really believe you can do it. And you have to if you believe he's innocent. They have to believe him.'

I pause, taking in her face, so full of certainty. But that pure feeling of belief I felt after I met him in prison feels unsteady, wavering, as though the earth is shifting beneath our feet.

'You still believe him, right?' Piera mutters.

'It doesn't matter if I do –'

'Of course it does. I know even if you believed he was guilty you would still do everything you could, but you know deep down that cases feel different when you believe in your client's innocence. The jury can feel it, they can see it. If they think that even you don't believe him, he doesn't stand a chance –'

'I know,' I say, kissing the side of her head. 'Part of me knows that even if he is guilty, even if he is lying about everything, unless he admits his guilt to me, I still have to represent him. I still have to put his defence forward. But I want so much for him to be innocent. When I spoke to him in the prison I really believed him. If he killed her and is lying to my face, what kind of judge of character am I? I can always tell when they're really guilty, even when they swear that they're not. But him . . . I believed him.' I sigh, frustration pulsing through me. 'I do believe him, it's just . . . Golding got in my head. I'm sorry. Let's not talk about it for now . . . Dinner?'

'Yes,' she says, moving away from me. 'It's just keeping warm. And then I guess you have work to do tonight?'

I nod. 'Yes . . . It's going to be a long weekend.'

She opens the oven and lifts out a tray, steaming, the smell of lasagne wafting across to the living room. 'Um . . . I was actually going to ask you to have Rose for a few hours tomorrow while I go to see Rachel? Just a few hours is fine, right?'

'You can't take her with you?' I ask. 'Has Rachel gone off her?'

She smiles, tilting her head in that way she does when she finds something amusing. I love it. 'No,' she guffaws. 'But she needs to talk to me about something serious . . . I think there are problems with her and Josh. And you know if Rose is there –'

'You'll have no time to talk. I know . . . You know I'd love to have her, but the first witness is on Monday morning. I need to be ready –'

'Look, I know how important this is, and I know that you need time, but you'll have the whole weekend, you've had the whole week, every night until now – it's just a couple of hours.'

'Piera, I can't be distracted while this is going on –'

She crosses her arms, a flash of anger in her eyes. 'Oh, so our daughter's a distraction now?'

'Hey,' I say standing, moving towards her, placing my hands on her elbows. 'Where is this coming from? You've done trials like this before, you know what it's like. I need to focus. Of course she's not a distraction, it's just that it's starting properly on Monday and I have to be ready.'

'You're right.' She nods, and for a moment the tension in my body releases. But then I see the look in her eye. 'I do know what it's like,' she continues. 'At least, I did until I put my career on hold to give you a baby.'

My mouth falls open and for a moment we stare at each other, the air between us crackling. But then she lifts her hand to her mouth, her eyes shimmering with tears. 'I'm so sorry. That wasn't fair –'

'It's okay,' I whisper.

'No, that was so unfair. I'm such a bitch.'

'You aren't, it's okay.' I pull her towards me and wrap my arms around her waist, exhaling as she buries her face in my neck, her breath soft and warm against my skin. 'I love you. And I'm sorry too. I'll have Rose –'

'No, no. I'll take her to Mum's. It wasn't fair of me to put that pressure on you with everything happening on this trial. I know it's important.'

'Are you sure?'

She nods, tilting her chin up towards me and pressing her lips against mine. 'I'm sure,' she says and then turns back to our dinner, busying herself with filling our plates with a generous pile of lasagne and salad, and then carrying them over to the table.

'Come – let's eat.'

But I can't get her comment out of my mind. She's never used having Rose against me. Not in an argument, or in any kind of decision about Rose or about our lives. She wanted to wait, and I didn't. I didn't want to wait to be a father until I was well into my forties. But we discussed it together – and we decided together.

So why did she say that? Is it really because I said I couldn't have Rose? Or is there something more, something bubbling beneath the surface that I can't see? I can feel something there, but I just don't know what it is. Anxiety turns my stomach, and my eyes lock on to Piera, watching as she takes a seat and scoops lasagne into her mouth. I've never felt like this before – not in our entire relationship. She is there. But I can't reach her.

*

I step into our bedroom, pausing with a wince as that same spot in the carpet creaks under my weight. But Piera doesn't stir. It's two in the morning, the house completely silent, my mind replaying the footage over and over, whirring with the facts of the case, the witnesses appearing on Monday and questions, questions, questions. Every possible line of questioning set out and explored. And worry – worry about Piera. I could have done with another hour of work but my body feels heavy, so weighed down with exhaustion that I couldn't even focus on the words on the screen.

I undress then creep towards the bed slowly, lowering myself into it carefully so as not to disturb the mattress. I settle in and let out a sigh. But now that I'm in bed – now that I'm finally in a position to fall asleep – my eyes just stare up into the darkness, tiredness refusing to allow them to close. Instead, I feel wired. Piera always tells me off. She says I need downtime between working on a case and climbing into bed. Reading, or watching something mindless on the television. Playing my long-neglected guitar. And she's right. It's so difficult to switch off, no matter how drained I am.

A bright light flashes from the centre of the bed. I glance over – it's Piera's phone, discarded beside her. She must have fallen asleep looking at it, or scrolling. I reach over to grab it and tap on the screen, ready to swipe down to dim the screen light. But the message that caused the flash in the darkness sends a strange feeling juddering up my spine. My eyes dance over the words again – maybe I misread them. But no. It is as clear as day.

Rachel:
Just got in from drinks . . . such a funny night.
So much to tell you.
Was great seeing you last week. I know you're busy but
I miss your face. We need to catch up again soonxx

Why would Rachel say that if she had just talked to Piera earlier tonight and they'd organized to see each other tomorrow? As much as my mind is trying to rationalize, I can only see one possible answer.

Piera isn't meeting Rachel tomorrow.

But where is she going?

And why did she lie?

7

The knock sends a jolt through me, an abrupt shove out of my thoughts and back into the courtroom. I stand, forcing my tired body to its feet, my head automatically lowering itself as the judge makes his way to his seat – moving on autopilot. I haven't slept much all weekend. On Friday night, I thought about waking Piera, asking her directly if she was really meeting Rachel and why did she feel she had to lie? But I couldn't. I've never not trusted her. And she's never given me a reason to think I'm unable to trust her. But on Saturday when she left, I couldn't stop thinking about where she was going. I should have asked her, but once she had gone and returned it felt as though it was too late. I couldn't figure out how to ask without sounding like I was calling her a liar. And while I should have been focusing on preparing for the first witness, the same questions have been running through my mind, over and over again. Do I ask her? And how?

'Good morning,' Hawthorne says, and I force the thoughts out of my head. I'm defending a murder trial. Snap out of it.

'Good morning, My Lord,' I say, Golding echoing the greeting a moment after.

'Any legal issues that have mysteriously arisen over the weekend that I need to turn my mind to before we bring in the jury?'

'No, My Lord,' Golding says. 'The Crown is ready to proceed with the first witness.'

'Very well.' He nods at the clerk and she rises to her feet, exiting swiftly.

I glance over to Frank. His shirt is now slightly creased beneath the jacket, his tie no longer perfectly centred. I roll my eyes, stopping myself abruptly as he looks up and greets me with a small smile.

'Are you ready?' I asked him just an hour ago down in the cells. 'Anything you want to ask me before we begin?'

'Yes . . .' He sniffs, pausing, then glances down at himself. 'Do you think I shouldn't wear the tie today?'

'Really, Frank?' I say. 'That's the first question you want to ask me? The first witness is on today, the Senior Investigating Officer. He's going to play the 999 call and show the jury the body-worn video from the officers who came to the scene. You understand that, correct?'

'Yes, I do, but I've seen the footage. I've heard the 999 call. There's nothing in there that I'm worried about or afraid of. What I *am* concerned about is that the prosecution painted me out to be a sociopath who is trying to manipulate the jury. So, do you think I shouldn't wear the tie today?'

'Do you not think that doing exactly that will play

94

into their narrative even more? Don't even think about it. She's baiting you and you're biting.'

He nods, but his eyes are still doubtful. 'Frank, don't do anything to what you're wearing. You look great and you're being yourself. Trust me.'

He just couldn't listen to me. He just couldn't leave his fucking suit alone. Maybe this is the real reason why Prior dropped the case. He is one of the best – he doesn't need any cases. There will always be another juicy trial awaiting him so he can pick and choose for himself, finding subtle ways out of them when they don't suit him or he takes a dislike to the defendant. And knowing Prior, Frank wouldn't have been his kind of client. A client who always knows best. But this is nothing. Whilst Frank might be a know-it-all who can't help himself, I've dealt with far worse.

And I'm not Prior. I don't have a choice. Not yet. Not until I prove myself.

The jury enter and I turn to look at them. The woman at the front of the line – Mendez, I think her name was, Frank's fan – strides in eagerly, her eyes bright. Some of them look apprehensive, others excited. A few wear expressions tinged with terror. The opening is one thing; it's story-telling, performance. It isn't evidence. It doesn't count. They could forget everything that was said to them by the prosecution in their opening speech and it wouldn't make a difference. But the first witness? This is where it truly begins.

'Thank you all for being prompt and ready to begin this morning,' Hawthorne says. 'There may be days where you have to wait for a little while before you are brought into the courtroom whilst the advocates and I discuss legal matters in the case, so I will thank you for your patience ahead of time. But for today, we are ready to proceed.' He turns towards Golding. 'Ms Golding –'

'Thank you, My Lord.' She lifts her chin. 'The Crown calls Oliver Noakes.'

I glance down at the time on my laptop as the clerk goes to fetch the witness.

10:03 a.m.

I wonder what Piera is doing.

I shake my head, letting out a deep sigh. Out of the corner of my eye, Golding snaps her head towards me. Was it that loud? Did everyone hear it?

Get it together.

The clerk returns with Oliver Noakes following closely behind. I've worked with Noakes before as a prosecutor. Thorough, hard-working, meticulous. He knows his cases inside and out.

He steps up into the dock. 'Good morning, My Lord,' he says to the judge.

'Good morning, Mr Noakes,' the judge responds, his face warming at the unforced politeness of his greeting.

Noakes automatically glances back to the clerk. 'I'll say the affirmation, please.'

Golding smiles. Some police officers are absolute professionals. So used to the formalities and processes of court that it no longer fazes them. For her it makes her job a dream. But for a defence barrister? It makes cross-examination almost impossible. They are difficult to rattle.

'I, Oliver Noakes, do solemnly, sincerely and truly declare and affirm the evidence I shall give shall be the truth, the whole truth, and nothing but the truth.'

Golding stands, the smile still fixed to her face but now directed firmly at Noakes. 'Good morning, Officer,' she says, making clear to the jury at once that this is no normal witness. This is a police officer. Depending on the jury, this is either a good thing or a bad thing. Do they inherently trust or distrust the people whose job it is to protect us? For now, the jurors are inscrutable, their faces full of trepidation or completely impassive.

'Good morning, Miss Golding,' he responds.

'Could you please state your full name and title for the jury?'

'Yes, of course.' He slants his body, directing his shoulders towards the jury, his lower body still directed towards her. But he meets their eyes, slowly making contact with each of them as he speaks. 'My name is Oliver Noakes and I am a detective inspector within the Homicide Unit and the Senior Investigating Officer in this case.'

'Mr Noakes, there are several pieces of evidence which you will produce in due course, but before we begin with those, I'd like to ask you a few questions about your experience and knowledge of the case.'

'Of course.'

'How long have you been a police officer?'

'I've been in the police since I was eighteen years old. So twenty-two years.' He smirks over at the jury. 'Feel free to do the maths.'

A few of them laugh, surreptitiously, like children who aren't sure if it's allowed, and he elicits smiles from the rest. They are warming to him, instantly. He's good.

'And you've been Detective Inspector for how many years?'

'Five.'

'And how many of your twenty-two years have been in the Homicide Unit?'

'I've been in the Homicide Unit for just over ten years now.'

Golding pauses, letting that information settle. A few of the jurors' eyebrows are raised, impressed by his level of experience. They will take everything he says even more seriously now.

'When did you become aware of this case?'

'Soon after the 999 call in. Uniformed officers attended but we were looped in shortly after that and I attended the scene.'

'Is it usual that the Homicide Unit are involved so early?'

'Not always. Often we aren't involved until it becomes clear that a homicide is in question.'

'Why were you involved so early in this case?'

'The means of death, the state of the scene, and Mr

Joseph's presence, meant that my unit was contacted straightaway by the officers at the scene.'

'What time was the call made?'

'You can see from both police systems and from Frank Joseph's call data –'

'Sorry, Officer, if I might pause you for one moment there. The call logs in question are behind Tab B of the jury bundle at page 17. The Crown asks that they are exhibited as exhibit ON/1. Please, continue.'

'Yes, from both the police systems and Frank's call data you can see that the call to the police took place at 6:17 p.m. and lasted for just under four minutes.'

'And is the 999 call available to be listened to?'

'Yes, it is.'

'At this juncture, the Crown asks that the recording of the 999 call is exhibited into evidence as exhibit ON/2.'

The judge nods, writing down the reference for his notes to use in his summing up. The clerk looks up from her screen. 'Exhibit ON/1 and 2 entered into evidence.'

'Thank you, Madam Clerk,' Golding says. 'I would ask that the exhibit be played now for the jury and also be made available for them to listen to again during their deliberations if requested.'

'Any objections?' Hawthorne asks, peering over his glasses at me.

'No, My Lord.'

'Very well. Members of the jury, we will now play the 999 call that was made on the twenty-first February of

99

this year. Please pay careful attention to the evidence as it will only be played once during this trial, but should you need to listen to it again during deliberations, this can be requested and I will decide at that juncture whether to allow it.'

The clerk waits for his signal before turning to her computer, the courtroom watching her in silence as she navigates to the file. She double clicks, the sound loud in the quiet, and white noise rumbles through the speakers. I inhale, holding my breath.

Here we go.

'Police emergency,' the voice of the call handler says. 'What's your location?'

'I-I'm in Hampstead, 10 Wheeldon Avenue,' Frank's shaky voice stutters. 'Not far from the Heath.'

'And what's the emergency?'

'I-I didn't know whether to ask for an ambulance or for you, but . . . my wife . . . my wife, I think, I think she's dead.'

'Okay, explain to me – what's happened?'

'She . . . oh god! She slit her own throat.'

'How did you find her?'

'I was in the house.'

'Did you see her do this?'

'Yes! I tried to stop her but I couldn't. Please, just send someone now!'

'Okay, police and an ambulance are on their way.'

'I've been trying to stop the bleeding but I think she's gone.'

'Are you applying pressure to the wound?'

'Yes, I have a towel –'

'Keep applying pressure and –'

'I am but she's gone . . . she's . . . Linda! Linda, please!'

'What's your wife's name?'

'Linda Joseph.'

'And your name?'

'Frank Joseph. Sorry, Francis. Francis Joseph.'

'They should be with you very soon. You should hear the sirens when they're close.'

'I can't hear anything!'

'They are two minutes away. What I want you to do – take Linda's wrist and place your index and middle finger on the inside – can you feel a pulse?'

Rustling sounds come through the speakers, clothing being jostled. Frank adjusting Linda's unmoving body.

'I don't feel anything. And she isn't breathing. My god, I don't know what to do. How can I help her? What should I . . . Oh, I hear the sirens! They're here.'

'Okay, Frank. You'll need to go to the door and open it for them.'

'I can't leave her –'

'The sooner they're inside, the sooner someone can help her and you. So go on, go to the front door.'

There is a loud thud – the phone dropping to the floor. More rustling. Quick, heavy footsteps. Muffled voices.

'She's in here –'

The phone call ends.

Golding waits, keeping the courtroom suspended in tension. The jurors' eyes dart from the officer, to Golding and then over to Frank, who is staring up at the ceiling, his lips pressed together, his eyes glassy in the light. What must it be like to have to relive the worst moments of your life over and over? To watch as other people experience those moments vicariously through a recording, their minds poring over every word, every inflection in your voice, doubting every waver of emotion, every crack as your heart breaks. To lose your wife, to try to save her, and to be blamed. How does anyone survive this? And what are the jury thinking? This 999 call is one of the strongest parts of his defence. Will the jury really be able to listen to this phone call and look at Frank in the dock now and think anything other than that he desperately tried to save her? Because there's only one alternative to that assessment: every second of that phone call, and every second as he sits in the dock, is an act. A carefully crafted performance.

'Thank you, Madam Clerk,' Golding says, her voice deferential and respectful, as though she is speaking at a funeral. 'Officer, at this point the phone call ended, is that correct?'

'Yes.' Noakes nods, once again directing his answers at the jury. 'The call cut out, so we believe once the paramedics and uniformed officers entered the scene, the defendant ended the phone call.'

'Can you confirm that, as we have heard in the

phone call, the defendant asked for police, not for an ambulance?'

'Yes, I can confirm that.'

'Were any of the officers who attended the scene wearing body-worn cameras?'

'Yes, they were. And I exhibit the footage as ON/3.'

The judge and clerk nod in unison. 'My Lord, the Crown would now like to play the body-worn footage for the jury.'

The clerk jumps into action, gesturing to the usher in the back of the room to assist her. Together they lower a large screen, and the jurors lean forward in anticipation. Once it is in place, the clerk returns to her seat, readying herself for the judge's signal once again.

'Members of the jury,' Hawthorne says, 'before we commence the footage, I will utter a word of warning. What you will see now is footage from the body-worn cameras of the first officers at the scene of the offence in question. As you know from the detail of the charge against Mr Joseph and from what was said by Mr Joseph himself in the phone call, what you are about to see is graphic. I understand that for some of you, watching this footage will be very difficult, but I urge you to give it your careful and considered attention.' He pushes his glasses from the edge of his nose firmly on to his face and narrows his eyes at the screen. 'Thank you, Madam Clerk.'

The screen comes to life and I brace myself. No matter how many times I watch this, scouring the footage for details, scrutinizing it for anything the prosecution might point out and say *Gotcha!*, the uneasy turn of my stomach never stops.

A gasp comes from the jury box as the front door opens and Frank appears. Whilst the phone call might have given them some sense of what the scene might look like, only the darkest of imaginations could have foreseen the image of Frank as he opened the door.

My eyes are pulled like a magnet to Frank where he is sitting now in the dock. His eyes are squeezed shut, his fists curled tightly into balls and pressed against his ears. But the jurors are watching, some with their mouths hanging open, others with hands clamped to cover their noses and mouths as though in prayer. A woman at the back is crying silently. I've seen those tears before. They are tears that simply can't be stopped. Tears of trauma – a complete and utter shock to the system. Tears of seeing something that can never be unseen.

'Mr Mason-Hall, any cross-examination?' the judge says as Golding takes a seat.

After the body-worn footage ended, the camera cutting abruptly as Frank was placed in handcuffs, the officer went on to introduce photographs of the scene into evidence. The kitchen, the bedroom upstairs, the holdall in the hallway. For now those exhibits will simply sit there, biding their time until a witness attempts to shed some light on their importance. The neighbour. Linda's sister. Frank.

I stand, lifting my notebook and placing it on the lectern. 'Yes, My Lord.'

I reach for the glass of water beside me and sip, using the momentary pause to look over the rim at the jury, gauging their mood, their reactions.

The footage will have shocked them. Some may be on his side – others won't be able to shake the image of him covered in her blood, her lifeless body on the kitchen floor. I don't want to push him or ask too many questions. We don't want to look too defensive, not yet. Not when what is on the table is a call and footage which can't be altered. 'Mr Noakes, thank you for your time and for being here today,' I say, offering him a respectful nod. 'I won't be taking up too much more of your time – I have just a few questions for you.'

He nods in return. 'Of course.'

'As you said, you've been a police officer for twenty-two years.'

'Yes, that's correct.'

'In approximately how many cases have you been the Senior Investigating Officer or a key investigator for a murder offence?'

He frowns, lifting his chin to look up at the ceiling. 'Um . . . I'd say between fifteen and twenty. Somewhere around there.'

'So you have significant experience in this field?'

He nods. 'Yes. And in policing in general.'

'In your experience, when victims or close family

members of victims report a crime, would you say that it is commonplace for them to be panicked?'

'Yes, of course. Everyone reacts differently to the experience, but of course there's panic there.'

'It would be fair to say that they aren't always thinking about every action they take or word they say as clearly as they would be if they were not in that scenario?'

'Yes, that's fair.'

Okay . . . we're nearly there. I've just got to land the point.

'So it would be fair to state that there is nothing to be inferred by Mr Joseph asking for the police rather than an ambulance when asked which service he required?'

Noakes pauses, glancing to Frank and then back at me again.

Come on, Noakes. Play fairly now.

'There could be an inference there –'

'In your experience, do people often ask for the police in response to an emergency scenario? Especially where a loved one has been injured or passed away?'

He sighs, almost imperceptibly. 'Yes, that is common.'

'Thank you, Mr Noakes.' I turn to the judge. 'No further questions, My Lord.'

'Are you sure you're okay?'

Frank doesn't look at me but instead continues to stare at the floor of the cell, unblinking. He clears his throat. 'Yeah . . . um . . . I'm okay.' He licks his lips and then raises a clenched fist to rub his eyes. 'I didn't watch it.'

'I know, but it can't be easy.'

He finally lifts his chin to meet my eye. 'I've imagined that moment so many times. And her . . . what she looked like lying there. But I just couldn't watch it knowing that they were also watching it. They were seeing it for the first time, but they will never feel what I felt when it happened. They'll never understand. To them it's just a piece of the puzzle they've been tasked with solving.'

'Trust me, Frank. They're human. It will have affected them.'

'Yes, because of Linda. But not because of me.'

I narrow my eyes. 'What do you mean?'

He sighs, blinking rapidly as though trying to discover the right words. 'I mean it will affect them because of how they'll feel towards that image of Linda. The violence, the blood, the horror of seeing someone like that. But when it comes to me . . . will they really be thinking of how I felt? Or will they just be trying to figure out whether it points to me being guilty?'

'I'm sure that anyone who has ever loved someone couldn't help but put themselves in your shoes at that moment. I think the evidence today . . . while it's the prosecution case, it only helps you. The 999 call, the footage at the scene – anyone can see how distressed you were. How much you were trying to help her.'

He nods. 'Maybe. Um . . . Harry?'

'Yes?'

'Could you do me a favour?'

'Sure.'

'Do you mind going to my house one day and getting me another suit? I can't wear this for the whole trial, and the laundry at the prison takes forever –'

'Frank, we should really ask your solicitors to do that.'

'Oh, once we get hold of them they'll say it's too late.'

'Then I can get an officer to go –'

'Are you joking?' He stares at me, shaking his head, aghast. 'No, no – I only trust you. Please.'

I take in his face, heavy with exhaustion, his slumped shoulders, almost defeated. I sigh. 'Okay. Just this once, though. And I can't go tonight, it'll have to be another day.'

'Tomorrow?'

'Maybe the day after.'

'Okay. Thank you so much.'

'How do I get in?'

'There's a key box by the front door. The code is 890427.'

'890427.' I retrieve my phone from my pocket, repeating the number in my head as I open my notes app. '890427 . . . Okay.'

'Thank you.'

'Is there anything else you want to ask me?'

'No . . . I guess I'll just see you in the morning.'

I stand and nod, pulling on my coat over my suit. 'Yep. See you tomorrow.'

I make my way out through the Old Bailey, and as the distance between myself and Court One increases, my mind begins to drift away, finding its path back to Piera and that text message. Why did she lie to me? But every so often, what Frank said echoes in my mind. Did the jurors truly see him? Or were they consumed by the image of Linda, her tragedy in a vacuum all of its own? What if they were so busy focusing on the victim that they failed to see what I saw? Frank kneeling beside her, desperately pressing an already blood-drenched towel to her neck, his face wet with tears and wracked with anguish.

8

'I'm going to bed . . . Are you coming?'

I look over my shoulder to the open door. Piera is watching me expectantly.

'Um . . . I think tonight has to be a late one, I'm sorry,' I say. 'The prosecution have switched the order of the witnesses –'

'Who are they calling next?'

'Eve Thompson, the victim's sister. They were meant to just be reading her statement but now they're calling her –'

She frowns. 'Oh. That's not good.'

I shake my head. She's right. It isn't good – Linda's sister's evidence was meant to be uncontroversial, but if the prosecution are calling her now . . . I just need to make sure it doesn't panic Frank.

'So I need to make sure I'm ready.'

'Of course.' She leans down, pressing her lips against mine. I hesitate as Rachel's message appears in my mind again.

She pulls away, her eyes tinged with concern. 'Is something wrong?'

I should speak to her about it now. I should just ask

her. There is something wrong, I know there is . . . But I can't bring myself to do it. Not now.

'No,' I mutter. 'Everything's fine. Just trial stress, you know.'

She smiles softly. 'I know. At least, I used to know all about it . . .'

I wince, her words stinging.

'Piera –'

'I'll see you in the morning.' She backs away, turning to head down the corridor towards our bedroom. She steps inside and closes the door.

Is that why she's been acting strangely? Is she worried about returning to work? Or does she resent me?

But neither possibility explains Rachel's message.

They don't explain the lie.

'What do you mean, they're calling her?' Frank demands. 'It was meant to be Geraldine first –'

'Yes,' I say, imbuing my voice with a firm calmness as I sit down on the bench in his cell. 'Your neighbour was going to be called first and she's here – we'll probably reach her this afternoon. But the Crown have decided to call your sister-in-law first.'

'I still don't understand why they're calling her at all. She's on my side –'

'Frank, I know you're frustrated, but I've explained to you before – witnesses do not *belong* to anyone. To either side. The Crown are just as entitled to call her if they think she has evidence of value for their case.

I will cross-examine her if she says anything that goes against your defence, but that isn't going to happen. Like you said, her statement supports your story.'

'But why have they decided to call her instead of reading out her statement? It makes no sense.'

'They probably want the jury to see her, so they have a face to tie Linda to. A victim –'

'*I* am a victim!'

His fists clench, his face brimming with barely suppressed anger.

'I know you are. But for now, in this case, you're the defendant.' I place my hand on his shoulder. 'It will be over quickly, I promise.'

'The Crown calls Ms Eve Thompson.'

The clerk nods at the usher, who has been sitting in the back corner of the courtroom, and he quickly disappears through the double doors which lead out into the back rooms where the witnesses will be waiting.

A low buzz runs through the room at the prospect of the first civilian witness taking the stand – and none other than the victim's sister.

The door opens, and I turn my head. The usher strides forward, cutting a path around the dock towards the stand, and a petite woman with greying blonde hair trails behind him, her eyes darting nervously around the room, her hands wringing together. But then, as though she can't help it, her gaze is drawn up to Frank. And for a brief moment, their eyes meet. Is this the first time they've seen each other since Linda's death? Or perhaps she has visited him. He said they were close while he and Linda were married. Friends. But her sister is dead. And Frank is being blamed. Does she truly believe him? Can she? There's a reason the Crown have decided to call her first. It will allow them to try to pre-empt us from using her in Frank's defence. They can ask her questions that will seem innocent enough to the jury, but in truth will help lay the groundwork against him. Brick by brick they will build their wall.

Her eyes fall to the floor and Frank does the same, clearing his throat softly, but it is picked up by the microphone and echoes faintly through the speakers.

She steps up into the dock, her legs visibly shaking. 'G-good morning,' she says quietly, peering sideways up to the judge.

'Good morning, Ms Thompson,' Hawthorne responds, nodding at her with a kind, gentle smile. 'Thank you so much for appearing here today and for your patience in waiting to be called. I understand that this is a difficult time, and on behalf of the court, I extend to you our sincere thanks.'

'Y-you're welcome.'

The clerk stands, moving along her bench until she is close to the dock. 'Do you wish to swear an oath on a holy book or make an affirmation?'

'Uh . . . oath, please.'

'On which holy book?'

'The bible.'

The clerk swiftly pulls out a laminated card and places it on top of a weathered black leather bible, before handing both to her. Eve holds them in one shaking hand, the other lifting to clutch a small cross that hangs around her neck.

'I swear by Almighty God that the evidence I shall give will be the truth, the whole truth and nothing but the truth.'

The clerk retrieves the bible and the oath card and returns to her chair. Hawthorne leans forward, his glasses lowered.

'There is a jug and water there on the stand,' he says. 'Please feel free to help yourself should you need it. And whilst it will be Ms Golding for the Crown and Mr Mason-Hall for the defence asking you questions today – and me, if I see fit – please direct your responses towards the jury. It is important that they hear and understand your answers.'

'I understand.' She nods vigorously, blinking rapidly.

The judge lifts his chin towards the prosecutor. 'Ms Golding.'

Golding stands once again, but before she begins she reaches for her glass and takes a sip of water. Eve reaches down and does the same.

'Ms Thompson,' Golding says gently, 'thank you once again for attending today. I will keep you no longer than is necessary. My name is Laura Golding and I appear on behalf of the Crown in this case. My honourable friend, Mr Harry Mason-Hall,' she gestures towards me, 'appears on behalf of Mr Joseph. I will ask you questions first and then, once I have concluded, Mr Mason-Hall may have some further questions for you.'

Golding pauses, but Eve does not respond. She simply waits, the glass of water in her hands, the surface trembling. Like that moment in *Jurassic Park* – a moment of foreboding, a sign of dangers to come.

'Could you please state your name for the court.'

'My name is Eve Thompson.'

'And Ms Thompson, it is correct that the defendant in this case, Frank Joseph, was your brother-in-law?'

She nods, her chin dimpling as she presses her lips together. 'Yes. He was married to my sister.'

'Your younger sister, Linda Joseph?'

'Yes, she's three years younger than me.'

'What was your relationship like with your sister?'

Eve drops her head, her fine fringe fluttering as she attempts to take several calming breaths.

'Take your time, Eve,' Golding says. 'We're in no rush.'

I glance over at the jury. They are all leaning in, some of them perched on the edges of their seats. Waiting. Ready for her to speak. This is why the prosecution have called her. She may not have anything bad to say about Frank – she may not say anything that will actually be of use, anything that couldn't have just been read from her statement – but her grief, visible and immediate, has drawn them in.

She lifts the glass to her lips again and gulps. Placing

it down, she grips the edge of the dock, her fingertips turning white with the pressure.

'My sister and I were very close. We always have been. Growing up, we were best friends, even when we reached teenager age and had separate friends. She was someone I could go to for anything. And she knew she could do the same. But life happens.'

'When you say life happens, what do you mean?'

'I mean, I went to university and she was still at home. And then when I finished and moved back home briefly before finding my own place in London, she left for university. By the time she finished, I was married and living with my husband. And she moved in with Frank. I had kids. You know . . . life happens.'

'Did you remain as close as you were when you were children and teenagers?'

'We were still very close. But it's never the same as when you are children, living in the same house.'

'How about your relationship with Frank?'

She falls still, blinking. 'My relationship with Frank?'

'When did you first meet him?'

'I first met Frank when he and Linda were in their first year of university together. I visited her for a weekend in the November of that first year.'

'What kind of relationship were Frank and Linda in when you first met him?'

'They weren't in a relationship. They were just friends. I actually believe he was with someone else at the time, one of Linda's friends.'

I glance at the dock. Frank is staring at me, his eyes dark.

'When did Frank and Linda begin their relationship?'

'The second year of university.'

'How long were Frank and Linda together before they got married?'

'Five years,' Eve answers.

'And they were married for ten years, correct?'

'Yes . . . they had their ten-year anniversary not long before she passed away. They . . . they went out for dinner. She said they had a nice time.'

'And how would you describe their marriage as someone close to them?'

She licks her lips, taking a shaky breath through her nose, her nostrils flaring. 'Like any marriage, it had its issues. But Linda really loved Frank.'

'When you say they had issues, what do you mean?'

'Linda could be . . . ever since university, she had struggled with her mental health. Every so often she would suffer with really bad bouts of depression. And that placed a strain on their relationship.'

'Where did that strain come from?'

She blinks rapidly. 'I'm sorry, I don't understand the question –'

'Rephrase your question, Ms Golding,' Hawthorne says. 'Or move on.'

'You have said the relationship was strained because of your sister's mental health. Was the strain caused by her behaviour or something else?'

Eve glances over at Frank, her eyes shining in the light before she lowers them, away from him. 'Frank . . . Frank didn't always know how to handle it.'

'How did he handle her depression?'

'He tried . . . I really believe that he tried. We all did. But it was hard. We just didn't know what to do a lot of the time when she was that low. I tried to help as much as I could, but that day —' She gasps and clamps her hand over her mouth, her eyes filling with tears.

'Please take your time, Ms Thompson,' Golding says.

I turn my head to assess the jury. They are on tenterhooks, avidly watching as this woman, this stranger, lays bare her grief before them, as though she is being cut open, her insides exposed to the world.

Eve lets out a shaky breath, her face still wet with tears. She doesn't attempt to wipe them away. '. . . That day I couldn't be there. Maybe if I could have been, I could have stopped what happened.'

'What caused Linda's depression? Was there a particular event or trigger?'

'Recently she had been suffering because she wanted to become a mum. Her and Frank had . . . they'd struggled to become pregnant and then she had a miscarriage. About a year before . . . this all happened. She couldn't cope with the loss.'

'And prior to the issues with becoming pregnant — was there anything else that ever caused her to have a depressive episode?'

'It began at university. In her first year, Linda and

Frank lost one of their closest friends. He was only nineteen.'

'How did he die?'

Eve lowers her head. 'He committed suicide. Linda struggled with it for years. Even in more recent times, she used to speak about him when the anniversary was approaching. And it was like she would . . . shrink.'

Golding nods, her face in a forced expression of understanding. Can the jury see through the feigned expressions? Or are they taken in all the same by the drama, the smooth and eloquent lines of questioning?

'Let's move to the day in question. Had you spoken to Frank or Linda that day?'

Eve clears her throat and reaches for the glass, but then pulls her hand away, changing her mind. 'Frank had called me, asking me to come over to watch Linda. He said that he had to go to the office, that he couldn't get out of it. But he was worried about her and didn't want to leave her on her own.'

'And what did you tell him?'

'I told him that I couldn't. It was my son's first day of school and I had to go in for a settling-in session after they had lunch. I wanted to help Frank, of course I did, but . . . I didn't want to let my boy down. I didn't want him to wonder why I hadn't come.'

'How did Frank sound to you?'

'He sounded desperate.'

'When was the next time you heard from Frank that day?'

'I didn't hear from him again. The next I heard –'
She stops speaking abruptly, her words cutting off
mid-breath.

'Ms Thompson?' Hawthorne says, craning his neck
over his bench, angling his body towards her. He peers
over at our bench. 'Ms Golding, maybe this is a good
time for a break?'

'No!' Eve says, her exclamation echoing out of the
speakers. She blinks up at the judge, her face pale. 'I . . .
I'm sorry. I'd rather go on for now, if that's okay.'

'Of course.'

Eve's gaze darts from the prosecutor to the jury and
then, just momentarily, to Frank. 'The next thing that
happened was the police came to the door. An officer
was there and . . . they told me that Linda was dead.'

'What else did they tell you at that time?'

'They told me that Frank had been arrested.' She
looks over at him again, but this time she does not look
away. Instead, she holds his eye, unwavering. 'They told
me that he was in the house when it happened and was
being investigated for murder.'

'How did you react when they told you that?'

'That my sister was dead? I –'

'My apologies, no. How did you react when they told
you that Frank had been arrested?'

'I . . . I didn't know what to think. I don't even
think I thought anything. You think you can imagine
how it would feel if you lost someone you loved in
that kind of way. To such violence. How you would

react. But really, when something like that happens to you, your mind does everything it can to protect you. It shuts down. Like a computer overloaded with too much data. So, I felt . . . I felt nothing. It was as though everything had switched off. It wasn't until later that it all hit me.'

'When it hit you – and you understood that the evidence was showing that Frank had been there when it happened – what did you think?'

'I don't know what you want me to say.'

The corners of my mouth tingle with the urge to smile or to frown, I'm not sure which. Golding is trying to edge Eve towards condemning Frank. So far, she is resisting. But will she continue to do so? Or will she turn on him?

'What were you thinking and feeling when you found out that your brother-in-law was being investigated for the murder of your sister?'

I glance once again at the jury.

'I was horrified. I mean . . . wouldn't you be?'

'Did you believe that Mr Joseph was capable of doing what he had been accused of?'

I rise quickly to my feet. 'My Lord, what Miss Thompson believes is not relevant to the question of whether Mr Joseph is guilty of this offence –'

Golding glares at me. 'It's relevant as to his character and whether those close to him, those who knew their marriage and knew their recent history, could believe he would commit such an offence.'

'Move on, Miss Golding,' Hawthorne says with a wave of his hand.

'We've had evidence introduced by the Senior Investigating Officer in this case by way of exhibits of the scene – your sister and Mr Joseph's house. The bundle is to your right, Miss Thompson. If you could go to Folder A.' Golding gestures towards the set of large folders containing the countless documents and photographs that make up the evidence in this case. She gestures at the jury to do the same. Eve tugs the folder out of its place and sets it down on the dock in front of her with a heavy thud. 'If you could turn to Tab C, page one, please,' Golding instructs.

Eve and the jurors open the folders and flip to the correct page, the sound of pages turning filling the silence.

'Can you please describe what you see in this photograph?'

'It's a leather holdall.'

'Do you recognize this bag?'

Eve narrows her eyes. 'Yes, I believe this is . . . was . . . Linda's bag. She used to use it for weekends away, that kind of thing.'

'And can you tell from the photograph where the holdall is?'

She blinks slowly. 'It looks like it's in the middle of the hallway.'

'Was your sister planning on going somewhere that day?'

My breath catches in my throat, my pen pressing into the page.

Eve's eyes skitter over to Frank but glaze over quickly. 'Not that I'm aware of.'

I hold back a sigh. Frank's case was that he was going to take Linda to her sister's house, for her to stay there for a few days to try to distract her. To try to lift her out of her depression.

'You previously said that Frank called to ask you to come to their house to look after Linda. But you didn't communicate with him again that day. That's correct?'

'Yes. I didn't speak to him again.'

'Where do you think your sister was planning on going?'

'My Lord,' I say, standing again. 'There is no relevance on where Miss Thompson *thinks* her sister might have been going. There is no evidentiary value to her guessing.'

Hawthorne nods. Golding grits her teeth. She leans forward and reaches for her drink, taking gentle sips. Biding her time.

'Miss Thompson, can you remember the last time you spoke to your sister?'

'She called me not long before she died.'

'If we turn to page thirty of the bundle, there are the call logs from both the phones of Linda and Francis Joseph. On page thirty, there is a highlighted phone call. Is that your number?'

'Yes, it is.'

'And as we can see, the phone call only lasted a few seconds.'

'Yes.'

'What was said on that call, if anything?'

'She was saying something but I couldn't hear her. So I . . .' She hangs her head, a tear falling on to the dock. 'I ended the call then tried to call back, but she didn't answer.'

'Before this call, can you remember the last time you spoke to your sister or saw her in person?'

Eve sniffs. 'Yes, I can.'

'When was that?'

'About five days before she died.'

'And how did she seem?'

'She had been depressed. So she seemed . . . out of it.'

'Was this normal behaviour when she was depressed?'

'Yes, absolutely.'

'Symptoms of being distant, reserved?'

'Yes.'

'Any other behaviours?'

'No, not really. Sometimes a bit strange. But mostly just a very sad woman.'

'Strange how?'

'As though her thoughts weren't clear. She described it once as feeling foggy. That last time I saw her, she was really quiet, not speaking much. And then she said, out of nowhere, "Did you get my last letter?" We used to write letters to each other, we had done since we were children. We used to leave them under each other's pillows or hidden somewhere in the room. And when we moved away from each other, the letter writing continued. Even though we used to see each other, the letters felt special. But she hadn't written one in a long time.'

'When was the last time you received a letter?'

'It must have been at least six months before she died.'

'What did you tell her, when she asked about a letter?'

'I told her she hadn't sent me a letter. I asked her what it said, but . . .'

'But?'

'She just went quiet again.'

Golding pauses. She turns back to the officer behind her and leans towards him, muttering something so low it cannot be heard, not even by me. He nods and notes something down.

'Did your sister used to talk to you about her depression?'

I tilt my head up towards the ceiling. Golding is going in for the attack now. Straight to the very heart of the defence: is this a woman who could kill herself? And is this a woman who could kill herself so violently?

'Only when she wasn't actually in it,' Eve says. 'Once she was out the other side she would speak quite openly.'

'And what did she say to you?'

'She said it felt like being in a deep, dark hole.'

'Did she believe she could get out of the deep, dark hole?'

126

Eve narrows her eyes. 'Yes, she did. That's why she was never hospitalized. She said she tried to think of all the good in her life. She knew she had a life worth living.'

'And –'

'My sister never spoke to me about hurting herself. Never. Not once.'

Eve turns away from the jury, her entire body rotating until she is facing Frank. 'I've tried to treat him like a brother. I've always been there when he – when they – needed me. But my sister never wanted to hurt herself. She wasn't suicidal.'

Golding nods, decisively. 'I have no further questions, My Lord.'

'Thank you Miss Golding.' His head turns, his eyes darting to the large clock hanging on the wall to his left. 'I think now is a good time for a short break. We will be back to continue the evidence of Miss Thompson in fifteen or so minutes, at midday.'

'Court rise,' the clerk calls out.

We stand and Hawthorne rises and exits swiftly. He'll return to his chambers and have a cup of coffee waiting for him. The jury are led out of the room – they will be taken along the corridors to the jury room, which is for now a space for them to take their breaks but will eventually become the place where their deliberations take place.

I remain standing as some of the courtroom retake their seats, others leaving for a comfort break or to stretch their legs. Golding has turned around to whisper closely with the Investigating Officer. I need to check on Frank, but my mind is full of questions and I scramble to scribble them down, my eyes flashing back and forth between my notes on Eve's evidence and my list of questions, readying myself for the coming cross-examination.

'Harry,' says a disembodied whisper from the speakers.

My head snaps towards the dock. Frank is staring at me, and gestures insistently.

I stand and slide awkwardly out from behind the bench and head towards the dock. I reach a gap in the glass.

'How you feeling, Frank?'

His face is pale, but there is a flush in his cheeks. 'She made out like all that was wrong with Linda was that she used to get a bit sad or something. You ask her – she knows how many times I tried to take Linda to the hospital. She knows that this was more than just being sad.'

'Don't worry – I know.'

'She just . . . she said it so definitively. "*My sister never wanted to hurt herself.*" What does she know? She wasn't there every day. She didn't see –'

'Okay, try to calm down, Frank. People are still watching you, remember.'

He lets out a long, rattling breath, rubbing his fore-head. 'I'm sorry. I just . . . I didn't think she would turn on me.'

'She didn't. She didn't say she thinks you killed Linda –'

'She directly implied that Linda wouldn't have done this to herself. What other assumption are the jury going to come to?'

'Everything she said is just her thoughts, her beliefs. And the jury cannot deal in emotions and beliefs. They have to deal in evidence. She doesn't have any. So just keep your cool. Don't let them see your concern.'

He sets an elbow on the panel of wood in front of him and rests his chin on his hand, his face inches from the glass. 'I understand.'

'Frank, just one question. These letters Eve was talking about . . . Did you ever see any? Could there be anything in there that's useful? I noticed the officer noting something down when they were mentioned.'

He shakes his head. 'No. It was just their sisterly thing. Gossip and stories and recollecting memories. All very nostalgic. But Linda hadn't written one for months.'

'Okay. I'll check with the prosecutor – see if there's anything disclosable.' I place my hand on the glass and tap it gently. 'I'm going to go back to my place. I'll speak to you very soon.'

I move quickly back to the bench, but before I sit down I reach across and grab the edge of the lectern. Golding pushes it towards me with a juddering scrape across the hundreds-years-old wood.

'Thanks, Laura,' I say.

'You're welcome,' she says back, her voice clipped.

I pick up my pen and begin making notes, my hand moving faster and faster with each passing word, my mind frantically trying to process the notes I made during Golding's questions to ensure I do not miss anything. The clock ticks, and with each passing minute, I envision myself standing, asking Eve questions, pushing her, but not too far, not to breaking point. As many times as I have done this, cross-examining a witness who is a family member or a victim always sets my nerves on edge. Anxiety setting off small bursts of nausea in my stomach, my chest crackling with energy.

One knock, followed by two.

'Court rise,' the clerk calls.

We stand once again in unison as Hawthorne returns to his seat. 'Thank you, Madam Clerk,' he says. 'Please bring in the jury.'

Within a few seconds, the door opens and the jury file in, the system working unusually like clockwork. They sort into their places, rearranging themselves into the right order to get into their correct seats. Soon enough this will become second nature: like school-children, they will take their place in line without even thinking about it.

Hawthorne retrieves his glasses and places them carefully on his face, then cracks his thumb in his fist briefly before picking up his pen and poising it above a fresh page, ready.

'Mr Mason-Hall.'

I stand, directing my gaze towards the jury, attempting

to meet each of their eyes in turn as I sweep over them before landing on Eve.

Okay. I inhale deeply through my nose. It is time.

'Good morning, Miss Thompson,' I say, lowering my head to her respectfully, then lifting my chin to meet her gaze. Kind but firm. She is a victim. She has lost her sister in one of the most horrifying ways imaginable. But she is also a witness. A witness who is claiming that Linda Joseph would never have hurt herself to escape her depression. So a certain level of challenge is required, even if I do not relish it. And it must be balanced, if not simply out of fairness to her, but for appearances. A defence barrister badgering the grieving sister of a woman who was theoretically murdered by her husband will do Frank no favours.

'Morning,' she responds, hesitantly.

'As Miss Golding set out earlier, I am Harry Mason-Hall and I am representing Mr Joseph. I have a few further questions for you, but I'll endeavour to not take up too much more of your time.'

'Okay,' she says, her eyes full of trepidation.

'You have said that on the day in question, Mr Joseph had asked you to come to the house he shared with your sister.'

'Yes, that's correct.'

'And he asked you to do that because he had to go to work and she had been suffering with a depressive episode?'

'Yes.'

'But Mr Joseph did not want to leave her alone.'

'Yes, that's right . . . But like I said, I had something I didn't want to miss.'

'Had Mr Joseph asked you to do that before?'

She frowns, her eyes flitting over to the prosecutor. 'Do what, sorry?'

'Had Frank asked you to come to their house to be with Linda?'

'Yes, he had.'

'Regularly?'

'Um . . . I don't know what you mean by regular.'

'Well, is it something that Frank asked you to do during these episodes?'

She picks up her water and takes a small sip. 'Yes, he had asked me a number of times.'

'And how many times had you gone? Let's take the most recent episode, for example.'

'Twice, I think . . . Maybe three times. Frank had been looking after her, he'd been staying at home, so sometimes he'd been there. But he just thought it would be good for her to have my company.'

'But your understanding was that Frank did not want to leave Linda alone.'

'Yes, that's right.'

I pick up the folder that is open on the table to my right, and place it on the lectern. I glance over to the jury and their eyes have automatically followed my lead, their attention drawn once again to the picture of Linda's packed bag.

'We've seen in the bundle that there was a holdall containing Linda's belongings.'

'Yes.'

'In the past, has Frank ever brought Linda to your house for her to stay with you?'

'A-a couple of times.'

'Could you tell us a bit about those times?'

'Um, once he had to go to New York for work. Instead of leaving her on her own, he brought her to me. She said that she was okay on her own, but we both said that it would be better for her to stay with me – I tried to play it off as though I wanted her to keep *me* company.'

'Why did you do that?'

'Well . . . she didn't think it was that bad. And I didn't want her to think I was judging her or trying to protect her.'

'Is it fair to say that she was fragile? You had to handle her with care?'

Her face drops, her lips parting slightly. 'Not all the time. Most of the time Linda was happy and strong. But during her depression . . . Yes, I suppose that's fair.'

'And the other time or times she came to stay with you?'

'This was a couple of months before she died. Frank called and said that he was outside. He asked if Linda could stay with us for a few days.'

'Was he going away?'

'No – he told me Linda was struggling at home and he needed help.'

'It's fair to say that Frank was good at asking you for help when he or Linda needed it?'

She presses her lips together, hesitating, then replies quietly, 'Yes.'

'You said in your evidence that you don't know why Linda's bag was packed that day.'

'Yes, that's correct.'

'But as you've just said, there were times in the past when Frank brought her to your house without forward planning. Spontaneously.'

'Um, yes –'

'So it is possible that Linda's belongings were packed so that Frank could bring her to stay with you?'

'I don't think –'

'Is it possible?'

She stares at me. 'Yes. It's possible.'

'And it's also true the reason behind Frank asking you to come over to their home or bringing Linda to you is he didn't want her to be left alone.'

'Well . . . yes.'

'He was worried for her safety if she were to be left alone.'

'I . . . I don't know what he was thinking.'

'Miss Thompson, were you made aware that Frank took Linda to hospital on a number of occasions?'

She brings her hand to her chest. 'Yes – I don't know how many times, though.'

'And you're aware that Frank had taken her as he was worried for her safety. He was concerned that he could not take care of her or stop her from hurting herself.'

'That's what he said, but like I said before, Linda never wanted to hurt herself. She was never sectioned and she told me that the doctors all said she was fine.'

'And yet you were so concerned about your sister's safety that you would look after her when Frank couldn't?'

She turns her head towards the judge, her mouth agape.

'Miss Thompson?' I say, making sure my expression is soft. Open.

Hawthorne leans forwards. 'Miss Thompson, you do need to answer the question.'

She sighs. 'I wanted to try to make her happy, if I could. I didn't want her to be lonely when she was depressed. But that doesn't mean I agree that she wanted to hurt herself.'

I look down at my notes. The next line is just one word, scrawled in capitals: *STATEMENT.* She has gone the very way I predicted, but the next step needs to be taken carefully.

'Miss Thompson, do you have a copy of your statement in front of you?'

'I . . .' She cranes her neck up towards the judge. 'I was told I couldn't look at it while I'm in here.'

'For your examination-in-chief, that is correct, Miss Thompson. But sometimes during this part of questioning it is necessary to refer back to what you said in your statement.'

'Oh.' She looks back at me slowly, her eyes narrowed. 'Yes, I have it here.'

'You have said in evidence today, both in your examination-in-chief and in answering my questions, that your sister would never hurt herself.'

'Yes, and I stand by that.'

'Could you please turn to the third page of your statement, and read the second paragraph down in full.'

The jurors lean forward, some of them arching forward in an attempt to see better, even though they have the best view in the house. Eve turns the pages and her eyes land on the paragraph, her eyes dancing over the words. Her jaw sets and she looks up again at Hawthorne. He nods.

'Um . . . *I have known Frank for fifteen years. He has always done everything he can to look after my sister. He would . . .*' She pauses, sniffing gently, and tears spill from her eyes. She wipes the page with one finger where her tears have wet the paper. '*He would never hurt her.*'

I swallow. Wait.

'Miss Thompson, I know this is difficult but can you please finish the paragraph by reading the last sentence.'

'No, it isn't what I believe.'

'It's what you said at the time of the offence and it is different to what you are saying here now in court, so it is important for the jury to hear.'

'No –'

'Miss Thompson,' Hawthorne says, his voice full of authority. 'You do need to finish the paragraph.'

'It says – *He would never hurt her. I can't believe she thought there was no other way out.*'

'Miss Thompson, when was this statement made?'

'The day after she died. But that's before I had time to process what had happened. It's before I knew everything.'

'You were not in that house when your sister died, were you?'

'No, I wasn't –'

'You did not witness what took place –'

'No, I didn't.'

'But what you do know is that your sister had been suffering from a serious depression.'

'Yes.'

'And Frank had attempted on several occasions to seek medical help for her.'

'Yes, but she didn't need it.'

'And you also accept that Mr Joseph rearranged his life to ensure that Linda wasn't left alone, and if he could not be there, he always made sure that you or another person could be there for her.'

Eve crosses her arms and lowers her eyes, staring at the empty space in front of her rather than defiantly at me. 'Yes, I accept that.'

'So both now and then, when you made that statement, you acknowledge that Mr Joseph did everything he could to look after your sister.'

She juts her chin towards me, her gaze hardened. 'Yes.'

'I have no further –'

'Until he killed her.'

Eve raises an eyebrow at me. I could go on. But I have extracted from her what I needed to, even if she gets to have the last word. If I continue, the jury could be drawn too firmly over to her side; she could be given too much space to embellish on her beliefs, on her changed opinions. No . . . better to stop now when the point I have made is still fresh in their minds.

'I have no further questions, My Lord.'

I sit down, my back clicking as I settle on to the bench. I look down at my lap but Golding is in my periphery. Will she ask more questions? Or leave it be?

'Miss Golding?' Hawthorne says.

Golding clears her throat. 'No re-examination, My Lord.'

'Thank you for your evidence, Miss Thompson,' Hawthorne says, with a small smile in her direction. 'You are now dismissed. You may leave the courtroom, but should you choose to do so, you may return to watch the rest of the trial at any time.'

She nods but doesn't say anything, her lips pressed into a long, thin line. Stepping down from the witness stand, she follows the usher out of the courtroom, her gaze lowered, avoiding everyone's eye as she leaves, never looking back.

'It is nearly twenty to one, so rather than bring in the next witness now, we will adjourn early for lunch and return promptly at two p.m.'

'Court rise,' the clerk calls.

My body moves automatically, without thought, taking me through the process of standing, lowering my head, retrieving my notes and placing them in a pile with my laptop and pen, ready to leave. But I am focused only on Frank. The escorts lead him out of the dock and away to the door that will take him down to the cells.

Did I do enough to defend him?

I lift my chin, attempting to catch his eye before he disappears.

But he doesn't look back.

9

I stifle a wide yawn as the jury enter the courtroom.

Another day. Another witness. Another unrelenting day of questions and answers, the prosecution moving their pieces about the board while I scramble to defend the king. We're on to the police who attended the scene. Then the paramedics. Then the experts: Linda's GP, the coroner's report, the Crown's psychiatrist and a psychologist will all be coming over the next week or so. The mental health practitioners will be difficult. The Crown are saying that whilst she was on antidepressants, she was never unwell enough to be sectioned. Never so unwell that she was suicidal.

I yawn again, my nostrils flaring as I clamp my jaw closed. All that cross-examination to come and I'm already exhausted. I tried to go to bed early when Piera went out, but my mind was racing, grappling with the evidence until eventually my eyes drifted shut. The next thing I knew I was being woken by my alarm and in a rush to get ready. I didn't even get to ask Piera about her night.

That was another reason why I hadn't slept – thinking about when she would be home.

We had been sitting on the sofa, cuddling Rose

between us while I gave Piera the run-down of Eve Thompson's evidence, when her phone rang.

'I've just got to take this,' she said. 'Sam is calling me. Do you mind?'

'Your clerk, Sam?' She nodded. I paused, the hairs on the back of my neck standing up. Is she lying again? Is that really Sam on the phone? 'No, of course not,' I said. Internally scolding myself. 'Go to my office. I'll put Rose to bed.'

'Thanks.'

I stayed on the sofa for a few minutes with Rose, holding her to me as she rested her head on my shoulder, her chubby little arms wrapped around my shoulders. I breathed her in, trying to calm the anxiety that was making my mind spiral – she'd just had a bath and smelt like cotton and bubbles, the way only babies can ever smell. I stood, walking towards the office so that Piera could say a quick goodnight to Rose. Rose babbled loudly as I knocked and then pushed open the door.

Piera paused, smiling as she gestured at her phone. I held Rose's hand and waved it.

'Night night, Mummy,' I mouthed, pushing down the angst that was swelling in my chest. *Who is she talking to?*

'Goodnight,' she mouthed back.

I closed the door then headed upstairs, forcing myself to focus on readying Rose for bed, changing her nappy before putting her into a fresh sleeping bag and into her cot, her muslin beside her. I sat in the chair just beside her and pulled one of her favourite books from the shelf. *Goodnight Moon.* She watched intently as I read, babbling along and smiling. God, I love her.

When I made my way downstairs, Piera was there. 'Is everything okay?' I asked, keeping the nerves from my voice.

'Yeah, actually . . . Um, that was Sam and he said the whole of chambers is going out for a drink this evening for JC's birthday and would I like to join.'

'Ooh, the big Jonathan Chance KC's birthday. That's nice . . . Are you going to go?'

'I think so . . . as long as that's okay with you?'

I stared at her, taking her in. I've looked at her so many times, watched how she moves, and how she speaks, her mannerisms . . . But now – I can't read her. It's as though she's a stranger and I'm trying to understand her all over again.

Her eyes widened – she noticed my pause.

'Of course it's okay,' I said, stepping forward and wrapping my arms around her waist. 'Go and have fun. I'll just get an early night.'

She quickly ran upstairs to change then came to where I was sitting on the sofa and kissed me. 'I love you,' she whispered.

'I love you too,' I said. 'Have a great time.'

'Thanks.'

The door closed behind her and I stared at it. What should have been the quiet peace of the house was suddenly unnerving. All I could think were questions:

where is she going? Who is she seeing? *Is she lying again?*

'Ms Golding, are we ready to call the next witness?' Hawthorne says, interrupting my chaotic thoughts. His voice is croaky. Maybe the exhaustion is getting to him too. Anyone who watches a criminal court case must think it's an easy day's work for a judge, that all they have to do is watch. Oversee. But they are constantly thinking, assessing, applying the law in their minds and intervening where necessary. Making silent decision after decision after decision. Ensuring that they don't miss a detail which would cause an error in their summing-up, or make a mistake which could open the case up to appeal. It must be mentally draining.

'We are, My Lord,' Golding says. 'The Crown calls Police Sergeant Gemma Portland.'

The clerk stands. The jurors ready themselves.

And we begin again.

I park my car and lean forward over the steering wheel, looking out at the leafy skyline of Hampstead Heath. I never come out here. I came once, during Bar school, to a friend's house, and a group of us threw a rugby ball around on the Heath, drinking beers out of cans during the heatwave of exams. But never again. It really is beautiful.

I get out of the car, locking it behind me. Frank's house is just down the road. I scan the houses, each one as beautiful as the next. Red brick, detached, stone driveways. I reach number 10.

Frank's house is still pristine, even after months of him not being here. Is he still paying a gardener? It wouldn't surprise me. And the windows are clean. The brickwork, perfect.

I walk up the driveway and come to a halt outside the glossy navy front door, its brass handle and number ten reflecting in the light. And there, just to the right of the door as Frank said, is a key box.

I pull open the cover and press in the code, not needing to retrieve it from my notes. I've always had a way with numbers – they seem to stick in my head no matter what. And this one is easy to remember for some reason.

890427

I turn the dial and the hatch opens, revealing a set of brass keys. I snatch them up and step towards the front door. Get in, get the suit, get out. I want to get home to Piera and Rose. I want to be with my wife, not picking up a suit for a client like a servant. But in truth, I also don't want to spend more time than I have to in this house.

I turn the key, which sticks slightly, but I jiggle it in the lock until finally it clicks.

The door swings open and I step inside. The footage from the body-worn camera flashes before my eyes: the officer following Frank down this hallway, the glances into the rooms that are now in front of me, him stepping into the kitchen to find Linda's body on the floor. The kitchen that is now almost visible through a set of double doors.

But I don't need to go down there. I don't want to. Instead I head straight for the stairs, taking them two at a time. All the doors are open, so I quickly glance through them. At the front of the house is a bedroom and a family bathroom. And at the back, what looks like the master bedroom and . . . a nursery. My stomach drops as Rose's face shimmers into view. How must it feel to lose a child? And for that loss to then cause you to lose your wife as well? I peer inside. There is a cot, pristinely made, and a chair beside it. Then a changing table, some loose items strewn on top. Some small socks, a tiny babygrow. And one of Linda's hair ties, a silk one, dusky pink. Piera has one just like it. Emotion wells up. I need to show Frank more sympathy. I couldn't imagine losing Piera. Never. And not like that.

I step backwards and pull the door closed then turn quickly towards the bedroom. I cross to the expansive wardrobes, opening and closing the doors, which reveal Linda's dresses and jumpers and shoes, all her belongings that she will never return to, until I find Frank's suits, of which there are many. I retrieve one, dark navy, and grab a spare tie and shirt just in case.

Now I just need to get out of here.

'Honey, I'm home!' I close the door behind me, my forced joyful greeting not allaying my frayed nerves.

But Piera doesn't respond. She isn't in her usual place on the sofa. I step inside the living room and peer across to the kitchen. She isn't there either.

'Piera?' I call out.

'I'm upstairs,' she calls out in a loud whisper.

I set down my bag and then climb the stairs, noticing the sound of running water, and remove my suit jacket, loosening my shirt collar. I push open the bedroom door and Piera is there, undressing.

'Hi,' I say, moving around the bed to kiss her. I always kiss her when we first see each other. Without fail. But she turns her cheek and continues to fiddle with her necklace. I frown. 'Are you okay?' I ask.

'I thought you'd be home earlier today.' She looks round, her eyes hardening. 'Did you go to chambers after court?'

I sit on the edge of the bed beside her, placing my hands on her hips. 'No, actually, I um . . . I had to go to my client's house to pick up a suit.'

She pulls a face. 'Pick up a suit? Seriously?'

'I know, I know . . . I promised him a few days ago when he'd had a bad day in court. I should have told you. I'm sorry.'

She sighs. 'It's okay.' She leans down to kiss me. 'Sorry to be in a mood. It's just Rose kept saying "da-da" over and over and I kept telling her you were coming and then I had to put her to bed without her seeing you, so . . .'

My heart sinks. I hate disappointing Piera. And I hate feeling as though my daughter misses me. 'I really am sorry.'

She nods. 'Anyway . . . how was your day?'

I wrap my arms around her waist and lean forward, resting my head against her stomach. 'It was fine. It was the uniformed officers who were first at the scene. Pretty easy day for us.'

Piera coughs, her fingers tangling in my hair. 'What happened with that letter the victim's sister mentioned? Did the police find anything?'

'No. The police went today and searched the house again. They couldn't find anything. Either she got rid of it or she never wrote it in the first place . . . Anyway . . . we don't need to talk about the case any more today. He's taken up enough time. How was your day? And how was last night? We didn't get a chance to talk properly about the drinks.'

She swallows and unbuttons her jeans, pulling them down to her ankles and then sitting on the edge of the bed to tug the fitted legs over her feet. 'It was really nice, actually. Good to see everyone and to celebrate Michael's birthday –'

My stomach sinks. She didn't say it was Michael's birthday last night.

'Michael's?' I ask. 'I thought it was Jonathan Chance's birthday?'

She frowns, crossing to the corner of the room to toss the jeans into the laundry basket. 'Did I say Jonathan's? Sorry, no, it was Michael's birthday.'

She's lying. Jonathan Chance and Michael are not two men who can be confused.

'Oh . . . How old is he now?'

148

'Fifty something, I think.'

'What, it didn't come up in conversation?'

'Do people actually tell you their age at birthday parties if it isn't the turn of a decade any more?'

I shrug, not responding. I don't know what else to say.

'Is there a problem?' she says, frowning down at me.

I inhale, readying myself for the challenge. I should say something now. But . . . I can't just outright call her a liar. How would we go back from that? 'No, of course not,' I say, hating my weakness. 'So it was a good night?'

'Yeah . . . it was good. And they didn't apply any pressure on me to go back, so that was great too.'

'And uh . . . how was seeing Rachel the other day? I didn't ask.'

My eyes are fixed to her face, checking her features for every micro-expression, for every small sign of a lie.

'It was good. You know Rachel . . . Oh, question, have you seen . . .' She pauses, like her mind has gone blank.

My heart sinks. She's just going to keep on lying. 'Have I seen . . . ?' I mutter, defeated.

'Um, what's the word . . . Rose's Sophie toy? You know, the chewy giraffe?'

'I thought it was on her play-mat? I can check –'

'No, it's okay, maybe I just missed it.' She sighs. 'Right, I'm going to jump in the shower.' With a glint in her eye, she raises an eyebrow. 'Want to join me?'

I force a smile. 'Um, as much as I'd love to, I'm exhausted.'

'Suit yourself . . .' she shrugs coyly and sashays out of the room dramatically.

I laugh, but as soon as she has closed the door, the smile falls away from my face and my eyes are drawn like a magnet to her phone which lies dormant on her bedside table.

I've never looked through Piera's phone. Never. Even after the whole issue with Rachel's text, I still didn't allow myself to cross that line. But . . . she definitely said it was Jonathan's birthday. We repeated it more than once. Maybe that was a mistake.

Or maybe it was a lie.

Maybe she said it was Jonathan's birthday to get out of the house, and today she forgot who she'd said and said Michael's name by accident.

If it was a lie, then who was she talking to on the phone last night?

I dart towards it, tapping on the screen quickly. It lights up, our faces – Me, Piera and Rose – shining out from the screen, our faces beaming. I swipe up to bypass the facial recognition and tap in Rose's birthday. The phone unlocks.

I navigate quickly to her call record, my eyes bypassing a phone call from her mum, one from Rachel lasting over an hour, and a missed 0800 number.

And there, the only call from yesterday evening: a private number.

But she said it was Sam. She has Sam's number, and chambers' number wouldn't be blocked. I scroll back further and there are a number of calls from this private number, including one just an hour ago.

Who has been calling her?

And where has she been going?

10

Two Weeks Later

'I have no further questions.'

I take a seat and meet Frank's eye. He nods, almost imperceptibly, and relief rushes over me. He has been on the stand for the past day and a half and his evidence went as well as could be expected. He presented well, answering my questions calmly and carefully. Showed how much he loved his wife. But the hardest part is coming next. The cross-examination. His defence, which has been established through careful questioning over the past two days, going through the prosecution's evidence and pushing back on their narrative, is about to be examined, picked apart, and potentially torn to bloody pieces.

Golding stands quickly, smoothing down her robe, and meets Frank with her steely gaze. But Hawthorne leans forward. 'I think that now might be a good time to break for lunch before continuing with Mr Joseph's cross-examination.'

Golding's face falls. She won't want to leave the jury with the picture of Frank and what happened that he and I have painted, not even for fifteen minutes, let alone for over an hour. His detailed, emotional evidence will stay with them, seeping into their subconscious. She'll have wanted to dive in straightaway, not allowing any thoughts to take root.

'I agree, My Lord,' I say, nodding sincerely.

Golding resists rolling her eyes. 'I could make a start now, My Lord, and then we could break at one?'

Hawthorne shakes his head. 'I don't think there's any benefit in getting in twenty minutes of cross-examination now and then breaking. Better to start afresh at two p.m.' He stands abruptly, dismissing her with a wave of the hand.

'Court rise,' the clerk calls, and we all stand in unison.

I let out a breath as the jury are led out, and turn nodding to Frank as he is escorted back down to the cells. Not long to go now. Just the cross-examination. The final climb, those last, most precarious moments before reaching the summit. And then the slow descent while we wait.

I pick up my laptop and my notebook and nod at Golding before leaving the room, pushing through the heavy door and then quickly descending the sweeping staircase to head to the robing room. I take off my wig and place it back in its box, then remove my robe. Pushing my hair back, I look at myself in the mirror. I should feel satisfied. Relieved that my part is largely over. But that feeling dissipates very quickly. The reflection that looks back at me now is drained. Empty eyes and sunken cheeks. I have spent the last two weeks consumed by this case and consumed by thoughts of Piera. Thoughts of her lies. Thoughts of her insisting that she isn't hiding a thing. I've wanted to push some more but I haven't been able to. I shake my head at myself, disgusted. *What's going on?* is all I would have to say. *I know that you're lying to me.* But I haven't been able to do it. I have lain next to her, night after night, unable to say the words that are just on the edge of my tongue. Am I really that weak? Am I really that afraid of what she might say?

Yes.

That's the truth. When I look at her, when I look at Rose, at our little family, I'm terrified that if I confront her, something horrifying will come out of her mouth. *I've met someone else. I'm having an affair. I don't love you any more. I'm leaving.* And so I've stayed silent. Ignorant and constantly questioning. But still with her beside me.

My fist curls, my body overtaken by a sudden urge to punch the wooden cupboard containing my coat and bag. But I stop myself. That isn't me. I'm not that person. I've never been the person allowing emotion to overcome them and I won't become one now. Not here in the robing room of the Old Bailey.

But I have to do something.

Once this case is over – once it ends, one way or the other – I will speak to Piera again. I just need some more reassurance. It's Piera. I've never doubted her before. She loves me. I know that she loves me . . . Don't I?

She has to.

I can't lose her.

I *won't* lose her.

Golding stands again and the courtroom, although quiet, seems to fall silent. I look behind me, craning my neck – I can't see the gallery but it is full. It's as though the presence of these people is radiating downwards, their energy so alive. This is what everyone has been waiting for. His examination-in-chief was one thing but the cross is where the drama lies. Prosecution versus defendant. This is where the show begins.

I press my pen into the fresh page of my notebook, readying myself.

'Mr Joseph,' Golding says, her voice low and demanding. 'May I call you Frank?'

Oh Jesus. She's already trying to provoke him. She knows that we refer to the defendants by their second name. He isn't a child. But she wants to test him. To see how easily he might bite back.

I meet his eye, desperately trying to reach him with just a look. Having spent four weeks with him, it's as though I can read his mind; I can already predict what he wants to say. 'If I can call you Laura,' I imagine.

Don't do anything stupid.

'You can if you'd like,' he says. 'But I'd prefer Mr Joseph.'

She nods. 'Very well.' She presses her lips together. 'Mr Joseph, we have all heard the 999 call you made on the day in question and also seen the footage from the body-worn camera. You were very distressed.'

'Yes, of course.' He stares at her. 'My wife had just killed herself right in front of me. I didn't know what to do.'

'You had come home from your meeting and went straight upstairs to see Linda.'

'Yes, that's correct.'

'And you say it was at that point you saw your wife had a number of open pill bottles next to her.'

'Yes, that's right.'

'But we heard from Mrs Geraldine Grey, your neighbour who you asked to check on Linda, who stated that she did not see any pill bottles next to the bed.'

'Geraldine must have not gone all the way into the room. If she just peered inside, she wouldn't have been able to see Linda's side of the bed.'

'If we turn to page fifty-four of the bundle behind Tab C, we can see that there is a clear view of the entire bed, even from the door –'

'Linda used to sleep facing towards the wardrobes, away from the door.' He stares directly at Golding, refusing to open the bundle. 'Maybe if she'd been lying on her back Geraldine could have seen past her to the bedside table and seen all the pills. But all she would have seen was her back.'

'But you heard her say in her evidence that she saw the bedside table and there were no pills there. Are you saying that Mrs Grey is lying?'

'No, not at all. I'm saying that she's mistaken.'

'Mistaken?'

'Remembering incorrectly. It was in the coroner's report that Linda had a huge amount of antidepressants and codeine in her system. And some sleeping medication. That wasn't an error or a mistake. That's fact, isn't it?'

'That is a fact, Mr Joseph, you're correct. But that does not mean that those pills were on the beside table as you allege. Who –'

'Then where did they come from? Thin air?'

She tilts her head, glancing at the jury as she takes a small, feigned sigh. 'You're the one answering questions, Mr Joseph.' She leans her forearms on the lectern. 'Who used to be responsible for giving Linda her medication?'

'I was.'

'Did you keep her medication away from her?'

Oh. I see where this is going. Be careful, Frank.

'I kept it in the kitchen.'

'In a locked cupboard, correct?'

'Yes.'

'If we turn to page fifty-six of the bundle . . . is that the cupboard you're referring to?'

Frank blinks slowly at her then turns his attention towards the bundle. He opens it, and it slams heavily on the dock. He flicks through the pages until finally finding the page. 'Yes, that's it.'

I glance down at the page. There are two photographs.

One of the cupboard as it was found: it is open, the shelves lined with various bottles and pill packets. The other shows the door closed, a padlock fixed to its front. But –

'But as you'll see,' Frank says, stealing the thought from my mind, 'the cupboard is unlocked.'

'Who used to keep the key to this cupboard?'

'I did, of course. Not much point in locking up her medication for her to keep the key.'

'And you kept it with the rest of your keys? As we can see in the photo on page fifty-seven?'

I turn the page. There is a bundle of keys – a car key, a garage fob, a number of house keys, all bundled together – but then a small gold key on its own loop.

'Yes, that's correct. But as I said before, there was a spare.'

'But the spare was hidden from Linda?'

'Of course. She must have found it.'

'Did you realize that she had found it?'

'No, otherwise I would have moved it.'

'So, it just so happened that on a day where you leave Linda alone, she finds the key, accesses the cupboard and takes a substantial amount of medication.'

'Yes. I didn't know where she'd put it, but like I said, the police found it in her cardigan pocket. It's in the bundle.'

Good. Well done, Frank.

'Had she ever managed to get into that cupboard before?'

159

'Not that I'm aware of, no.'

Golding clicks her pen, just once, then strikes something from the page in front of her. Point one ticked off her checklist. 'Mr Joseph, Linda wasn't prescribed codeine, was she?'

'No, she wasn't.'

'She was prescribed antidepressants and sleeping tablets but no painkillers.'

'Yes, that's correct.'

'The codeine was yours, correct?'

'Yes.'

'Why were you prescribed codeine?'

'I injured my back earlier this year. I was given codeine for the pain but I only took one of the packs and then stopped.'

'Why did you stop?'

'Because I know they're addictive. And strong.'

'They can make you extremely drowsy, correct?'

'If you abuse them, yes.'

'Was the codeine kept with the antidepressants?'

'Yes.'

'Is that right?'

Frank narrows his eyes. 'Yes. I think the second box is in the photograph –'

'Yes, that's correct. But there is also a photo on page sixty-seven of the bundle . . .' Golding pauses and waits. Frank turns the pages, his eyes not leaving her, and the jurors follow suit, their fingers scrambling to find the page so she might continue. 'That photograph was taken in your office. The empty pack of codeine you mentioned. All but one pill taken. Why was that pack in your office if you kept the codeine together with her medication?'

Is that a faint flush on Frank's cheek? He still seems calm but his face is beginning to shine, and he shifts his weight from one foot to the other. Keep your cool, Frank.

He clears his throat. 'When I was first prescribed them and was taking them, Linda was okay. She was depressed but not to a level that I was concerned about her safety. Once I was starting to worry that she might hurt herself, I locked them away with the rest.'

'Had she ever asked you for codeine before?'

'No.' Frank shakes his head firmly. 'Never. And I wouldn't have given it to her even if she had.'

Golding reaches forward and grips the glass of water that is balanced precariously on the edge of our bench. The court is so quiet, I can hear her thirsty gulps. And I can imagine her thoughts, the feeling of momentum building, of giving pause but not wanting to lose the pace, or give him time to think.

'Mr Joseph, if you turn to page seventy-two of the bundle –'

The jury turn the pages quickly, the sound like falling rain.

'– you will see photographs of a handgun and bullets inside a safe.'

'Yes, that's correct.'

'That safe is in your office?'

'Yes.'

'Did Linda have access to that safe?'

'She did, yes, but –'

'Would you not agree, Mr Joseph, that committing suicide using a readily available gun would have been a much easier death for your wife than even an overdose?'

'I would agree, yes. But my wife hated guns. I know it's easier, quicker, but I'm sure there are a lot of people who would prefer the idea of taking pills and passing out, never waking again, over having to hold a gun to your head and find the nerve to pull the trigger. She thought that the overdose would work. Clearly.'

'But she had the nerve to slit her own throat?'

Frank flinches, then takes a steadying breath. 'By then I was in the kitchen with her. She knew she couldn't get to the office.'

'She could have tried, no?'

'I would have stopped her. It's at the front of the house, and she'd have to unlock the safe. I would have stopped her.'

'Mr Joseph, you've described coming home from your meeting, and we've seen the brief footage from your doorbell camera of you entering your home at five thirty-three p.m.'

Frank looks up to the ceiling for a moment, disorientated by the classic tactic deployed in cross-examination: a sudden change in direction. 'Yes.'

'And as you said in your evidence, you went up to the

bedroom, found Linda unconscious, made her be sick, that's when she went downstairs, you followed and she then killed herself with the knife.'

'Yes, that's correct.'

'Why didn't you call the police until six seventeen p.m.?'

Frank blinks. 'I don't understand the question.'

'You entered the house at five thirty-three p.m. The police weren't called until six seventeen. Are you telling me that the events you described took forty minutes?'

'Well, it must have because that's what happened.'

'From the way you've described it, I'd estimate that only taking ten minutes. Fifteen at a push – wouldn't you agree?'

'No, I wouldn't. Realizing what was happening, getting her to be sick, trying to stop her from killing herself – it all felt like it was flying, but if it took forty minutes, that's how long it took because I called 999 straightaway!' His voice breaks and he covers his mouth. I bite on the inside of my cheek. This is where she is going to try to break him. This is where she fully sets out the prosecution's vision of what happened behind the closed door of 10 Wheeldon Avenue that late afternoon.

'We heard from the evidence of your sister-in-law that Linda made a phone call to her sister that lasted a few seconds.'

'Yes.'

'Linda made that call at five forty-seven p.m.'

'Yes.'

'What did she say?'

'I didn't see or hear her on the phone. In everything that happened, she didn't actively make a call. It must have been accidental, in the rush. That's why nothing was said.'

'Mr Joseph, can you please turn to page seventy of your bundle?'

Frank sniffs and nods, flipping through the pages slowly as he catches his breath. But as he reaches the page, he gasps – a short, sharp intake of breath.

I glare at Golding and get to my feet. 'My Lord, might I please remind my honourable friend that there are many photographs in this bundle that are graphic and to ask Mr Joseph to turn to a photograph of his wife without forewarning is simply not fair.'

'He has seen all of these photographs before, My Lord –'

'It is a purposeful move to cause him upset and unnerve him as he answers very difficult and emotional questions.'

Hawthorne nods. 'Ms Golding, please, before you ask the defendant and the jurors to turn to a photograph, warn them of the contents of the exhibit.'

'Apologies, My Lord,' she says, nodding at him deferentially. 'Apologies, Mr Joseph, I will make sure to warn you going forward.'

Frank lifts his chin, his face now covered with tears. He nods, but does not engage her with a response.

'As we can see from this photograph, your wife had vomit on her hands when she died.'

Frank slams the bundle shut. 'Yes,' he says, his voice quiet but cold. 'Like I've said, I had to make her sick.'

'But as is clear from the coroner's report, she had vomit under her nails when she was examined, not just on the skin.'

Frank's eyebrows raise. 'And?'

'And that would be an indication that your wife made herself sick. Not you. That's what happened, isn't it?'

'No, that isn't what happened. I made her sick. But when she realized what was happening, she was thrashing around, covering her mouth, scratching at me, hands flying everywhere. That's how it got there. I had vomit on my hands and under my nails too.'

'Mr Joseph, if you could re-open your bundle and turn to page seventy-one, please.' She places her hands on the edge of the lectern. 'I can confirm it is not a photograph of the victim.'

Frank clenches his jaw but does as she says. 'I'm on the right page.'

It's a photograph of the knife. Long and covered in blood, some drying, some still slick and wet.

'Can you remember the last time you used that knife?'

He shakes his head. 'No . . . But I used to use those knives every day. I did all the cooking while Linda was unwell. So, probably earlier that day, or the night before.'

'Do you wash your knives after using them?'

'Yes, of course,' he says. 'But I also put them away.'

Golding pauses – her next question already pre-empted. Frank is not a stupid man. He knows exactly where she is leading him.

'Your fingerprints were all over the knife, weren't they?'

'Yes, like I said. I use them every day. And when I wash them, I have to touch them again to put them away. So of course, yes – my fingerprints were on them.'

'And –'

'And so were Linda's.' Frank pauses. His legal training hasn't worn off, even having never practised – using silence for effect. 'Linda's fingerprints were on the knife too.'

'If you turn the page again, Mr Joseph,' Golding says, moving on quickly, 'there are photographs of you shortly after your arrest.'

'Yes.'

'As you can see from the close-up photography, there are several injuries on you. Firstly, scratches on your left cheek, and the right side of your neck.'

'Yes.'

'Then bruising to your upper chest and the area around your collarbone.'

'Yes.'

'As we've heard from the coroner's report – these are described as defensive injuries. Linda gave you those scratches and bruises as she tried to protect herself from you, didn't she?'

'No –'

'You had been in charge of Linda's medication and decided to murder her by giving her sleeping pills combined with her antidepressants and an excessive amount of your prescription of codeine –'

'That isn't right.'

'You had intended that Mrs Geraldine Grey would find her dead and you would have the alibi of being out of the house –'

'I had a work meeting and had no idea she could get into that cupboard, otherwise I wouldn't have left –'

'But when you returned home, not only was your wife still alive, she had made herself sick –'

'I made her sick.'

'And she was packing a bag, desperately trying to escape before you got home –'

'I packed that bag to take her to her sister's house.'

'She attempted to call her sister, then, in fear, ran downstairs with the bag, but you blocked the door and that's when she dropped the bag in the hallway and ran to the kitchen –'

'No, that's not right.'

'Your wife knew that you were trying to kill her, and as she tried to fight you off, she scratched, and hit, and punched, and did everything she could to get away, didn't she?'

'No –'

'Wouldn't you agree that your injuries in those photos were sustained by a desperate woman who wanted to live?'

'No – my injuries were caused by a suicidal woman, desperate to die.'

For a moment it is as though the court freezes, Frank's statement suspended in time and space, destined to repeat over and over.

'Whilst that's a very believable narrative that you've put together there,' Frank says, his voice gentle and low, 'and it might be more believable than the truth, what it misses out is that my wife was a very sick woman, who had suffered with her mental health for such a long time that she would do anything to have what she wanted. Even if that meant using extreme violence against me and against herself.' He stares defiantly at Golding. 'Linda wanted to die. And she hated me because I wouldn't let her.' His voice breaks, and he wipes his eyes with his fists. 'I tried with everything I had to stop her. And I failed. I couldn't save her.'

My eyes glaze over but I blink rapidly, forcing myself to focus on Hawthorne's voice as he sums up the evidence to the jury, taking them through the law that they must apply to their consideration of everything they have seen and heard throughout the duration of the trial. My mind wants to switch off, to allow it to be over, but if he makes a mistake, I need to correct it. I need to make sure they're being properly instructed. And even with a judge as brilliant as Hawthorne, I can't stop working now. We're so close. So close to the end.

My back is aching, my shoulders curling forwards

over the bench as I take notes. Golding questioned him for almost four hours. Even after his heart-stopping, emotion-fuelled speech, she began again, never letting him go. The pace was unrelenting, even for me. And after that I re-examined for a further hour, making sure he had a final chance to show the jury his side. Frank was on the stand for nearly two days. I look across to him, but I can't see his face. His head is hanging down, his hands clasped together between his knees. He must be exhausted, even more than me. He laid himself bare, refusing to hold back any emotion, defending himself as hard as he could. He did so well.

But now it is down to the jury.

'And finally,' Hawthorne says, looking up from his extensive notes, and removing his glasses, 'it is my duty to implore that, as with the trial, while you are in deliberation you must not discuss the evidence in this case with anyone outside of your twelve. You are the only ones who have heard the evidence, seen every photograph, heard every word uttered by the witnesses and the defendant. No one outside of your twelve has had the insight into the case that you have. Only you can decide whether the prosecution has met the threshold for you to convict the defendant: you must be sure that he committed the murder of Linda Joseph and intended to kill or grievously wound her. If you are anything less than sure, you must acquit. That is your duty. I thank you all for giving over your lives, minds and efforts for the last four weeks.'

He stands, lowering his head towards them.

'Court rise.'

We stand, all watching as the jury file out from their benches and then out of the room. Some of them do not look back, their eyes fixed ahead of them, the relief palpable. Others throw glances at me and Golding, and others stare at Frank, taking a final look at him before leaving to decide the rest of his life.

Frank gazes back at them, his eyes empty. Drained. Nothing left to give. He must feel me watching him because he drags his gaze over to me, and gives me a single, tired nod.

I nod back.

Now, we wait.

11

'Harry?'

I turn to look over my shoulder at Piera, her hair still tousled, Rose balanced on her hip.

'Yeah?'

'Do you think it'll be today?'

I shrug. 'Who knows? Hopefully.'

She nods. 'Okay . . . Well, let me know what happens. And good luck.'

'Thanks. I will.' I step forward, crossing back over the threshold, and kiss her. Her hand touches my chin and I breathe in deeply, all of my still unanswered questions hanging precariously in the space between us. Can she feel them too? Or is she utterly oblivious? Am I really so inscrutable that she doesn't see that there is something wrong? That I don't believe her? Is that her fault? Or mine?

'Bye,' I say with a small smile, then step back out and trot down the steps to the short path before the pavement.

'Love you,' she calls after me.

'And you,' I call back, my heart heavy.

I walk down the path and out towards the car,

shaking my head as I try to tear my thoughts away from the prospect of losing Piera and back to the trial.

The jury have been deliberating for almost five days now. The judge sent a note down after three days saying that they can come to a majority verdict – only eleven of them need agree, rather than a unanimous verdict of all twelve. But still we wait. That isn't a good sign. If they can't decide at all, it'll be a hung jury, and this trial will have to start all over again. A fresh batch of twelve strangers, the evidence recounted all over again, the same questions asked with possibly different answers. My life will rewind five weeks and begin again. Part of it, at least. Some things cannot be erased.

'Thanks, James,' I say to the man from the coffee shop down the street from the court as he hands me a large black coffee. The coffee in court is bitter, and it's impossible to stay in there all day with the endless waiting, not knowing if it will be any minute that we get the nod, or not at all.

'You're welcome, as always,' he says.

I turn to take a seat in the window seat behind me, but as I set my coffee down on the high table, my heart stops.

My phone is vibrating.

'Hello?'

'Mr Mason-Hall, it's Paul, the usher from Court One –'

'Is it in?'

'Yes, Sir.'

'I'm on my way.'

I grab my bag and run straight for the door, the bell ringing as I yank it open.

'Harry, your coffee —'

'I've got to sprint! Don't worry, see you soon,' I shout over my shoulder.

I run up towards the court, just one hundred feet away, my feet pounding on the pavement as I dart through tourists who are loitering on the pavement outside, craning their necks upwards to take photographs of Lady Justice perched on top of the central dome.

'Excuse me,' I say, sliding between two women and then through the doors.

I pass through security as quickly as I can, and then keep running, pushing through the door to the robing room to grab my wig and gown. I tug them on, glancing at myself quickly in the mirror before heading back out and then up the stairs, two at a time, and crossing the vast hall to Court One.

I make my way down to Counsels' bench and Golding greets me with a nod, her face serious and focused.

'Afternoon, Laura,' I say, smiling.

'Afternoon,' she responds with a sigh. 'Hopefully this isn't them saying they can't come to a majority verdict.'

'That had crossed my mind too.'

'What a fucking nightmare that would be.'

I nod, surprised by her sudden lack of formality. 'Yep . . . a fucking nightmare indeed.'

'You ran a great first defence as a KC.'

My eyebrows lift, my cheeks flushing. 'Thank you. That means a lot coming from you.'

'While I hope your man goes down, you did a great job representing him.'

I laugh. 'Thanks.'

She nods kindly.

'You —'

I am interrupted by the signature signal for the judge, one knock, followed by two.

'Court rise.'

I inhale deeply, and Golding and I stand together.

He enters quickly, his robe sweeping behind him, and takes a seat.

'Good afternoon,' he says.

'Good afternoon, My Lord,' we reply in unison.

'Is the defendant on his way up?'

'Yes, My Lord,' the clerk says.

'Very well, as soon as he's in the dock, go ahead and bring them in.'

A creak sounds from the back of the room and I peer over my shoulder. Frank enters, led by two escort officers. He heads towards the dock, his hands hanging limply beside him. Could this be the last time he has to be brought up to the dock? Could he be leaving it a free man?

I raise my hand at him, catching his attention. 'You okay?' I mouth. He seemed fine this morning, but he had entered that false state of ambivalence that many defendants reach where it seems that every day will be just another day of deliberation. Hearing that the jury have come to some type of decision can come as a shock.

He simply nods.

The clerk enters, the jury filing in behind her. I stare at them as they take their usual seats, scanning their faces, trying to read any sign of which way they have gone, or if they have failed to come to a decision at all. But it's impossible, as always, to tell. Predicting a jury's movements is a losing game.

'Good afternoon,' Hawthorne says.

'Good afternoon,' a few of them mutter in return.

The clerk retreats behind her desk but does not sit. 'Mr Joseph, could you please stand?'

Frank rises to his feet, his fingers gripping the edge of the dock.

'Will the foreman please stand?'

The man in the front row, on the end closest to the judge, stands. I grip my pen tightly, my jaw clenching.

'Have you reached a verdict upon which you or a majority of you are all agreed?'

'We have,' he says.

Golding and I throw glances across to each other. A verdict. Not a hung jury after all.

'For the offence of murder, how do you find the defendant?'

The foreman turns his head to stare directly at Frank. Frank closes his eyes. My stomach drops.

'Not guilty.'

My fists clench triumphantly in my lap, but my face remains passive. It isn't for an advocate to outwardly celebrate. This is justice. Not a football match or personal vindication. But satisfaction rings inside my chest as I look across at Frank who is staring about in disbelief, his face awash with relief. They believed him. We did it.

I grab my phone from beside my laptop and hold it beneath the bench, navigating quickly to Piera's name:

Frank = NG.

'Members of the jury,' Hawthorne says, his voice booming through the low murmurs around the court, 'thank you once again for committing yourselves to this service – you will now be escorted out, and are relieved of your duty. Good afternoon.' He turns to focus on Frank. 'Mr Joseph, you have been acquitted. You are now free to go.' He stands.

'Court rise,' the clerk calls, and the court stands again, and we lower our heads for the final time.

It's over.

Frank is free.

*

'Thank you so much for everything,' Frank says, holding out his hand earnestly.

I grip it tightly. 'You're welcome.'

His eyes dart around the unlocked cell, his face full of disbelief. 'I can't believe I get to go home. I haven't been back there since . . . since that day.'

'I know it will be difficult, but take each day as it comes. You're free. It'll be hard to process life without her after everything you've been through. Just take your time.'

He nods, but his eyes are drawn to something behind me and I turn at the sound of quiet footsteps coming to a halt.

An officer is standing there, a bundle of papers outstretched in his hand. 'Frank, these are for you.'

'Thanks.' He takes them, and the officer steps out, waiting to escort him out of the back, avoiding him having to collide with press and jury members. Frank steps towards me and reaches out once again, passing me a small piece of folded paper. 'My number. In case I can ever return the favour.'

'Just doing my job,' I say with a shrug.

'It was nice knowing you, Harry.'

I smile. 'Enjoy the rest of your life.'

'I'll try.'

He steps out of the room, and is gone.

Another case over. My biggest trial yet. And an acquittal.

People always ask me how I defend guilty people.

How do I sleep at night knowing I might defend someone who is guilty? And I tell the same spiel that every barrister knows and understands: every person deserves a defence. Without it the whole system would come collapsing down around us. But with some defendants it feels different. You don't question whether they are telling you the truth when they insist they are innocent. You simply believe them. And Frank is one of those. I believed him. And so did the jury.

But it's the foundations of my belief in someone else I need to secure. Piera. I'm no closer to knowing what is going on with my wife. Nor understanding why she has been lying to me. And now that this trial is over, it's finally time for me to know the truth. I need to know.

I climb up from the cells back to the courtroom to gather all my remaining belongings from the court. It is empty now except for the usher waiting to lock up – Golding has taken her stuff already, the prosecution pile of bundles cleared by the police. This infamous room, which less than an hour ago was teeming with people and tension, is now devoid of anything. An empty space ready to be filled with whoever's tragic story needs to be heard next.

'Thanks, Paul,' I call out to the usher.

I push open the door but pause as his voice calls out behind me.

'Oh Mr Mason-Hall, I'm so sorry, I almost forgot.'

I turn and he is holding something between his fingers. 'This was left in the dock. Must be your client's.'

Frank's prayer beads. Linda's prayer beads. He's been holding them the entire trial, clinging on to them for dear life.

'I'll get them back to him. Thanks, Paul.'

He nods, smiling. 'See you soon.'

I throw a final wave over my shoulder and then head back to the robing room. I place my robe carefully back in its bag and place my wig back in its box, then pull my coat on before pulling out my phone and calling my instructing solicitor. Maybe they can come and sort out Frank's beads.

No answer.

I could post the beads, I suppose.

I call again – no answer.

I pull the folded piece of paper out of my suit pocket, narrowing my eyes to decipher Frank's slanted scrawl before tapping his number into my phone.

But it doesn't ring. Maybe he hasn't turned it on yet.

I glance at the time. It's still quite early. Only 3:30 p.m. Piera won't be expecting me back any time soon. I'll just take them myself. It'll take me an hour, no more.

I leave the courtroom, nodding at familiar faces as I pass them, then clamber into my car, adjusting the rear-view mirror as I pull out.

My phone connects to my car. I scan my notifications for her name but there is nothing. She hasn't messaged back. Disappointment settles in my stomach. She usually would have sent something by now. Congratulations or commiserations, but always almost instantaneously. I tap Piera's name. It rings and rings but she doesn't pick up. She's probably feeding Rose.

I come to a standstill at a set of traffic lights and pull my phone out of its holster, glancing around me quickly to make sure there are no police around. I tap out a message.

Just quickly have something to do and then I'll be home. Should only be an hour. Love you.

I sigh. As long as there isn't traffic, it should only take me twenty minutes or so to get to Hampstead. Drop off his beads or post them through the letterbox, then go home.

All trials take over a barrister's life to some extent. But this one has been different. This one has consumed me, drawing me away from Piera and Rose. I shake my head – that isn't right. It's Piera who has been pulling away from me. But now this is over, I am going to get back to my life. Whatever has been unknowingly broken, I will fix. I have to. Piera is the axis around which my whole world turns. She always has been. So it's time for this to be over.

The end of R v Francis Joseph.

And then on to the next.

I park the car and get out quickly, my eyes fixed on number 10, about two hundred metres down the road on the opposite side. I grab Frank's beads from the central well of the car and climb out, striding quickly down the pavement, keeping an eye on a gap in traffic so I might cross.

I stop at the junction of Wheeldon Avenue and an adjoining street as a car flies past me. I'm about to dart over but something catches my eye. Something so familiar that it makes my stomach turn.

Piera's car.

But that makes no sense. Why would Piera be here? It must just be the same car.

I narrow my eyes at the licence plate.

It's Piera's car. It's definitely hers.

Why is she here? Does she have a friend who lives around here that I don't know about? What possible reason –

My mind falls quiet as the pieces slot themselves into place, locking together with an abrupt click. Her lies about where she is going. Her strange behaviour. High emotion. It all began when I got Frank's case. The phone call she said was from chambers was from a blocked number. And so was the call she said was Rachel.

Prisons block phone numbers.

I stare across the road at his house, the beautiful building suddenly seeming dark and sinister. As traffic passes, blurring before my eyes, there is one more detail niggling away – something that is somewhere in my memory but won't click.

I close my eyes, squeezing them shut.

Until finally –

The hair tie. The one in Frank's house, in the nursery. Dusky rose pink silk.

Piera's.

She has been inside his house.

Is she in there right now? Is he home yet?

I pull out my phone and tap on Frank's unsaved number in my recent calls. I hold my breath, expecting it to remain disconnected.

But it begins to ring.

'Hello?' his gruff voice says, a level of surprise in his voice at an incoming call. Must be alien after a year of only outgoing communication.

I swallow hard, trying to clear the lump of emotion in my throat. 'Frank, it's Harry.'

'Harry? Oh hi – did you really miss me that much already?'

'Not yet, but maybe soon.' I force a laugh. 'You left your prayer beads at court. I'll post them back to you, okay?'

'Oh shit. I must have been so overwhelmed with the verdict that I didn't even think of them. Thanks, Harry.'

I lift my hand to cover my eyes, the road swimming in front of me. 'Well, I hope you have a great rest of your day . . . Have you made it home yet?'

'Thanks. I'm nearly there, just out of the station. Man, it's surreal –'

'Well, enjoy it,' I interrupt. I need to move. If he's just out of the station, he's less than five minutes away. 'Have a great life, Frank.'

'Thanks, Harry. Maybe catch you again one day.'

'Yep, maybe.'

I end the call, my heart racing as I dart down the pavement, back towards my car, and throw myself inside. My breaths are ragged, my hands shaking as I desperately try to slow the adrenaline that is pounding through me. But even with all of this relentless frantic energy, my insides feel cold. Empty. Like everything I thought I was has been carved out, leaving me hollow.

My gaze fixes to the side mirror. Soon enough I will see him walking towards me. I grip the steering wheel, my knuckles turning white.

What the fuck is going on?

The world seems to slow as suddenly he appears, a small figure in the distance, slowly growing in stature. He crosses the road, and as he gets closer to his house, I look away, out of the passenger window, afraid he may spot me if he glances back towards me. But in my mind I can still see him as he approaches his house, as he goes up the path, as he lets himself into the house, his hands trembling with anticipation.

I slowly look back across to his house, and he has gone. He is inside. And if Piera is in there too . . .

What are they doing?

If he touches her, I swear . . . I'll kill him.

No. God – what am I thinking? There may be an explanation to all of this. And even if there isn't – even if my worst fears are true – I am not that person.

I step out of my car again and fly back down the road, and then cross, the horn of a car wailing as it passes me, but I can't think. All my thoughts are scrambled as my mind tries to make sense of what is happening. How is Piera tied to Frank? What is she doing here? Why didn't she tell me?

I can't lose her.

Not like this.

And not to him.

I climb the steps, ready to pound my fists on the door and demand answers, but I notice something which makes me pause, my hand raised. The door-bell camera – it isn't lighting up. Not a single blink of light. The battery has gone. Which means he won't know I'm here yet. My eyes flicker to the key box. What if . . .

I open the hatch and punch in the code –

I gasp, my fingers freezing as the hatch unlocks and another piece slots into place.

890427.

Piera's birthday – year, month, day . . . and I didn't

even realize. But why would I? Why would my mind make that connection when it had no reason whatsoever to join the dots between my wife and the man I have been defending?

I grab the key, my fingers fumbling as I push it into the lock and turn it slowly. It unlocks and I inch the door open. There is nobody there. But I can hear voices drifting down the hallway from the back of the house.

They're in the kitchen.

I push the door slowly, being careful as the lock clicks back into place. I pause – nothing. They are still talking, their words muffled. I creep down the corridor, past the stairs and the living room, an office, and come to a halt outside the double doors, one slightly ajar.

My hands are shaking, my heartbeat so loud in my ears, I almost can't hear anything at all. But I press my hand over my mouth as Piera speaks, her voice as familiar to me as sunlight.

'You would have done the same for me –'

'Oh, Piera, take your credit where it's due,' Frank's voice says, sounding so different to the voice I've been listening to for the past four weeks. This voice is low and brimming with confidence. He clears his throat. 'Without your help, I'd be in prison for the rest of my life.'

I gasp as his words plunge me into freezing, turbulent waters, my blood running cold before my chest begins burning with a growing rage. Just one thought finds its way through my blurred, whirring mind and mutters:

I do not know my wife at all.

The Wife

13

The phone rings and I reach for it, expecting Harry's name on the screen. He's been at court all day and was going to chambers afterwards. Maybe he's leaving soon.

But it's an unknown number.

I ignore it and turn my head to breathe in the clean scent of Rose's head, her new baby scent still lingering. I kiss her a few times on her cheek, whispering that I love her before placing her in her crib.

The phone buzzes again. I step out of her room quickly, pulling the door shut quietly as I glance at the screen.

The unknown number again.

I roll my eyes and answer the phone, ready to hang up at the introduction spiel of a tele-salesperson.

'Hello?'

'Piera. It's me.'

I fall completely still, my entire body almost paralysed as a voice from the past echoes through the phone.

Francis Joseph.

I haven't talked to him in fifteen years. I never thought we'd speak again. Not after Oxford. Not after everything that happened. My heart swells. Even with all his flaws, he was my best friend. The first love of my life.

'Frank?' I mutter in disbelief.

'I need your help.'

'I'm hanging up –'

'Don't. Please. I helped you once, remember?'

The *please* and his tone are at odds. He isn't asking me for help. He's demanding.

I quickly descend the stairs, distancing myself from Rose's bedroom. I sit on the bottom step, unable to enter my living room with him. It feels like a betrayal.

'What is it?'

'I . . .' He inhales deeply and falls silent.

'Just say it, Frank, or I'm hanging up –'

'Linda is dead.'

My body falls still, my hands shaking.

'What?'

'Linda . . . she killed herself.'

Linda . . . Linda is dead. The words just don't feel right – they sit uneasily, as though they could never be true. I haven't seen her in years, not since Oxford, but she was my first friend at university, my first real friend. And now she's dead.

'Oh my god . . . Frank, are you okay? I . . . I don't know what to-to say –' My words catch in my throat, my mind unable to process. Linda is gone. 'When did it happen?' I whisper.

'No, Piera, you're not understanding. She killed herself just now.'

Creeping dread stretches its fingers up from my stomach and grips me by the throat, my breathing tight and shallow. 'What?' I mutter. 'You're not making sense.'

'She just killed herself now. Right now. I'm standing in the kitchen with her body.'

I squeeze my eyes shut but I can't stop the image of her lying dead in her kitchen appearing unbidden in my mind.

This can't be real. Linda really struggled after . . . after everything. But has she struggled all these years? Was she that alone? Would she still be alive if we had remained friends?

'Jesus, Frank . . . are you . . . is the ambulance on its way? The police?'

'No, I haven't called them yet.'

'Why the hell not? Why are you on the phone to me?'

'Because I need an alibi.'

No. No, no, no. He can't be asking me to do that.

'Frank, I can't . . .'

'Piera, I need you to do this –'

'What do you mean? If she's killed herself, just call the police and explain!'

'No, it'll look like I've done it –'

'Why?'

'Because she slit her own fucking throat!'

The hairs on the back of my neck stand on end. 'She did what?'

'She . . . she tried to overdose but when I came home

I found her and made her be sick. Then she came into the kitchen and slit her throat. But no one will believe me if they know I was here, they'll think I did it, so I'm going to delete the camera footage and say I was with an old friend from university –'

'No, Frank, you can't delete camera footage. Is it a doorbell camera? Or a CCTV camera with physical footage?'

'A doorbell camera. Why –'

'The police can retrieve that – deleting it from your app doesn't make it magically disappear! It's stored elsewhere and they'll search your phone and see you deleted footage, they'll know you're hiding something and they'll ask the company for the footage.'

'No, if you give me an alibi –'

'Frank, even if the camera wasn't an issue, I can't give you an alibi. I can't be dragged into this.' My heart is racing, pounding against my chest, the sound ringing in my ears. 'I have a child, I'm a barrister, my husband's about to be made a KC. I can't lie to the police, I can't lie in a court –'

'I helped you! I've kept your secrets for years! I'm asking you to help me, just this once –'

'I can't say we were together!'

The call falls silent, my loud, panicked breaths the only sound.

'Then you give me no choice. I didn't want to threaten you, Piera, but if you don't help me with this, I'll have to stop protecting you.'

'Frank, you're not thinking clearly –'

'If you don't help me, I will tell the truth about you. About what happened. You'll lose everything. Your career. I don't suppose your husband has a clue. You'll lose them all. Him, your daughter –'

'No!'

I shake my head slowly, biting down hard on my bottom lip to stop my voice from breaking. He'll hear it – the weakness. He can always tell.

'No!' I repeat, firmly. 'You've kept it a secret, Frank, you and Linda, and I've always appreciated that. But you have no proof –'

'Oh, but I do.'

The hairs on the back of my neck stand on end, as though the temperature has plummeted below freezing.

'What?'

'I have proof. I've always had proof. I've just never needed to use it until now.'

'H-how?'

There is a brief moment of silence, the sound of static as he adjusts the phone against his face.

'There was a camera. And I've got the footage. So the police would have the evidence needed to put you away for a long time. And your husband –'

'I'll tell him myself –'

'And you think he'll believe a word you say after you lied to him all these years? You have hidden everything about yourself from him – and you think he'll just believe that he should trust you?'

'Frank, please –'

'Are you going to help me or not?'

What do I do? Does he really have proof? Or is he bluffing? I can't risk it. And I can't tell Harry. Frank is right – Harry is all about trust, honesty. I've always told him he knows me, he knows everything about me. And yet all I've done is lie. He'll take Rose away and I'll lose everything. That can't happen. I can't risk even the slightest chance of that happening. But I can't give Frank an alibi, that simply isn't possible. The police will realize within the first twenty-four hours of investigating that he is lying and that he was in the house when it happened.

Wait.

'Frank . . . they won't know when it happened. They'll know you came home because of the CCTV footage, but they won't know when she did it. You can just say that you came home and found her dead –'

'Don't you think I already thought of that? But she . . . she made a phone call. She spoke to someone.'

'When? What did she say?'

'Piera, I don't have time to discuss all these details, I just need to know whether you're helping me or not.'

An overwhelming sadness washes over me. Linda's laugh rings in my ears. But her shining eyes turn increasingly sad. How can I do this?

Harry and Rose appear in a flash, a clear picture of what is most important to me in the whole world: my family. My hands shake, the phone trembling next to my ear. 'I . . . I'll help you.'

'Oh,' he sighs. 'Thank you.'

'I can't give you an alibi –'

'You –'

'An alibi is only going to make you seem more guilty. Please, believe me. I've prosecuted hundreds of trials and an alibi that is so easily disproved will only make them think you're guilty. But . . . I can help you make sure the evidence at the scene is clear that she did this to herself.'

'O-okay.'

'She . . .' I pause, my heart racing. Linda's smiling face is still right there, before my eyes. Her hair shining in the sun as we lay in the park. That first autumn as friends. The four of us . . . It was magic. 'She did do this to herself . . . Right?'

'Of course she did,' he says, his voice firm. 'You knew back at university how hard she was finding everything. That hasn't gone away. She wanted to die.' He pauses. 'After everything we went through, you and me, do you really think I could kill Linda?'

'No . . . no. I'm sorry. It's just the shock.' I puff my cheeks out then exhale, readying myself. 'Right . . . You said she tried to kill herself with pills. Where are the pills kept?'

'In the kitchen.'

'Does she have access?'

'No, they're locked away. But she must have found my spare key.'

I frown. 'Where did you keep it?'

'In the safe.'

'Does she know the code to the safe?'

'Yes.'

I stand, unable to stay seated any longer. 'Okay, good. Where is the spare key now? Does she have it on her?'

'No, it's here on the side.'

'Right . . . There must be empty bottles or packets from what she took?'

He pauses.

'Frank?' I say, coming to a sudden standstill. I glance out of the front window, at the peaceful evening, so at odds with what is happening now, inside my house.

'Yes. They . . . They're here too.'

'Okay, so she took the overdose in the kitchen?'

'She . . . she must have.'

I resume my pacing, down the hallway towards the back door and then back again. 'Where did you find her when you made her sick?'

'In the bedroom.'

'Right . . . you're going to take those empty bottles and packets and put them on her bedside table.'

'Why?'

'The kitchen is already going to hold a lot of evidence. Distancing the pills from the scene looks more like an intentional overdose. She took the pills from the cupboard, and actively took them upstairs to overdose in her bed.'

'But my neighbour came in to check on her – will they ask her if she saw evidence of an overdose?'

I pause, chewing my lip, my brain racing. 'Would you be able to see Linda's side table from the door?'

'No, I don't think so.'

'Then that's fine. Now listen, what is she wearing, does it have a pocket?'

'Uh, a cardigan, over her nightdress.'

'Does it have a pocket, Frank?'

'Yes.'

'Okay . . . take the key,' I swallow, the back of my throat thick with guilt. 'And put it in her pocket.'

I hear movement, footsteps, then rustling.

'I've done it.'

I inhale deeply, my thoughts swirling around my mind as I try to imagine a house I have never seen, a traumatic event that I was not there to witness.

'Right – do you have blood on you?'

'No . . .'

I lift my hand to my forehead, my eyes squeezing shut as I try to make sense of his response. 'No? Are you lying to me?'

'No . . . I . . . I changed my top, I panicked –'

'Why did you do that?'

'I thought you would give me an alibi, I didn't know what to do!'

'So there's blood on your top? The one you were wearing when it happened?'

'Y-yes, some, splatters, but how will that help me?'

I take a steadying breath. 'Frank, when she did this to herself, what did you do? You tried to help her . . . right?'

'At first I was frozen to the spot, you have no idea what that feels like to see something like that happen! I didn't know what to do!'

'Okay, listen to me, you're going to hang up the phone and then . . .' My stomach plummets. 'Wait, what number have you called me from?'

'What?'

'Please tell me you have not called me from your main phone –'

'No, no – it's a spare I have –'

My heart races, my breath quickening with panic. 'Is it connected to you? Will the police be able to tie this number to you?'

'It's a burner.'

'Why do you have a burner?'

'Jesus, Piera!'

'Frank, you've asked me to help you!'

He sighs loudly. 'I use it to get coke, Piera, okay? Is that what you wanted?'

'Jesus.' I force myself to take a steadying breath. 'What you're going to do, is hang up the phone. Then you are going to destroy it. Get rid of the sim, get rid of the handset so nobody will find it. And then you're going to change your top back and go to Linda, and you're going to get more blood on yourself. And on a hand towel. It'll be much easier for them to believe she did this to herself if it's clear you tried to save her.'

'O-okay.'

'And then you're going to call 999. Straightaway. Understand?'

'Yes.'

My bottom lip trembles, my vision clouding over as tears fill my eyes. 'Okay . . . I need to go now. All right? . . . I'm hanging up now –'

'Piera?'

I bite my lip, suppressing a cry. 'Yes?' I choke out the word.

'You believe me, right?'

I swallow, Linda's face flashing once again before my eyes. But then Frank appears – the Frank that I once knew, the Frank from the very beginning – and I nod.

'Yes,' I whisper. 'I believe you.'

'And if I need your help again, you'll be there for me, right?'

I lick my lips, unable to respond.

'You'll be there for me . . . just like I've been there for you.'

'Y-yes,' I stammer. 'Now go.'

The call ends and my hands loosen, my phone dropping to the floor and sliding across the stone tiles.

Linda is dead. Frank is terrified. And somehow, after all these years, our secret is being held above my head, the trust between us so tenuous that it could break at any moment and bring my life down around me.

Them

Fifteen Years Earlier

The bell rings out across the courtyard and Piera Roman, a phone pressed to her ear, darts across the square to the building on the other side, set back from the pavement and framed by trees.

'I'm nearly there,' she says into the phone. 'Shit, I hope they let me in.'

'They will,' her best friend Linda says with a soft chuckle. 'You'll smash it, all right?'

'Thanks, Linda. See you later!'

Trust you to be late to your first intra-college competition, her father's voice says in her head as she shoves her phone into her coat pocket. It couldn't be helped – something went wrong and her bus was at a standstill for twenty minutes. She tugs her bag, which has her advocacy folders inside and is sliding down her arm, back up on to her shoulder. It pulls on her long hair but she doesn't waste time freeing it, pushing her way inside the building. But there's no need to panic. It's just a moot competition – to test budding barristers' advocacy skills – it's not serious. Right?

She opens the door carefully but it lets out a groan,

as if bemoaning the weight of the heavy wood on its hinges. She dashes to the small row of desks at the top of the hall, past the other students, already sat in their places, some relaxed, others with a frantic look in their eyes.

A short woman dressed in a black robe is waiting for her at the top desk, her glasses poised on the edge of her nose, her mouth downturned.

'Miss Roman, I presume?'

The voice, drawling and slow, is paired with a pair of icy blue eyes, throwing daggers up in her direction.

'Yes. I'm sorry, my bus was delayed –'

'If you are lucky enough to become a criminal advocate at some point in your future, Miss Roman, these types of excuse will not hold water with a judge or a jury, or an instructing solicitor who is paying your fees. And they won't hold water with us. We will forgive this one occasion. But if you are talented enough to proceed, if you are late again you will be disqualified.'

Piera swallows, ignoring the heat that is flushing her cheeks, ignoring the stares of the other students all sitting at their desks which encircle the room in a large U shape, their heads turned towards her. Ignore it all – it's the first round. Soon enough, it will all be forgotten.

'I understand.'

'Fantastic. Now take your place. It isn't quite obvious which one is for you, as another student has succeeded in being even later than you were.'

'Does it matter –'

'No. They aren't fixed, so just choose one.'

Piera nods and heads to the left of the large U, taking her seat at a desk two places down from the scolding woman.

'Well, with all but one of you arrived, I think it's best we begin.' She gestures to two other professors in black cloaks who take their seats either side of her. But as she clears her throat to speak again, the door to the room slams and all the heads turn towards the sound as one. Piera blinks at the newcomer – hopefully it'll replace their collective memory of her tardiness with something new. There is a boy standing there, a wonky smile set across his face. No sense of apology in the way he is carrying himself. No apology forthcoming at all.

'Mr Joseph,' the woman drawls once more. 'You are late.'

'Well . . . Thanks for waiting for me.' He smiles even wider and dimples appear, pitting his cheeks.

'Take a seat now, and be quiet.'

'Yes, Ma'am,' he says with a mock salute. He shimmies his way behind the desks on the right side of the U, taking his place across from Piera.

She looks down at her lap, suppressing a smile. At least there's someone here with a sense of humour. He might cause trouble for himself, but at least he'll be fun.

'Ah yes,' the woman says. 'My two latecomers sitting across from each other – undisciplined and disorganized. As I told Miss Roman, you will do well to not be late to this competition, Mr Joseph, if you proceed.

Understood? Right – back to where we were before the interruption.'

Her words fade as Mr Joseph catches Piera's eye.

'Miss Roman?' he mouths.

Piera nods.

He tilts his head to the right, offering her a slight bow. That mischievous smirk still glued to his face.

'Name?' he mouths silently.

'You need to concentrate,' the girl next to him mutters, glaring at him sideways as she scrawls notes on to her advocacy papers.

He rolls his eyes, which glint in the golden-hour light, and shakes his head in amusement. 'Name?' he mouths again.

Piera raises her eyebrows. This one will be interesting. 'Pi-E-Ra.' She moves her lips carefully, exaggerating each syllable even in silence. His eyes move from her eyes and down to her mouth. Her stomach flips.

'Again?'

'Pi-E-Ra.'

He shakes his head, his long, dark blonde hair, which until now has been pushed away from his face, falling haphazardly into his eyes.

She holds up a finger – just one moment – and picks up her pen. She writes her name in big capital letters, her face burning. He is still watching her, she can feel it. Glancing once again at the judge, she turns the notebook towards him.

His eyes move from her face and down to the paper.

One eyebrow lifts upwards, and he tilts his head again, just like before.

'Nice.'

Piera nods her head towards him – *your turn*.

He smiles, his teeth gleaming white. He looks at her for one second longer, then drops his eyes down to his paper, scrawling quickly. He lifts the notebook and turns it towards her, not even turning to check on the judge again.

Francis.
You can call me Frank.
In fact, call me whatever you want.

Piera giggles, her shoulders lifting, her feet shifting beneath the desk. She nods at him. Then turns away, facing the three judges purposefully. She really needs to concentrate. She wants to be here – she wants the others to take her seriously. So, with that little encounter over, she can focus. But his eyes are still on her face, and she can somehow feel that smile beaming towards her.

Her eyes flicker sideways before she can stop herself. And there he is, his head propped on his hand, watching her. He catches her glancing his way and beams. *Made you look.*

Piera blushes.

And for the rest of the evening, for the next two and a half hours, even as Piera completes her prepared arguments, winning her case and proceeding to the next round, the dance between them continues. Francis looks at her with his shining eyes – his golden skin, and that smile – and Piera realizes her very first instinct about him was right. This boy is going to be one thing and one thing only.

Trouble.

14

The café is bustling, almost all of the tables full. I glance around the space, smiling at another mum at the table just next to mine, cradling a newborn. She has a harassed look on her face, her hair scraped up into a messy bun on top of her head, wearing a hoodie stained with milk. I remember those early days – the exhaustion, the forcing yourself out of the house in order to save your sanity but finding the effort to go out into public even worse. I smile over at Rose, who is sitting up in her pram, and I unbuckle her straps and lift her out, straightening her legs to manoeuvre her into the high chair.

'Here, want a sandwich?'

I tear the ham sandwich into tiny mouthfuls and place them on the tray in front of her, laughing as she scoops them up and rams them into her mouth.

'She's lovely,' a voice says.

I glance over – the woman at the table next to me is watching us, her head tilted.

'Thank you,' I say, beaming. 'How old is your little one?'

'He's three weeks . . .'

'He your first?'

She nods. 'It's . . . it's hard, isn't it?'

'I promise it gets easier. You're doing amazingly for only being three weeks in. Try not to be hard on yourself.'

She smiles. 'Thank you.'

My phone vibrates on the table next to me and I glance at it.

Private number. Who even calls on a private number any more?

Dread swirls in my stomach. It couldn't be . . .

'Sorry,' I say, gesturing at my phone. 'I need to take this.'

'No worries,' she says, turning her attention back to her baby who is now grizzling in her arms.

I pick up the phone and stare down at it for a moment, then lift it to my ear.

'Hel—'

'This call is from a person currently in a prison in England,' an automated voice interrupts. 'All calls are logged and recorded and may be listened to by a member of prison staff. If you do not wish to accept this call, please hang up now.'

A phone call from prison. There's only one person I know who could possibly be calling me from prison. Unless . . . unless it's work related. But that's highly unlikely. Even when I was practising, I didn't get these kinds of calls – I'm a prosecutor. It's my job to put bad people behind bars – not to help them back out again.

I tap the screen.

'Hello?' I say hesitantly.

'Piera,' his voice says.

It is him. Frank.

I pull the phone away from my ear, my finger flying towards the red button to end the call. But it curls inwards, into a fist.

It's been nine months since Linda died. But I haven't heard from him since that day, and I haven't seen anything about it in the press. I thought what I had told him to do had worked . . . So what does he want?

I glance around the café, at all the people busying themselves with their day-to-day lives, while Frank is invading mine.

'Hi,' I say back. I pause, waiting. But he stays quiet. 'Are you okay? Why are you calling?'

'Oh, so now you're concerned about me?' he mutters. 'You've made no attempt to check on me since that day –'

'Frank, I thought if you needed something you would find me. I had no way of contacting you, I thought everything was okay –'

'Well, it's not. I was charged.'

I hold my breath, my eyes watering as they dart around the café.

He continues, 'I just thought you might like to know that I got rid of the barrister who was representing me yesterday.'

'What? Why did you –'

'And I've heard of a brand-new KC who's meant to

be brilliant, so I've asked my solicitors to brief him. I think you might know him quite well –'

'Frank, what are you doing?'

'I'm briefing the best advocate I can get.'

I shake my head, my hands clammy. 'No. He has a trial.'

'I think his clerk said it was only meant to last three days. So it should be fine.'

A lump forms in my throat and I swallow hard. 'Why are you doing this?'

'I just want the best. I always wanted your husband to represent me. I just needed a way out of my current representation and now Harry Mason-Hall KC is going to be my advocate. I thought you'd be happy for me. Aren't you happy for me?'

I pause, a chill taking hold of my shoulders.

He's done this to make sure I know he's still out there. I helped him and at any moment he could turn my life upside down. I shudder. 'Yes. I'm happy for you.'

'Good. I knew you were a good friend even though your advice still led to me being prosecuted for murder.'

'I tried to help you, I did the best I could, but you must have known that there was a possibility they weren't just going to believe your word –'

'Well, we're here now. And if Harry is as good as I hear he is, then I'll be fine.' He falls silent, and all that is audible is my panicked breaths, muffled between my cheek and the phone, pressed to my face. 'Won't I?'

'Y-yes.'

'You better make sure of it.'

My body falls cold. Not quite a threat. But close enough.

'And, P?' he mutters.

'Yes?' I whisper.

'A good friend would come to the first day of the trial.'

This is about control. It always has been. 'Frank, I –'

'See you soon.'

The call ends and I set my phone down on the table. I stare slowly around the room again. Just moments ago it was a place of safety, comfort. Happiness. A casual afternoon excursion with my daughter. And now?

Now it is entirely changed.

15

Harry leaves the kitchen to go to Rose and I wait, a steaming forkful of curry still in my hand, listening as he makes his way out of the living room and up the stairs before I let my mask drop. My hands shake violently as adrenaline runs through me, the lies sending my body into overdrive.

Harry has recounted the case to me in detail, each point landing like a blow as Linda's face refuses to disappear from my mind. I had to receive each piece of information as if it was brand new, intriguing, another fascinating legal case, rather than repeated waves of grief lapping over me again and again. But there was one detail I hadn't heard before. Harry mentioned a bag.

What bag? When Frank called me that day, he never mentioned packing a bag for Linda. Why didn't he mention the bag? And what will happen when they meet? Will Frank play nice, or will he tease that we know each other, a cat playing with a mouse?

I need to calm down – Harry will be back soon. I can't let myself cry again, he'll know something is wrong. And he can't know.

I freeze at the sound of his feet treading carefully

down the stairs. I reach out quickly and grasp the bottle of wine, busying myself. He appears and I point at it.

'No, I'm good for now,' he says. 'So . . . hell of a case, right?'

I set the bottle down. 'What a defence.' I try to stay in the room, in the present, but my mind drags me back to that phone call, the manic questions, the hasty creation of a story. I blink rapidly, pulling myself back. 'What's your gut say? Think he did it?'

'I mean, it's an outlandish defence, definitely, but surely it isn't one you just pluck out of thin air. *What if* he's innocent? What if it really was her?'

'But to slit your own throat?'

'People have done far worse when their mind turns against them.'

I nod, closing my mind against the image of my old friend – her pale skin, blood streaming down her neck, staining her clothes dark red. A knife dangling limply in her hands.

But then, replacing her in the darkness of my mind, I see Frank. Not as he is now, but as he was then. His smile breaking open his face, his cheeks full and spiked with dimples, his eyes shining with life and laughter and fun. I had a thousand reasons for wanting to leave. And he had his reasons for choosing Linda. She had her reasons for wanting him when she knew what it would mean for our friendship. We all have – had – our secrets. But at one point Frank was the centre of my entire world. My best friend. Even with everything that

216

happened, do I really believe he is capable of killing his wife?

'Well . . .' I say, 'either way, it doesn't really make a difference, does it? If he's guilty, it's very unlikely he'll ever tell you, and it's your duty to represent him. And if he's innocent . . . If he's innocent, then he needs the best defence he can get. You can do this.'

'Thank you,' he says. 'I love you.'

'I love you too.'

He leans across the table and kisses the side of my head. I look down at my plate and push the food around, the horror of what I'm doing making the room swim before me. I've never lied to Harry. Well, not directly. Only by omission. This is different. This is active dishonesty. And he is my whole world now. He has stood by me through everything. Through countless nights of working late, the complete dedication to progressing in my career, the sudden disorientating switch to motherhood . . . He has always made sure I am happy. And I'm doing this to him.

My eyes glaze over and I stare emptily ahead.

I don't know Francis any more. And he doesn't know me. I don't know who his friends are, what his hobbies are, whether he still loves Chinese food or still hates horror movies. And he doesn't know anything about me. But there are some things we do share. Things that I don't share with anyone else. Not even Harry.

Secrets.

16

'Right, give me that gorgeous baby and enjoy your coffee.'

I smile at my friend Rachel as she holds her outstretched arms towards me. 'She's happy playing –'

'Yes, but you're watching her like a hawk instead of relaxing!'

'Okay, okay,' I laugh. I pick up my latte from the side table and sip. 'Ahhh, a hot coffee.'

'See – you need to chill.'

Rose babbles along to our conversation, bashing her toy giraffe against Rachel's armchair.

I settle back into the sofa, gripping the mug, relishing the warmth across my palm and my fingers.

'So is maternity still going okay? Or are you ready to go back to work?'

I sigh, placing the mug back on the table.

'Tough question, huh?'

'Just not straightforward . . . I really want to go back, but –'

'You're scared to leave her?'

I shrug. 'Partly it's that. But also . . . I'm so scared of what being off for a year will have done to my career. I know it shouldn't make a difference, but I've had so many friends who struggle to get back into it with as many cases as before, and if I'm not being briefed then I'm not being paid. It's just terrifying. I spent years building a career, a practice, and . . . what if it's all gone?'

'What does Harry think?'

'Harry . . . he tries to be supportive, I know he does, he's the best . . . but he just doesn't get it. I put everything on the line because he wanted to have a baby. You know? I could have waited. I wanted to wait. But I did it for him. And then I've been off and his career has just exploded, he got made a KC, and I'm so happy for him, but –'

'It feels like you sacrificed your success for his.'

I nod, chewing on my bottom lip at the words that have always been inside me and Rachel has just spoken into existence. Harry would hate it if he knew I felt this way.

'Anyway . . .' I clear my throat and flash my teeth at her in a false smile. 'What's going on with you? Have you seen Louisa recently? I haven't seen her in a little while.'

But as Rachel begins to speak, ranting about an argument she'd had with Louisa because of her boyfriend Joshua and his drunken weekend antics of which Louisa vehemently disapproves, my mind is transported to Wormwood Scrubs where Harry is meeting Frank. They are meeting each other for the first time, sitting across a table from each other, discussing his defence. The defence that I helped him stage. A rush of nausea passes through me, and I swallow hard.

'. . . so now I don't really know what to do. I don't want to fall out with Louisa, but I know that she genuinely can't stand him. What would you do?'

I cough, blinking rapidly as I try to remember what she was talking about. 'Rachel, you know my thoughts on Josh.'

'Yes, but you wouldn't accuse me of being jealous of your relationship – and you have the most perfect husband in the world. Even if sometimes it doesn't feel like it.'

I smile, that sick feeling still in my chest. 'I know.'

And I do know. It took a long time for me to let Harry in. As soon as I saw him for the first time, when he met my eye across the room in chambers, I felt it. That frisson of energy. That deep-down knowing feeling that this was a person who was going to change my life. He was going to be special.

But I had felt that exact feeling with Frank. So there was only one response to feeling that way again.

Run.

And that's what I did. For months I avoided him, wouldn't look at him, even, exchanging the bare minimum of polite conversation when I absolutely had to. But over time, I began to trust him. He became my friend. He showed me that it didn't have to be an intense, toxic, whirlwind relationship to be worthwhile. He was patient. And kind. And the first time he kissed me, his face breaking into a smile as he realized I had let him break the personal barrier – not moving away as

he stepped over the line between friendship and something more – I knew that he was different.

He isn't Frank.

My phone, which is pressed between my leg and the
arm of the sofa, vibrates loudly.

'Speak of the devil,' Rachel says.

Harry.

Con finished. Call me when you're free.

So that's that. He has met Francis. They have sat face to
face; Harry has been closer to Frank than I have been
in more than fifteen years. But what does he know?

'I'll just quickly pop out and call him. Watch her
for me?'

'Sure,' Rachel says, lowering herself off the armchair
to sit beside Rose.

I stand up and head through Rachel's kitchenette
and through the back door into the garden. I open
my phone again, and our faces beam out through the
screen. I love that photo. We took it on a quick stopover
in Paris – a spontaneous trip which resulted in us running down the Champs-Élysées in the rain, stopping by
the river to take a photograph: me cradled into Harry's
chest, his hand extended as he captured the moment.
Soaked to the skin. Clothes sticking to our bodies. But
our faces lit up with joy. Our smiles breaking open in
laughter. That was a great trip.

I tap his name and lift the phone to my ear, listening
to the rhythmic ring.

'Hello, gorgeous,' his warm voice says.

'Hey,' I say, trying to prevent my voice from going upwards in pitch like it does when I'm anxious. I fail.

'You okay?'

'Yes, I'm good . . . Just with Rachel.'

'Ah, how is she?'

I chew on my bottom lip. *Stop with the questions, Harry.* 'Yeah, she's good – she's had a bit of a falling-out with Louisa because of Josh. He's such a prick.'

'Be nice, Piera.'

'I know, I know . . .' I sigh. 'Anyway – how was it with your new defendant?'

'It was . . . you know, he's a broken man, P. He really is.'

My breath catches in my throat. Broken. But Frank never breaks. Even when any other person would shatter catastrophically, Frank remains solid. At least he did when I knew him. He was unshakeable.

'That bad?'

'His wife has died, Piera. In a horrific way. I'm strong, but if that happened to you . . . God, I can't even think what I'd do. I don't know how I could go on.'

I nod slowly, squeezing my eyes closed. But in the pulsating darkness, Frank is there. Crying. I only ever saw him cry once. And Linda was there, too –

'Piera? Are you there?'

'Yes, I'm here, I . . . So what do you think? Innocent? Guilty?'

'You know I don't normally deal in belief. But . . . I

believe him. I do. While I was with him in that room, I believed him.'

Hmm. Frank will do that to a person. I exhale heavily. 'And now that you're out in the cold light of day?'

'I know that a murderer will come up with a story if they can. I get that. But I really did believe him. I think his defence could really stand up to scrutiny. And if it can, then a jury –'

'Then a jury must acquit.'

'They have to. If there's the slightest doubt –'

'Yes, I know how the burden of proof works, thanks, Harry,' I snap.

A silence falls around us, crisp like the late autumn air.

'Why do I feel like I've done something wrong?' Harry asks.

'No, you haven't. I'm . . . I'm just tired. Sorry . . . So it went well.'

'Yes. It's just going to be a tricky one. I'll essentially have to use his wife's mental health against her. She's been suffering with depression since her first year of university. It's so sad.'

A shiver runs down my spine, my eyes filling with tears. Linda always struggled. Sadness followed her from the beginning and it has haunted her all this time. She must have felt so alone. I swallow, trying to force the lump in my throat away. 'Oh really?' I say, keeping my voice as neutral as possible.

'A friend of theirs died and she couldn't cope. Ever since then, it just kept rearing its head.'

My stomach plummets. *A friend of theirs*. A friend.

A sudden movement through the glass catches my attention, and I blink rapidly at the door. Rachel is gesturing at me, mouthing words. *Rose is crying*.

'Harry, I actually have to go. Rose is crying and I think Rachel doesn't know what to do.'

'Okay.'

'See you later. Bye!'

'Okay, see you at home, love you –

I jab at the phone, ending the call. My hands are trembling, my heart racing. But his face flashes in front of my eyes before I'm able to suppress it.

A friend of theirs died.

Richard. Tall, handsome, wild. And wildly optimistic.

He was my friend first.

Them

Piera pushes her way through the heavy wooden doors and is immediately hit by a wall of noise, sweat and the smell of alcohol lingering in the air. She's never seen a pub so busy. Not in her home town in the suburbs of outer London, where pubs are frequented by men in their sixties and seventies, resting half-pints on wonky tables while eating pork scratchings and shouting at the football. Her sights had always been set on Oxford, from when she was a young girl and her parents would rave about their time there, telling her she was smart enough to get there too, but she hadn't expected how different it would feel to her usual life in the country-side. Oxford was its own world entirely.

But the Lamb and Lion is nothing like that. It is full of students – laughing, shouting, dancing. Music is playing, and a group of girls around a large table in the window sing along. The air crackles, alive with electricity.

Piera scans the mass of people, searching for his face. But he isn't here. Not yet. She's already fifteen minutes late, but she texted him and said she was running behind. Has he decided against it? Is watching each other from across their tutorial room, sharing text conversations that span the entire day and long into the night, as far as this is going to go? He seemed keen but . . . he's a boy. And boys are fickle.

Richard came to see her as she was getting ready – knocking on her door with his standard rhythmic rap of the knuckles.

'Getting ready for your date?' he said, his eyes scanning her swiftly, his neck flushed. They had briefly had a thing at the very beginning of the year when they met at their college's Freshers events, but Piera had realized very quickly that Richard just wasn't the kind of boy she wanted. She needed something more – someone for whom she was willing to risk it all. If she'd wanted a small love in a small place, she would have stayed at home.

'Just be careful – I've heard of his . . . reputation.'

Piera rolled her eyes. 'His reputation doesn't mean anything. He's . . . There's something special about him.'

She pushes her way through the crowd and slides into a small gap at the bar, between two groups of lads. One is deep in debate, something about an upcoming boxing match, but the other group all turn to look, their eyes dancing over her. They jostle each other towards her, jeering, but she avoids looking at them, trying to block out their lewd comments. She knew she shouldn't have worn this dress. But . . . she thought that Frank would like it.

'Leave her alone, lads,' the woman behind the bar

says, with a stern look. 'She clearly isn't comfortable.' She catches Piera's eye, offering her a warm smile. 'Would you like something, love?'

'I'm just waiting for a friend –'

'She's with me, Erica,' a voice says from just behind her. His voice.

She turns her neck, and there he is, so close that if she tiptoed upwards, she could kiss him. He smiles, placing his hand gently on the small of her back whilst he leans forward to kiss her on the cheek.

'Evening, Piera.' His voice is raspy, his eyes sparkling. His eyes flicker down her body and then back up again. But when he does it, it doesn't make her skin crawl like those other boys. Instead, her stomach flips, the back of her neck flushing.

'You look bloody gorgeous.'

She beams. 'Thank you. You look great too . . . I love your shirt.'

Usually in class, he dresses more casually, but still with purpose, his jeans ripped, a baggy T-shirt, a chunky ring on his thumb. But tonight, his jeans are fitted but not skinny, the denim dark, and worn with a black leather belt. His white shirt is tucked in, the collar open, the buttons undone to the top of his chest, his collarbone exposed. Her stomach flips again. What kind of power does this man have? She's never felt like this – never has she been so physically drawn to someone. A magnet dragged powerlessly towards its opposite.

'Did you make all this effort for me?' she whispers, blinking up at him coyly.

'Did you expect me not to?' he whispers back. 'It's the first time you've agreed to meet up with me outside law school – you only get one first impression in this life.'

'Well . . . bravo. And how am I doing? Be honest.'

He allows his eyes to fall down her again, but this time slowly, his eyes returning to her face but resting just for a moment on her lips. He meets her eye. 'You give me butterflies.' He raises an eyebrow. 'Honest enough for you?'

Piera blushes, and unable to bear the intensity of his gaze for a moment longer, she blinks down at the floor. 'Shall we get a drink?'

He smiles. 'Sure . . . You go and sit down and I'll grab them. What would you like?'

'A glass of rosé, please.'

'Sure.'

He turns back to the bar, but as she walks away, aiming for a small empty table nearby, she glances at a mirror hanging on the exposed brick and catches him looking over his shoulder to follow her with his gaze. She catches his eye, and he smirks as he realizes he's been caught, then turns back to the bar with a shake of his head.

A smile stretches across her face. But as she takes in her giddy expression beaming out at her from the mirror, she lets out a slow, controlled breath. *Play it cool, Piera. He's just a boy. You've been with boys before.*

But not like him, a small voice whispers in response. *Not like Frank.*

'. . . And that was when I told her I just couldn't do it any more. That it would be best to end it there –'

'Just like that?' Piera gawps. 'Didn't that feel cruel?'

He looks at her, his mouth quirking. 'Isn't it better to be honest?'

'Well –'

'What would being kind have achieved? She would have felt cheated in the long run. I just . . . I always think it's best.'

'Be cruel to be kind?'

'I guess,' he shrugs, but for a moment his eyes turn dark. 'Dishonesty is far crueller.'

Piera wants to ask more questions, to delve deeper, but she doesn't want to push too hard. He has opened up to her so much – more than she had ever expected. She'd thought this first meeting would be all flirtation and banter, jokes and tension. But he had revealed truths about his childhood, his past relationships, his life. He had revealed himself.

Enough for now.

'Do you want another drink –'

'What about you?' he interrupts, his eyes warming once more.

'Do I want another drink?'

'No, no.' He shifts in his chair, his knees turning so that they are pressed against hers. 'When was your last relationship?'

'Well . . . I . . .' Piera uncrosses her legs then recrosses them, momentarily moving away from him. But he shifts once more, closing the gap. Her face turns hot. 'I haven't really had an actual relationship.'

His eyes narrow. 'Never?'

'I mean, I saw guys. I had things with guys but never a real relationship. Never anything that felt more than . . . shallow.'

'But you're not a shallow person.'

'Exactly. There was never anybody who showed me anything that would make me want to go further. I was working hard, I wanted to succeed. I had good friends and went out, and did whatever I wanted. Why give up my freedom for someone who doesn't even feel like a fully formed person?' She shrugs, her hands landing loudly on her knee, her fingers close to his own.

'And what about me?' he says in a low voice, leaning closer. 'Do you see anything more in me?'

Piera swallows. Suddenly, her throat feels tight, her mouth dry. She licks her lips, her eyes flickering to his intense stare, waiting for an answer.

'Maybe,' she whispers.

'Just maybe?'

She nods slowly, a smile stretching across her face, from cheek to cheek. He lifts a hand to tuck a strand of hair behind her ear before holding the back of her neck, his eyes on her face all the while. And then – just like that – he kisses her.

And for the first time, the first time ever, there is something there. A feeling like no other. An intense yearning deep inside her. Call it lust, or infatuation, or obsession, but this was the feeling she had been searching for.

17

'Very well,' the judge says, his voice as clear as a bell, even up here in the public gallery. 'Let's begin.'

I lean forward, my eyes scanning the jury. Harry will be directly below me, doing the exact same, assessing each of them in turn. Will they be helpful or a hindrance? Which will be swayed by emotion? Which one will try to lead the others? Which one will be led wherever the others tell them to follow? Which ones have already made up their minds?

The seats surrounding me are full, every place in my row and the rows in front of me taken up by a complete stranger. When I first arrived, I made my way to the back corner, to where I could be sure Harry wouldn't be able to see me. But I searched the faces of the people who had already taken their places, looking for a familiar expression, a smile that looked like Francis, or a tilt of the head just like Linda's. But I never met any of Frank's family . . . Even if they are here to support him, I wouldn't know. And Linda's only family is her sister, and she can't be here as she's a witness.

Maybe nobody is here. Nobody at all.

My body deflates with sadness. If I was gone, I

would have friends, family, making sure that justice was done. Watching every moment. But if it was me down there, the one on trial, who would come to rally behind me? Could friends really be relied on or would they fade away? Really there's only one person who would remain steadfast at my side, even from afar, even from up here in the gods, elevated above Court One.

Harry.

Or maybe he wouldn't. He's too good. Maybe he would leave. After all, I haven't told him the truth after all these years because even though I know he loves me, I'm not sure how he would react to the truth? If he knew me, really knew me – would he stay?

How would he feel if he knew I was here? I should have just told him – I wanted to, as I watched him readying himself to leave, it was just there on the tip of my tongue. I *might come to watch*. That's all I would have to say. And he wouldn't have minded – he might even have appreciated it. It's been a long time since I came along to a trial to support him. And this is his biggest yet, the pinnacle of his career. So if I told him I wanted to be there for him, he wouldn't have pushed back.

I peer forward, my eyes falling once again on the dock. When they brought Frank in, he sat down and listened to the judge. But as soon as Hawthorne finished speaking, he lifted his head towards the gallery. Looking for me. My heart sank for him – his face is sallow, his usually golden skin almost grey with worry. His forehead wrinkled in fear. But he caught my eye, and for a few moments, the clouds surrounding him cleared, and he shone. There he was: the Frank that I knew. He tilted his head forward, just slightly, such a slight movement that no one except me would have noticed it. But I knew straightaway what he was saying.

You came.

I shrugged my shoulders, knowing that even after all this time, he will still be able to read my meaning. *You called.*

His eyes softened. Then he broke away, and his worried expression quickly returned. But, at least for a moment, I granted him some kind of relief. That's why he wanted me here, after all. To be here for him when he needs me. Even if forced. But in truth I'm here to keep him on side. To have him believe that I will do what it takes, that I am here for him, that I still care. And I do. But it's always been the same way with Frank, and it always will be.

Handle with caution.

I always knew that. And Linda did too, I suppose. In her own way.

Did she not handle him carefully enough?

'Alison Aldridge,' the clerk calls out.

The clerk's shout pulls me out of the darkness of my thoughts. I can't think like that. Frank would never kill Linda. She was a woman filled with sadness. A sadness so all-consuming that there was only one way out. I have to believe that. By helping Frank, I am helping her. She loved him so much.

A woman makes herself known and heads to the benches, taking the first seat.

'Paul Hanawawe,' the clerk calls again.

'Uh . . . Thank you,' a man says, then shakes his head in confusion at his own words.

The juror slides along to the second seat.

'Oscar Norbury,' the clerk calls.

I suppress a sigh. Harry will be down there, his hands clenching more tightly with each man called from the group. It's three to one now. With each man they call, the tension inside him will be rising as he watches the balance shift in the wrong direction.

I sit back in my seat, adjusting my position, the hard seat already uncomfortable. I close my eyes and cross my arms as the clerk continues to call out names. I need to block out the calling of the jurors. I can't control it, nor can Harry. And focusing on each one will only make it worse. But as the sound of the clerk's voice blurs, I stifle a yawn. I couldn't sleep last night. It took Harry a while to settle, and I could tell he was thinking over every last detail of the case, the evidence, the defence. Every so often he would sit up, his phone lighting up in the darkness as he frantically wrote down a random thought that had come to him which he would need to remember. He had to write it down or it might disappear in the night. And what if that was the detail which could win the case? He's always like this, with every single trial, but this one is different. This isn't just perfectionism. This isn't just wanting to do the best job he possibly can. He's doing it for himself – to prove a point. To prove that he deserves to be the youngest criminal KC there has ever been. To prove that he deserves this kind of case. He doesn't want to falter.

My stomach turns. And that's what it was doing last night. Even after Harry finally drifted off to sleep, his hand still clutching his phone, I stared up at the ceiling. I know that today is just the beginning, that nothing too important or eventful will come to pass, that the first day never really amounts to anything. But still . . . it's the first day. The opening of Frank's murder trial. The jury will be chosen, the prosecution will set out the case against him. The twelve chosen strangers will be shown the peak of the mountain, and the Crown will navigate them up the precipice, guiding them through crevasses and weaving them through precarious passages until they are at the summit. The case is at its strongest at the end of the prosecution's opening speech. But then they have to prove it. And that's when Harry will storm in, sending tremors through the ground, hoping that an avalanche will sweep it all away.

'Thank you, Madam Clerk.'

The judge's voice breaks through my imaginings and I open my eyes, blinking back into the artificial light of the Bailey. I shift towards the edge of my seat and stare down at the jury's benches, now both full. Fourteen people – they've called two reserves. Standbys, just for the opening – in case a juror becomes too squeamish or an emergency takes place. But soon enough they will be dismissed and the twelve will be locked in. My eyes focus in, drawn to one man in particular. During the clerk's reading of the summary he looked faint, as if he might be sick at any minute. I'm sure Harry was hoping he wouldn't be called or he would ask to be excused. But he is there. What effect will he have on the group? Will his sensitivity push them towards conviction? Whilst some jurors hold power, really it's the balance that matters. Old and young. Class. Conservative and liberal. Male and female.

My eyes focus, scanning the group quickly.

I count.

My cheeks burn and I turn towards Frank. He is staring up at me again and he raises his eyebrows, meeting my eye with the smallest of smirks, the corner of his mouth barely lifting. He knows what this signifies.

Seven women. Five men.

The first triumph.

18

'So, she'll want to nap in around an hour,' I say, stroking Rose's hair as my mum hoists her out of my arms and into her own. 'Please make sure you put her down –'

'Piera, I did raise you, you know.'

'I know you did, but if she doesn't nap this morning then she won't nap this afternoon when she comes home because she'll be overtired and then I'll have a horrendous night. She has a routine and I –'

'I promise I will put her down to nap,' Mum says, placing her hand on my shoulder and giving it a reassuring squeeze. 'Now go. Have fun catching up with your friend.'

I lean in, pressing a kiss into Rose's forehead, breathing in her powdery clean scent. She smiles at me. 'Mama,' she babbles. It makes my heart soar every time she says it.

'I love you, sweetheart. See you soon.'

I step out of the front door and down the steps and on to the path, glancing back over my shoulder to wave at them both – a pang of guilt rushing through me. I always feel guilty leaving her, even though she is with my mum, and she will have a lovely morning with her grandmother. Even though I know that I deserve my own time and space. I am still a person, after all. Not just a mother.

But the guilt today is much worse because of the argument. Looking at myself in the mirror this morning, I was disgusted at what I'd done, turning the scenario on to him because I couldn't bear the feeling of being the bad one. Being the liar. The lie I told isn't the first and nor will it be the last. But it is this lie that is eating away at me as I say goodbye to Rose. The same lie I told Harry last night and when I left the house this morning and he kissed me goodbye from where he was sitting at the dining table, his papers spread out, his eyes tired from a night of note-making and strategizing.

The lie that I am seeing Rachel.

The visitors' hall is loud and busy, every table occupied with one or more visitors – family, friends, children, all coming to see a loved one who has been locked away from them. Away from society. My eyes are drawn to the sad-looking toys stacked in one corner of the room, a small toddler playing with a threadbare doll, its face covered in pen marks. Who is she here to see? Her father? When will he be out? Will his decision mark her life forever? Rose appears, hazy in my mind, and my stomach sinks with sadness.

I glance around, my mind unable to stop itself from taking in each person awaiting the arrival of the prisoners and imagining a whole life for them, a whole story for why they are here, and what the other half of the tale has done to be inside here.

The woman at the table beside mine must be no more than twenty-one. She is on her own, staring about the room with a frenetic gaze, her mind clearly trying to cope without the distraction of her phone or any of her belongings. They remove them from visitors as we enter – belongings are searched and placed into lockers. People have found simple yet ingenious methods for smuggling in anything from chocolate to hard narcotics. But what is this girl thinking? She looks scared, worried, her eyes full of fragility. Is she visiting a boyfriend? Was he violent? Abusive? Her shoulders are curled over, as though she is carrying a heavy weight. Does she feel guilty that he is here? Does she wish she hadn't called the police? That she had forgiven him one more time?

I tear my eyes away from her and focus on a table on the far side of the hall. There is a man and woman sitting on the bench, so close to each other that his arm is curled around her waist, their sides touching without a hair's breadth of space between them. They are old, I'd hazard a guess at late seventies. His hair is greying and her face is carved with the lines of a hard-fought life. Parents. Their son is inside. Do they feel ashamed? Guilty? Exhausted? Do they blame themselves? Do they question every decision that they have made, every time they scolded him or let something slide? Do they wonder if he was born this way or if it was them?

The heat of someone's gaze burns into my cheek and I glance back at the table next to me. The girl quickly averts her eyes. But she was watching me. Was she doing the same thing as I am? Was she keeping her mind busy by inventing a life for me? A story? I wonder what she imagined. She'll probably have noticed the ring on my hand so she'll assume that I'm visiting my husband. When he comes out, will the sight of him and me together make sense in her mind? When we were younger, my entire body used to tingle at the reaction to Frank and me as a couple. *You two make such a beautiful pair*, people at university would say. *There's something about you when you're around him*, my friends from home had exclaimed. And there was – but that was Frank. He did it to everyone, but especially with me. He made me shine. Like he was holding a spotlight and directing it my way, bathing me in light.

Until he wasn't. And everything went black.

A door behind me clangs loudly and my head snaps to look over my shoulder.

There they are – a line of prisoners, checking in with the officer standing by the gate who releases them one by one into the hall.

I stand, the backs of my knees knocking into the hard metal bench. I rub them, my neck still craning to get sight of Frank. My stomach flutters and I shake my head, scolding myself at the anxiety he still gives me.

A large tank of a man, at least six foot six and the

width of two men, steps into the hall, moving past me to reach his visitors, and suddenly he is there. He looks so different in prison clothing, the loose tracksuit hanging from him, the pale grey somehow making him less imposing. Smaller. Frank has always been so careful in the image that he portrays. Now, with his tailored clothes and perfect styling, and at university with his long hair and black clothes portraying a mystery that drew everybody in. Especially me. But now, in here, he has no control over how he appears to other people. To the people in this hall seeing him for the first time, he is just another prisoner. They won't even look twice.

He checks in with the officer, who points in my direction. His eyes flash towards me and as they meet mine, he smiles, his lips still pressed together, those deep dimples settling into his cheeks. And there it is again. My stomach flipping. Like I am eighteen once more, seeing him for the first time.

But Harry's face shimmers into view and my body turns cold. Harry: the stable foundations upon which I have built my entire life. A man who would do anything for me and ask nothing of me in return, other than for me to love him. My relationship with Frank, while full of intensity and passion, always felt transactional. If you give me this, I'll give you that. That isn't what I want. Not now. I'm not eighteen any more.

He walks towards me, his eyes never leaving mine. Heat rushes into my cheeks as I take in that same glint in his eye. *You are trouble*, I used to whisper to him whenever he looked at me like that.

Right, Piera: centre yourself. In just a few more moments he'll be before you, and this is your turn to take control. He wants to have power over you. Like always. But you can make the tables turn.

'Morning, Piera,' he says as he reaches me, his voice raspy. He lifts his hands towards me and I glance over at the officers.

'We can't,' I mutter.

'I'm allowed to hug you, Piera,' he says, a mocking smirk on his face. 'We've both been searched.'

I tilt my chin up at him and he steps towards me, one step and then another, pausing just for a moment before wrapping his arms around my waist and tugging me towards him. I place my hands gently on his back, my body stiffening. My heart is pounding. Just being this close to him feels . . . feels like another betrayal. But he feels so familiar – my head fitting just so into the space next to his collarbone, his skin giving off that same scent, even with the prison-washed clothes and prison-bought body wash. Even with the fifteen years that have passed. Frank is Frank. Warmth spreads over me and I begin to relax into him.

No.

I pull away from him with a tap on his shoulder blade.

'Oh wow,' he says, looking down at me. 'The classic friend-back-tap.'

'Well, that's what we are, Frank,' I say, manoeuvring

my way back around the table to the bench on the other side. 'Friends – remember?'

'Oh, I remember. You're married and I was married too. And I really like Harry. But it's . . . it's you. It's us.'

I shrug, crossing my legs as I take a seat. 'It wasn't us when you left me for Linda.'

'You know I didn't leave you for her. That's not what happened. She needed me. After everything that happened, she needed me. But that didn't mean I wanted her more. You know that.' He leans forward, his gaze insistent. I tear my eyes away. 'Don't act like it isn't the same for you,' he says, sitting down directly opposite me, our knees touching under the table. 'What we had was different. It always will be. Right?'

I glance up at him – there is an unnerving look in his eye. A cross between playful teasing and something else. A warning. Don't push too far.

'I know,' I say, forcing myself to meet his gaze. 'But I'm here as your friend. I'm doing everything you've asked of me because you're my friend. No matter what we've been through.'

'Thank you.'

'Frank . . .' I glance around, lowering my voice, even though the noise of the visitors' hall is drowning out any decipherable conversations. 'Why didn't you tell me about the bag?'

He frowns. 'The bag?'

'Harry said that there was a bag packed. Linda's bag. You didn't mention it when you called –'

247

'Fucking hell, Piera, my wife has just killed herself and I was panicking. What do you think I was hiding?'

'I don't know, I just . . . if she packed the bag you can tell me.'

I watch his face carefully as he reacts to my comment. He narrows his eyes slightly but otherwise there is no change. No shock or anxiousness or shame. Nothing. But he's always been good at hiding his emotions, at conveying something that maybe isn't there. I always thought he was so emotionally open when we were together, but when it ended I couldn't help but feel that maybe I had just been under his spell. Am I still under it now? Was Linda trying to leave? Was she making one final, desperate attempt to leave him after all those years and he stopped her in the only way he could?

'She didn't,' he says calmly. 'I packed it for her. To take her to her sister's house. Why would she pack a bag when she was planning on killing herself?'

I swallow as he fixes me once again in that stare – the stare that's impossible to escape.

'You don't believe me.' He shakes his head, the colour draining from his cheeks. 'After everything we've been through, everything I have done for you. You know that Linda would have told everyone what you did if I hadn't kept her quiet. The only thing that stopped her was how much she loved me – she'd never do anything I didn't want her to do. I've helped you without question for years and now you don't believe me –'

'No, I do!' I reach across the table and grab his hands, squeezing them. His lip trembles and guilt churns inside me. Did Linda really want to tell people what happened? I thought that she had kept our secret out of loyalty to me. Maybe out of shame or guilt for taking Frank from me. Was it really just because he told her not to? Is that the level of control he wielded?

I shake my head. No matter what I think of Frank, he wouldn't kill Linda. He loved her. He always did. 'I'm sorry,' I whisper. 'I just . . . I was confused because I didn't know anything about it. I'm sorry. I'm here for you.'

He pauses, staring at our hands linked together on the table, until finally he nods. 'I appreciate you coming. And I appreciate that you turned up yesterday. I wasn't sure you would.'

'You asked me to. And I wanted to be there for you. But I didn't like lying to Harry –'

'Grown a conscience all of a sudden, Piera?'

My mouth falls open slightly. His nerve never fails to shock me.

'A conscience?' I mutter.

'It's not like you haven't lied to him before. I mean, he has no idea who I am –'

'Why would I tell him about a relationship I had at eighteen? Everybody does that in a new relationship. You're asked about an old partner or lover and you act like it was no big deal or pretend they never existed! You don't go into the details, especially the sordid ones. It's

249

not like it's normal for your ex to wander their way back into your life and hire your husband as their defence barrister!'

'Okay, just calm yourself down.'

A growl rumbles in the back of my throat. 'Don't. Tell me. To calm down.'

'Piera –'

'You're infuriating! Why did you do this?' The words burst out of me before I can stop them. His eyebrow lifts in surprise.

'Why?' he repeats, his eyes narrowing.

'Yes. You had another barrister, a good one. Why did you have to drag me into this? To punish me? To control me? Why?'

He doesn't answer, simply stares, assessing me.

'Frank, just –'

'Prior wanted me to change my plea,' he says finally, disdain seeping through his skin. 'He didn't think I stood a chance.'

'He wouldn't have said that, he's a brilliant barrister –'

'Well, he said it in other words. And that's not what I needed. I needed someone who would do anything to help me. Who would fight to get me acquitted.' He sits back in his chair, the disdain leaving his face, replaced by something else. A smirk. 'And you weren't available. So . . .'

I scoff. 'So you dragged Harry into this.'

I inhale deeply through my nose, my hands clenching into fists in my lap. I let the breath out, slowly, as I close my eyes, forcing my mind which is raging red to flood with calming blue.

'You never know when to stop,' I say, my voice still shaking. 'I am here for you, aren't I? I helped when you asked me to. I came when you asked me to. I came *because* you asked me to. And I lied to my husband to do it.'

'I didn't ask you to lie to Harry.'

I roll my eyes. 'You know I can't tell him –'

'Funny . . . Do people tend to hide things as big as this from their partners or –'

The calming blue in my mind evaporates, consumed entirely by burning frustration. I stand abruptly. 'I'm leaving.'

'Piera, stay –'

'No,' I seethe, only the glances of other visitors and the stare of the prison officers preventing me from shouting so loudly that my cries reverberate up to the high ceiling. 'You don't know what it was like for all these years to have to keep this secret to myself. You and Linda had each other. You could rely on each other. But me? You left me outside in the cold and I couldn't tell anyone. So don't talk to me about hiding things from my husband. I had no choice!' I step over the bench and wheel around, my heart pounding in my ears. I can't do this. He never knows when to stop –

'Piera.'

I come to an abrupt standstill, his tone the grip of an icy hand, turning me entirely cold. My head turns slowly. His face is still, but his eyes are lifeless, no warmth emanating towards me.

I pushed too far.

'Sit back down,' he says. Not a question. Not even a request. A command.

I step back over the bench and sink on to the hard metal, staring at the table between us. I can't bear to look at him. But his gaze, which was so cold just a moment ago, is now burning into me.

'You say you're here as my friend. And you say you're here for me because I asked you to be. But we both know the truth, don't we, Piera? You're not really here for me. You're here for yourself.'

'That isn't true –'

'Oh spare me,' he says. I peer upwards and his mouth is curved into a disbelieving smirk. 'You're here because you have to be. When I called you, I didn't want to outright blackmail you if I didn't have to, but you had to push back. So I thought we had the implicit understanding that I won't keep lying if you don't do as I ask. If you keep trying to run off like this –'

'Maybe I don't need your protection.'

'And now you're just going to lie straight to my face?' He smiles. 'Because that's what that is, Piera. And you know it. A bold-faced lie. I've protected you. And I'll continue to do it. I'll keep your secrets like I have done all these years.'

'And I've kept yours –'

'They were *your* secrets, Piera. I was just there.'

'You were the one who –'

'But now,' he interrupts, holding his finger up towards me, 'if I need your help, I need to trust that you'll be here for me.'

'As you said, you've got a great barrister,' I whisper. 'And you're innocent. You don't need to threaten me –'

'But if I need your help again, you'll do it. Right? Because we know what will happen if I'm found guilty and I have to tell Harry a few home truths about his perfect wife.'

My lip trembles. I should stay silent but I can't help myself. 'What will happen?'

'You know what. Well . . . he certainly won't trust you any more. Definitely not after he sees that video. I mean, I know you didn't mention me when you were telling your husband about university. But does he even know about Richard? Does he know anything about your life before you met him?'

'He –'

'There's no need to lie.'

'Frank . . .' I wipe my eyes quickly, tears stinging in the corners. Finally, I look at him once more, my eyes wide and pleading. 'I'll do whatever you say.'

'Good,' he mutters, sitting back in his chair, his face softening. 'Let's keep it that way –'

My breath catches as his eyes once again turn cold.

'– or your husband will never look at you the same way again. And you'll lose your daughter forever.'

Them

'Piera!' a voice shouts, and she and Frank jolt away from each other, his hand still clasping the back of her neck, his fingers tangled in her hair.

Piera blinks, her vision blurred, breathless. The club is crowded, the dancefloor packed. She and Frank had hidden away in a booth in the far corner, completely lost, as usual, in their own world. As if no one else existed. But now Richard is standing over them, his red hair glinting under the overhead lights, Linda by his side. Piera had introduced them after she had decided she wasn't interested in Richard, hoping that he and her new best friend might hit it off. But instead they had become more of a trio, a musketeer-style friendship. Except, as time had passed, Piera was spending less time with them and more and more time with Frank. And she hadn't introduced them. She hadn't wanted to. Not yet. She wanted her and Frank to stay cocooned away. Happy. Falling in love.

But apparently Linda and Richard had decided that it was time.

'So, this is lover boy?' Linda grins, reaching forward to playfully ruffle Piera's hair, which she avoids with a swift movement to the side.

Frank coughs, throwing Piera a quick smile, his dimples deep in his cheeks. She blushes furiously, her cheeks burning. 'Yeah, I guess that must be me,' he smirks.

Piera smiles, reaching up to cover her mouth. Is lipstick all over her face? How long had they been watching?

'And you must be Linda and Richard,' Frank continues. 'It's good to meet you.'

'Yeah, good to meet you, mate,' Richard says.

But Linda doesn't respond with the same courtesy. 'I've heard a lot about you from this one.'

'Oh, have you really?'

'You seem to have gotten into her head.'

Piera hangs her head. 'Jesus, Linda –'

'I'm just saying. Aren't you the one who's always preaching about honesty?'

Frank places his hand on Piera's leg. 'So you've been talking about me to your friends, have you?'

'Just a little bit?' Piera gestures with her fingers, an inch apart.

He mimics the movement. 'Just a little bit.'

'We're sorry to interrupt you,' Linda says, her eyes sparkling sarcastically. 'We can leave if you want –'

'No, shut up,' Piera says, gesturing to two empty seats at the table behind them. 'Sit down, you idiot.'

'Thanks.' Linda waits while Richard retrieves the chairs, placing them down either side of Piera and Frank, then leans towards Piera, waggling her fingers at her, gesturing at her to come closer. Piera glances over at Frank but he's chatting to Richard, the two of them seemingly connecting over something or other.

'He's really hot –'

'Linda!' Piera laughs, and leans in even closer. 'I did tell you –'

'Just . . .' Linda glances away.

Piera frowns. 'What is it?'

Linda sighs. 'Don't get mad at me, okay?'

'What is it?'

'It's just I've heard some stuff . . . about Frank and girls. Apparently it doesn't always turn out that well for the girl.'

Piera chews on her lip. She has heard the rumours about Frank. And the nicknames. Heartbreaker. But that isn't how he is with her. What they have . . . it's special.

'Well . . . we'll see.' Piera blushes again. 'He's different with me. And he makes me happy –'

'Just be careful, okay?' Linda says, resting her hand on Piera's forearm. 'I don't want you to get hurt.'

'I know. Neither do I. I just want to have fun –'

'Cheers to that!'

They chink their glasses together. Piera smiles at Linda but can't help but glance nervously across at Frank. Is he going to break her heart? She knows that she is a romantic – she always has been. Her parents painted such a beautiful picture of their own love story, and they met here, at Oxford. Is she being a fool for hoping that she could have the same?

She shakes her head, blinking rapidly as Frank turns his attention back to her and grips her hand, running his thumb across her knuckles. *Stay present, Piera*, she thinks.

And a few more drinks, some shots and dancing later, the four of them are bonded, in the way only a night out in your twenties can bond a group together. And as she watches them all swirl before her, their movements blurring with the flashing lights and pounding music, Piera hopes that the rest of the year will be just like this. This perfect night.

Her and Frank.

Richard.

And Linda.

19

'Then what happened?'

'Nothing,' Harry says, shrugging his shoulders. 'Golding didn't re-examine, so she left.'

My chest tightens, anxiety swirling in my stomach, but I smile at Rose who is playing on the floor in front of us, babbling up at me. 'How did your client react?'

'I didn't get to speak to him until the end of the day . . . He was a bit cold with me. As though I hadn't done enough. But I did everything I could.'

'I'm sure you did. There's only so much you can push the victim's sister –'

'Exactly. I pushed her as far as I could without breaking her. The jury have the idea that potentially this was a very depressed woman who wanted to kill herself. That's all I could do. She was always going to hit back.'

'Sounds like it was tough,' I say.

He sighs. 'Trying to challenge a woman into accepting that her sister might have killed herself by cutting her own throat is . . . not easy.'

My breath catches in my chest. I reach for my mug on the side table and gulp down the cold tea that has been sitting there since just after lunch. An old barrister's trick to buy yourself some time. A moment to steady your thoughts. I place it back on the table and exhale slowly. Silently – so Harry won't notice.

'But she did accept that Frank looked after her, that he took her to hospital,' Harry continues, unaware. 'She even admitted that the last time she spoke to her she'd been acting strangely.'

I frown. 'Strangely how?'

'Apparently they used to write letters to each other but Linda hadn't written one in months. But she asked if Eve had received her letter . . . I think the police are going to look into it.'

'You think it could have something that would help Frank?'

'Or hinder him. Who knows if it even exists?'

I shift in my seat, tucking one foot beneath me. 'Who gave evidence after her?'

'The neighbour. She went in to check on her while Frank was out.'

'And that was okay?'

'Yes, fine. She said she went in, Linda was asleep and she left. I had to cross-examine her on what was visible to her as she insisted there was no evidence of pills in the room. But she caved quite quickly.'

I lean forward and pick up Rose, placing her on my lap. She collapses into me, resting her head on my chest, her chubby hands clenching and unclenching against me. I breathe her in. 'What's next?'

Harry leans towards me and rests his head on my

shoulder, his face close to Rose's. 'Next is the police who attended the scene.'

'And after that?'

'After that is the endless medical evidence, psychologists, Linda's GP. And then Frank. It's funny, isn't it . . .'

I turn my head to look down at him and he peers up at me through his eyebrows.

'A murder trial, and there really isn't all that much to say. It's listed for six weeks . . . I'd be surprised if it takes four.'

'Well, they were the only ones there. Frank . . .' I stop myself but it is too late. Harry is looking at me, waiting for me to finish. I cough.

'What were you going to say?'

'I was going to say . . . Frank is the only one who knows what happened.'

He nods, the stubble on his chin scratching against the bare skin where my jumper has fallen away from my shoulder. 'He's the only one who will ever know.'

Frank's words echo in my mind. *We know what will happen if I'm found guilty.*

'It's just so sad that she thought there was no other option,' I whisper. 'And so sad for him too, having to witness that.'

I scan his face as he stares into mid-air, checking for any minuscule change in his expression, trying to read his thoughts. What is he thinking? What does he believe? I can't ask him outright.

He sighs and sits up, holding out both hands towards

me and waggling his fingers. 'Gimme,' he says, smiling at Rose.

I smile back, my heart warming at the way he looks at her. So full of love. 'Here, go to Daddy,' I say, kissing her on the side of the head.

He takes her, placing her on his lap so she is facing towards him. He holds her gently by the wrists and tips her backwards. Only by a fraction, but laughter bursts out of her, like always. She loves this game. I chuckle along with both of them. This is all I want. For us to stay like this. How is it that someone miles away, locked in a cell with no freedom at all, could threaten everything?

My phone rings, vibrating next to me. I pick it up, my stomach dropping at the *Private Number* on the screen. I glance at Harry but he is still laughing with Rose, bending forward to blow raspberries on her tummy. She shrieks with laughter and he throws his head back joyfully, his face splitting clean open with a grin.

I look back at my phone. Is it him? Were his ears burning? It's as though he could tell we were speaking about him, that I was thinking about him.

'I've just got to take this. Sam is calling me,' I say, gesturing at my phone. 'Do you mind?'

'Your clerk, Sam? . . . No, of course not. Go to my office. I'll put Rose to bed.'

'Thanks.'

I stand quickly and stride towards the office, closing

the door firmly behind me. I answer the call but say nothing. I simply press the phone to my ear and wait.

'This call is from a person currently in a prison in England,' an automated voice says. 'All calls are logged and recorded and may be listened to by a member of prison staff. If you do not wish to accept this call, please hang up now.'

I hold the phone away from my ear, my chest rising and falling heavily. My body is tingling, every instinct telling me to hang up, to ignore, to take away his power. But angering him is not a good idea.

'Are you there?'

I breathe in shakily. 'Yes, it's me.'

'How are you?'

His voice sounds strange, forced. He wants something from me. But what?

We're being recorded. But he's clever. Whatever it is, he won't say it outright.

'I . . . I'm okay . . . What do . . .' I stop myself from saying *what do you want*. If he needs to be subtle, so do I. 'How are you?'

'I'm fine. I'm calling to ask a favour.'

'Okay.'

Here we go. I bite down on my lip, nerves churning.

'Linda used to write letters. To me . . . to *other people*. I want to make sure they're . . . safe. Could you go round to my house and check?'

Letters . . .

There is a knock on the door. I jump. It swings open

slowly and Harry is standing there. I smile at him and point at the phone still pressed against my face. He takes Rose's hand and waves it at me.

'Night night, Mummy,' he mouths.

'Goodnight,' I mouth back. He backs out, closing the door quietly behind him.

'Are you still there?' Frank says, his voice even more gravelly than usual through the weak phone line.

'Yes, I'm here.'

'Could you?'

'Um . . . yes. I could go tom—'

'As soon as you can.'

I try to swallow but my mouth is dry. 'Okay . . . How do I –'

'You will know the code. Some things never change. Remember?'

My mind is racing but I want to be off this phone call. 'Yes. O-okay.'

'Thank you,' he says.

The dial tone blares.

I sit down in Harry's office chair, my hands shaking. He wants me to go to his house, the one he shared with Linda, and let myself in. I'll know the code? What does he mean? And he wants me to look for letters. Letters . . .

What was it that Harry just mentioned about letters? Something that Linda's sister said in her evidence.

I sit up, my mind suddenly falling quiet as the pieces click into place. Eve Thompson mentioned that during her last conversation with Linda, Linda said she had written her a letter. But Eve never received it. She has assumed that Linda was just lost in her depression and had never actually written to her in the first place. But that isn't what Frank believes. Clearly, he thinks that this letter might be real, and he doesn't want anyone else to find it. There was something in the way he said that he wants to make sure the letters are *safe* . . .

He wants me to find the letter. And he wants me to destroy it.

Them

'Happy birthday, dear Piera, happy birthday to you!'

The group finish singing and Piera leans forward, squeezing her eyes tightly shut as she blows out her candles and wishes.

'Hip-hip –' Frank shouts, gripping Piera's shoulder.

'Hooray!' Linda, Richard and Frank shout together.

'Hip-hip –'

'Hooray!'

'Hip-hip-hooray!'

Piera opens her eyes and beams around at them. This is what she has wished for. For everything to stay exactly like this. The four of them. And at the centre of their group, her and Frank. Together. Always.

'Happy birthday, P,' Linda says, wrapping her arms around her from behind, her cheek pressed to Piera's.

'Thank you, Linda.' She looks around at Richard. 'Thank you all, this is the best birthday ever.'

'And it's just beginning,' Richard says, lifting a bottle of vodka from the table and adding more to her half-empty glass of vodka and orange juice. 'Let's have a couple more here and then go to Matrix to meet everyone else.'

'Sounds great,' Piera says, lifting her glass and taking a large gulp. She winces. 'Cheers.'

Richard laughs, leaning down to press a kiss to her cheek.

'Mate,' Frank says, nudging Richard's shoulder. 'Can you pour me some more too?'

Richard sloshes some vodka into Frank's glass. Some splashes on to the floor. 'Sorry, mate.'

'Whatever.' Frank nudges Richard out of the way and pulls Piera to her feet. 'Come with me,' he whispers in her ear.

'Where are we going?' she says, giggling as she throws a glance over her shoulder at Richard who rolls his eyes.

Frank guides her out of the living room towards his bedroom. 'I just want to give you your birthday present.'

'My birthday present?' She steps inside his room, which is dimly lit, just a side lamp and a candle throwing a warm glow across the space. 'You already gave me my presents.'

'I've decided to give you one last one.'

He retrieves a small box from his bedside table and then flops down on to the bed, patting the space beside him. She settles next to him and they face each other, both propped up on one elbow, their knees touching. He hands her the box.

She smiles at him, taking in his face. He's just so beautiful.

'Come on, open it –'

'Okay!'

She pulls the lid off the box, her eyes widening as she takes in what's inside.

A small silver key.

'Is this –'

'The key to here. Yes, it is.' His lips purse together, his dimples appearing.

'You want me to have a key?' she whispers.

He snakes his arm around her waist, pulling her closer to him so that their hips press against each other. 'I don't just want you to have a key,' he says in a low voice. 'I want you to move in with me.'

'Move in?' Piera's stomach flutters. Living with Frank would be a dream – he's her best friend, her everything. She wants to be with him all the time. But it's so soon . . . And they're so young.

'I love you. I want to live with you. Don't you love me?'

'Yes, of course,' she whispers.

'So, you'll do it?'

Piera stares at him – his wide, excited eyes, his beaming smile. And all she wants to do in that moment is make him happy. Keep him happy.

She nods.

'Yes!' He leans forward quickly, smothering her face with kisses. She laughs, high-pitched, joy spilling out of her. This is why she loves him. She can't help but do anything else.

'I'll need the code, too, for the door downstairs,' she

says as his excited kisses slow down and he moves to her neck.

He gives a muffled laugh. 'You already know the code.'

'No, I don't,' she says, confused, trying to think but unable to focus on anything other than the feeling of him kissing her skin.

'I changed it the week after I met you.'

'But you didn't tell me. I don't know it –'

'You do,' he whispers. 'It's the most important day of the year.'

'What day is that?'

'Today.'

Her birthday.

20

I grip the steering wheel, my eyes fixated on the house.

You will know the code. Some things never change. Remember? After all these years, the code to get inside Frank's house is still my birthday.

Jesus, Frank.

Number 10 Wheeldon Avenue. I've never been inside, but I remember friends talking about it after we left university. Frank had always resented his father, but it didn't stop him from accepting a house in Zone 3, a house that Linda moved into soon after. I drove past once – before I met Harry and was consumed by him, his love expelling the feelings that still remained for Frank – and I stared over at it from the road opposite, just like I'm doing now. Could this have been my life? If we had survived, would this have been me?

My phone pings with a message and Harry's name lights up my screen. I lift it up to my face and it unlocks, his words revealing themselves.

Enjoy drinks. I hope you enjoy seeing those guys again. Don't let them force you to come back if you don't want to though. If I don't see you tonight or in the morning before I leave, goodnight. I love you xxx

I needed a reason to leave. And I had told him it was

chambers calling. So I told him it was one of the clerks, Sam, who had been my friend, inviting me out for a barrister's birthday. But whose name did I say? Now I can't remember. I kissed Rose goodbye, already asleep in her cot, and then kissed Harry too, guilt turning my stomach as I told him I loved him.

But I need to do this. Soon enough, this will all be over. And I'll never have to see or speak to Francis Joseph ever again.

I catch my reflection in the rear-view mirror and force the worry from my face, steeling myself. In and out. That's all I need to do. Find the letter. And get out of there as quickly as possible.

I pull my hood down low over my forehead, then tug my scarf up tightly around my nose and mouth. I check my mirror again. All that's visible is my eyes.

I get out of the car, closing the door quietly, pushing my weight against it until the lock clicks into place. My feet move quickly beneath me, my breaths short and shallow as I race towards the front door, my eyes scanning for people walking down the street or prying neighbours. But the road is quiet and dark. The privilege of a quiet village in London.

The camera is there, fixed to the door. I drop my head even though it surely must have run out of battery by now.

Now to get inside. And to do it quickly.

I keep my head lowered but peer out from beneath

the hood, scanning the door porch for anything that might require a code. An electronic lock or a key safe –

Yes. There it is. A key safe.

You will know the code.

I step forward, my fingers shaking as I use my nails to open the cover to expose the keypad. I press the keys quickly – 890427.

The lock clicks open. I pull open the door and there it is: a key.

I grab it and close the key safe, and then rush back to the door, struggling to push the key into the lock while still keeping my face hidden. Finally, it slips in and I turn, but it gets stuck, the door remaining firmly closed. A low growl escapes my mouth and I clench my fists. I pull on the door with one hand, and then try again. And –

It opens.

I pull the key out of the lock and step inside, wincing as the door slams behind me.

A panicked whimper leaves me as relief floods my body. I am in.

I am in: inside Frank's home. *Linda* and Frank's home.

Linda.

She died here.

My eyes adjust slowly to the darkness as I stand frozen in the hallway, unable to move from the space just inside the door. The stairs are straight ahead. To my left is a living room, and on my right, an office. Beyond that there's another door but I can't see what's inside. And then at the end of the corridor, double doors. They must lead to the kitchen. The stairs, painted black, a cream wool runner leading the way up to the rooms above, draws my eye. How many rooms are there?

Where on earth do I begin?

I walk forward slowly, the wooden boards creaking beneath my feet. I wince, as though the sound will wake some deep-sleeping monster. But I am alone here. I peer inside the first room. Frank's office. I can tell it's his by the forebidding masculinity of the desk – a metal monolith in the centre of the room. The dark wooden cabinetry on the walls. The photograph of Linda on the desk. Her face sends a shudder down my spine. I haven't seen her in so long. She looks the same as she did at university, her eyes unchanged, her hair a slightly darker shade of blonde. But the same. Her laugh – deceptively low and filthy for someone with such a high-pitched sing-song of a voice – echoes in my mind, so clearly it's as though it's echoing through this house. When was the last time she laughed here? Was she happy? Or were her recent months nothing but sadness?

I step inside, scanning the room. His office would have been searched thoroughly for evidence. Computers, telephones. And why would Linda keep a letter here?

I go to leave but something to the right of the door

catches my attention. A cupboard door, a different shape to the others. The others are rectangular but this one is square, bespoke. It looks just like the cupboards in hotels which hide –

A safe.

I rush forward, throwing myself to my knees. I pull open the door and there it is, sleek and black. Surely the police would have checked inside here? But I can't help myself. My fingers reach towards the buttons and I tap in the same code. 890427. It flashes green and unlocks.

My mouth drops open. My hand is trembling but I reach forward and open the door.

It is empty except for one thing. A rectangular metal box and some papers secured to it with an elastic band. I reach for it and pull off the papers, tossing them aside to open the box.

A gun. There is a gun inside. A lengthened handgun.

My hand scrambles for the papers which just moments ago I discarded without a second thought. I open them –

A licence. He had a licence for a firearm. Did Linda know about this? Did it scare her?

I pull it from its secure foam casing and hold it between my hands. It is heavy, cold. But strangely comforting. If Frank had wanted to kill his wife, wouldn't he have done it with a gun? Her committing suicide with the licensed gun they had in their home would have been far more believable than her slitting her own throat.

I put the gun back in its box and return everything to its original place, paperwork and all, then quickly run my hand around the sides and back of the safe, checking for anything else. I close the door and the safe locks and I stand, my fingertips tingling, the feeling of the gun still lingering, like a phantom limb.

I move down the hallway and to the next room along. There is a small living room, like a snug, a small sofa tucked into the corner next to a fireplace and a bookshelf. I move along to the double doors and push. But as they open, revealing a large living area and adjoining kitchen, I freeze, unable to step beyond the boundary. This is where it happened.

Nausea rushes up from my stomach to my throat and I clamp my hand across my mouth. I thought I was numb to things like this, years of working in criminal law hardening me to any kind of emotional or visceral reaction. But this is uncontrollable. The thought of Linda lying just there, her blood pooling rapidly in the kitchen, her heart pumping hard in a desperate attempt to keep her alive, but only draining her of life all the quicker . . . I can't. I can't go in there.

I close the doors quickly, the slam vibrating through me. My fingers grip the handle and I breathe in deeply, trying to rid my body of wanting to be sick.

Just walk away. Go upstairs. Get as far away as possible.

I turn quickly and make my way towards the stairs, taking them two at a time. At the top of the stairs there are four rooms: two bedrooms, the doors opened, and then two others, the doors closed. I reach for the closed door closest to the stairs and turn the handle. The bathroom. The door to my right is open and I peer inside. This room is pristine, the bed perfectly made, no belongings left on bedside tables or on the windowsill. No markings of a life lived inside its walls. That must be the spare.

I head to the two doors at the back of the house and stand in an open doorway. Inside is a large room, a queen-sized bed up against the left-hand wall, one bedside table still laden with belongings. This must have been their bedroom. On the side closest to the door there is a glass, watermarked, a book on World War One beside it. Frank's side of the bed. He drank from that glass, read that book, lay in that bed and fell asleep not knowing that the next day his entire world would end. My eyes flit over to the other side. All that is there is a photograph, mirrored glass. Frank and Linda beam out at me, their faces full of joy. He, in a tuxedo. Her, in a beautiful white dress, her hair flowing down her back, a veil catching in a breeze behind her.

She looks so beautiful. Happy.

'Are you sure you're happy, P?'

I shiver as her voice echoes in my mind, so clear it is as though she is in the room with me. But it isn't her. It's a memory of her.

We lay together in the park, our favourite spot. Once spring came, the two of us would meet on Wednesday evenings, after our final lectures, without the boys. If the weather was good she would bring a bottle of wine and I would bring food, and we'd sit in the park, under the branches of a hanging willow tree.

'Are you sure you're happy, P?' she had muttered, seemingly out of nowhere. I paused with a frown, shocked at the sudden change in conversation. We had been talking about our weekend plans.

'Am I happy?' I repeated back at her.

She rolled on to her side, turning to face me. 'I mean . . . with Frank.'

'Of course,' I said, mirroring her position, our knees almost touching. 'I'm really happy . . . Why?'

She sighed. 'It's just, everything has happened so quickly. And it's so intense . . . he is so intense.'

'You don't like him? I thought you liked him?'

She shook her head, her brow furrowing. 'No, I do, you know I do. Frank is . . . he's a special guy. I just don't want you being swept away by it all and not being able to turn back —'

'I don't want to turn back. But if I wanted to, I could —'

'Do you really believe that, Piera?' She sat up, her hair falling forward as she looked down at me. 'He has a power over you. Over people. You know he does.'

I pushed myself up, the feeling in the air changing, the lounging on the ground no longer feeling comfortable. 'Frank loves me, Linda,' I said firmly. 'That's all that matters.'

She offered a small smile. 'I'm just trying to be a good friend. That's all.'

I looked into her eyes, searching for some underlying intent. Malice. Jealousy. But in that moment I couldn't read her. So all I said was, 'I know.'

'Just be careful.'

Her voice echoes again as I tear my eyes away from the photograph.

Be careful.

For so long after it was all over and Linda and Frank were together, I thought that her words were born out of wanting Frank for herself. That she wanted to break us up so he could be hers. But what if she wasn't under his spell yet? Was she trying to warn me? To usher me away from Frank before it was too late?

Then the same thing happened to her. She fell into his grasp. And before she knew it, it was too late.

I exhale deeply and then cross the room to the bed and quickly open the bedside drawers, first on one side, then the other, rifling through the contents. But no letter. I drop down to my knees, but beneath the bed is empty. I open the wardrobes, my hands flying, my movements becoming more frantic as I plunge into the pockets of coats, sliding my hands between folded jumpers and T-shirts, searching through rolled up pairs of socks. It feels dirty. As though I am pillaging their past. Their life.

But there is nothing. No letter.

The police would have searched this room, though. They would have found it.

I go back to the door, surveying the room one last time before I take a step backwards, into the hallway, where somehow the air feels clearer. I move towards the final closed door and push it open.

All the breath in my lungs escapes me, as though I have been punched. Winded. I step inside, my eyes filling with tears, my hands dragging through my hair, pulling my hair loose before I'm able to take control of myself. I was expecting another bedroom, maybe a small space for Linda to do whatever it was she did now, but I wasn't expecting this. This . . . this is too much.

A small crib in the centre, a mobile suspended above it. A small chest of drawers. A bookshelf hanging on the wall.

A nursery.

The atmosphere in here is even worse than the bedroom. A room never inhabited but somehow so alive. The grief palpable. A vision of Rose plays in my mind and my lip trembles, tears threatening to spill. She was so desperate for a baby. The loss must have hit her like a wave, the grief hitting her over and over again. An endlessly turning tide.

If it's anywhere it would be here. They may have looked, but their search would have focused on the spaces Linda and Frank shared their lives, and where the tragedy took place. Their bedroom. The hallway. The kitchen. Not an unused nursery, the air thick with sorrow.

And if Linda was trying to hide something from Frank, surely this is where she would have done it?

I take a few small steps inside the room, my fingers tracing the pale sage-green of the walls. She must have been so excited when they decorated this room. After years of marriage, finally a baby. A family. Finally. And then all taken away, in just a flash. Without a thought.

I stop before the dresser, pulling the hair tie off from where it is tangled around my fingers, and slowly open the drawers. Inside the top one there is a pile of tiny vests, stacked one on top of the other. A packet of unopened dummies. A soft-bristled brush. Minute socks.

No letter.

The drawer below is mostly empty, a blanket sitting alone on one side, its material so soft I want to press my face against it. Rose had one just like it, hers a blush-pink. I unfold it – it feels wrong to move it. But there is no letter in its layers. I fold it back carefully and replace it in its drawer.

The final drawer has a few babygrows and a raincoat.

No letter.

If Frank is acquitted, what will he do with all this? Will he leave it here, unable to touch it or remove it? The room locked away, a memory – never to be acknowledged but never erased? Or will he get rid of it all, simply not able to bear it? Or maybe he will find someone else. And before long they will move into this house and take Linda's place. Their child will take this child's place.

I cross to the rocking chair, sliding my hand around the edge of the base cushion – maybe she wrote it sitting there and tucked it down the side, forgetting about it until she spoke to her sister. But there is nothing.

I walk towards the door, breathing a sigh of relief to be leaving that sad room. But . . .

I turn back quickly and stride over to the crib. It is made up with a soft cotton sheet, a teddy placed just so at the top, where a baby's head might have lain. I pick up the teddy then lift the thin mattress.

And there, hiding all along, a folded piece of paper.

I pick it up, the paper shaking in my hand as I unfold it. My eyes feast on it hungrily, taking in each word, devouring them –

My hand lifts to cover my mouth, my breath catching. Heart hammering against my ribs.

I fold the letter again, trying to draw in oxygen, my eyes fixed to the page, heavy with Linda's terrified slanted thoughts. And the final paragraph.

I can tell. This man who I once called my friend, then my lover, then my husband. He wants me gone. I've become a nuisance, a problem, a poorly dog he just wants to put down. I'm scared. If I don't leave now I really fear . . . this man will kill me.
This man will kill me.

She was scared. She felt she was in danger. And I have been the world's biggest fool – tangled in Frank's web once again.

He didn't want an alibi because he was scared of being blamed for something he didn't do.

He killed Linda.

And I helped him cover it up.

Do NOT

21

My phone vibrates, my heart sinking at the sight of *Private Number* flashing up on the screen.

I answer the phone, my eyes blurring as I listen to the automated message I almost know by heart now. The line clears, the static of the call buzzing in my ear.

'P?'

'Hmm,' I say, unable to say anything else.

'Did you find it?'

'Yes, I found it.'

'Is it *safe*?'

I know what he wants me to do. He wants me to destroy it. He doesn't even know what it says, but he knows that it won't be good. The last shred of hope within me that Frank is innocent and this is all a big mistake disappears instantly, a light going off and plunging me into darkness.

I can't show anyone. I can't tell anyone. I can't take that risk.

'Yes,' I whisper. 'It's safe.'

I turn on the shower, holding my hand under the water until it turns from cold to hot, steam filling the bathroom. I need to wash this day away – I need to clear my thoughts. I've spent all of today looking after Rose, trying to focus on her, but completely absorbed by Linda's letter.

Frank killed Linda.

And I've been helping him. So much happened between me and Linda, but she was my friend. Before anything else, we were Linda and Piera. How can I ever undo what I have done?

Is that letter enough for him to be found guilty? Does it *prove* that he killed her? At the very least, it proves that she was afraid of him, that she was scared he was going to hurt her. But she never sent it. She hid it, instead. If I give it to the police anonymously, Harry will probably argue that this is just another sign of Linda's depression, of her desperately needing help, which wasn't given to her. After all, that's what Frank would tell him. If I give the letter to the police, will Frank know that it was me? When he inevitably calls, I could tell him that I didn't find anything . . . then maybe he would believe that the police found it. But that's not right. The police would have to disclose that it was given to them. That they didn't discover it at the scene. And Harry would argue that it's unfair to use it in the trial if they don't know where it came from.

No . . . the only way for this to be used against Frank is for me to tell Harry that I found it. And for me to do that, I would have to admit everything. My history with Frank. The lies that I have been telling him. And everything else –

'Honey, I'm home!'

'Suit yourself,' I force myself to say with a coy smile as I saunter out of the room. But as soon as I am out of sight, the two of us separated by the bathroom door, I crouch down, covering my mouth so he can't hear my ragged breaths.

Lies. I have told so many lies that I can't even remember what lie I have told. What if he sees someone from chambers and asks if it was Michael's birthday? What if he doesn't believe that that was an innocent mistake?

And he's been inside Frank's house. Why did Frank send him there? To wind me up? To remind me of his power? Of how easily he could upend my entire life?

I sit back against the door and rest my forehead on my knees, the steam from the shower filling the entire room and consuming me.

If I don't tell Harry about this letter, Frank might be acquitted.

But if I tell him, I might lose him.

What is worse? A world where a murderer is free because I didn't do something to stop him? Or a world without Harry?

I can't live without Harry. But if Frank is found not guilty, do I really believe that he will simply disappear out of my life? No. That isn't his nature. He'll always be there, lingering, threatening to ruin my life if I try to turn against him.

And if he's capable of killing Linda . . . is he capable of killing me?

Them

'Piera!'

Richard and Linda beam at her from the door, their arms full of drinks, their faces flushed from the winter chill which is still lingering into the beginning of spring.

'Come in, come in,' Piera says, gesturing excitedly.

'Look at her inviting us in, like it's her place,' Richard says teasingly as he and Linda step inside, his Prince Charming smile – teeth perfectly straight and white – shining in the low light of Frank's flat.

'Hello, darling,' Piera says, leaning in to Linda and kissing her on the cheek, relieving her of one of the bottles of vodka she has cradled in her arms. She steps forward and reaches up to hug Richard as well, having to stand on her tiptoes, even in high heels, to manage to wrap her arms around his neck. 'Well, actually . . .'

'Have you moved in here?' Linda gawps.

'Maybe . . .'

'Oh, you two are love's young dream, aren't you?' Richard shouts.

'We are!' Frank's voice says from behind Piera, his arms snaking around her waist as he buries his face in her neck. She giggles, her chest fluttering as it always does when he touches her, her feelings bubbling out of her uncontrollably.

She is in love. Truly. There is nobody like Frank.

'I'm really excited for you both,' Linda says, handing Richard the other bottle of vodka as she unwinds her scarf from around her neck. 'But isn't it a bit quick? I mean, Piera, you still have your room in halls. We're only nineteen!'

'I'm twenty,' Frank says, releasing Piera's waist and resting his hand on her shoulder instead. 'Thank you, Linda, for your concern –' he leans down and smacks a kiss roughly on the side of her head – 'but we are very happy.'

'Is that all I get?' Linda says. 'Do I not get a hug?' She reaches up to hug Frank, her hands around his waist. He rests his chin on top of her head, winking at Piera.

'Come,' Piera says, ushering them towards the two small sofas crammed into the corner of the apartment, glasses and ice already set out on the coffee table alongside a large bowl of crisps and another of popcorn. 'Let's sit. I'll get the drinks.'

Linda and Richard flop down on to one sofa, though there is an awkward distance between them, Linda's body turning in towards his, while his arms are crossed and he leans forward, away from her. Piera narrows her eyes as she pours a beer for Richard and Frank, and vodka lemonade for herself and Linda.

'Here you go,' she says, handing out the drinks,

before settling down on the other sofa with Frank, nestling in tightly against him, his arm crossing over her lap, his fingers gripping her thigh. 'Cheers,' she says, raising her glass.

'Cheers,' they all echo.

They simultaneously lift their glasses and drink, but Linda's eyes dart sideways to Richard then lower to the floor.

'So what's going on with you two, then?' Frank says, a cheeky smile spreading across his face.

Linda lifts her gaze quickly, blushing. But she doesn't say a word. She doesn't push back. She is waiting – what will Richard say?

'What do you mean?' he responds, shifting forward again on the sofa, his jeans squeaking on the faux leather, his knees almost touching the table. 'We're friends – aren't we, Lind?' He jostles her with his elbow, the very image of forced casualness.

Linda sniffs loudly. 'Yeah, of course. We're just friends, guys. Not everyone is in love like you two.' She takes a long gulp of her drink before sinking further back into the sofa. 'And I couldn't compete with Richard's crush, now could I?'

'Linda!' Richard's head snaps towards her, his eyes glaring.

Frank smirks. 'You haven't said anything, mate.'

'It's nothing, Frankie, honestly.'

'Nah, you can't do that. No secrets in this group. Who is it?'

'Nobody, I don't even know what she's talking about –'

Linda laughs, throwing her head back as she cackles. 'Well, he wouldn't tell you, would he, Frank?'

Frank's eyes narrow. 'Why? What does that mean?'

'Well, it can be a bit awkward if your mate fancies your girlfriend.'

'Fucking hell, Linda – what is wrong with you?' Richard shouts into a momentary silence.

Piera grits her teeth as Frank's hand moves from her lap. She has never seen this look on his face before, or the coldness in his eyes. He looks . . . different.

'You fancy Piera?' His voice is low, barely more than a whisper.

'No, Frank. I don't.'

'I mean, I know you had something for her before we met, but –'

'That was nothing! She's your girlfriend and you're my mate.'

'Then why would Linda say that?' Frank spits.

'I don't know,' Richard says, standing up then leaning forward, his body towering over Linda, who shrinks quickly, her body curling inwards. 'Why would you say that?'

'Because –'

'Because what?'

Piera's eyes dance back and forth between them – Linda looking so small in her corner of the sofa, Richard looming above her, and Frank staring, unblinking. Her triad of best friends. Her only friends. They've spent so much time together, their closeness as a group bonds them in a way that excludes others. But something like this has never happened before. There's never been this feeling hanging in the air between them. She holds her breath.

'Because I was joking!' Linda shouts, a hysterical laugh escaping her. 'Jesus, since when can't you lot take a joke?'

'You were joking?' Frank mutters.

'Yeah! Of course. Come on, Frank, Richard's your mate —'

'Piera's like a sister, Frank.'

Piera is frozen, awaiting his reaction. She doesn't care if Richard likes her or not. She doesn't care if he has been pining over her this entire time or if this was Linda's weird idea of fun. All she cares about is what Frank is thinking. Is he going to let this go?

He throws his arm around her shoulder, dimples appearing in his cheeks. 'You're both a pair of pricks.'

'Blame her,' Richard says, 'not me!'

Their conversation buzzes around her, and more drinks are poured, laughter billowing out of them. But Piera is fixed on the tinge of coldness still lingering in Frank's eyes. And on Linda. Because whether she meant to or not, Linda has revealed a chink in the armour of their indivisible group.

Jealousy.

22

Two Weeks Later

I hold my breath as I unlock my phone, the message from Harry hidden from sight.

He always messages with a verdict. Every trial. His entire career.

But this verdict. This one is different. I always want Harry to win, but if Frank is acquitted it will be because of me.

Last week I went back into the court. I snuck my way on to the back row of the public gallery without anyone seeing me, just like that first day of the trial. But this time, not even Frank knew I was there.

And I watched. I watched as he gave his evidence, as Harry took him through the story that I had unwittingly helped him fabricate, the evidence I had helped him secure and destroy. And I watched as he defended himself during cross-examination. He played the grieving husband so incredibly well. I almost believed it. I did believe it.

Until I saw that letter. And now it is hidden in my bedroom, just lying there. Linda silenced once more.

But nothing can bring Linda back. Nothing can save

her. Not even her letter. But if he is found guilty he could destroy me. He *will* destroy me, I know it. And he'll do it for one reason and one reason alone. Because he can.

Every day since the jury went out for deliberation, I've been unable to think about anything else, my mind consumed with the decision they are making. Guilty or not guilty? I've been trying to distract myself – today I arrived on Mum's doorstep so early that Rose hadn't even had her breakfast yet. But nothing is working.

I click on the message and the text appears. And just like that, everything blurs, my mum's voice in the background as she makes a snack for Rose, the living room becoming almost unrecognizable, even my own breathing. I am plummeting downwards, the world forever changed because of me. Because of all the things I did. And didn't do.

Frank = NG.

The jury acquitted. With the long deliberation, the note going down to the jurors that they could deliver a majority verdict and still no decision for days, I really believed it would be a finding of guilt. Or at least a hung jury. But they have acquitted.

By the end of the day, Frank will be out in the world. A free man.

Free to wreak whatever havoc he wants on my life.

This changes everything.

I was so focused on keeping him content, keeping

the peace between us while the trial was ongoing, that I didn't think about the consequences of him being acquitted. He holds all the power.

But . . . does he?

He knows my secrets. But now I also know his. If he can hold our shared history over my head, then I can hold what he has done over his. I'll keep his secrets, if he will keep mine.

I need to end this once and for all.

'Mum, I just got a text from Harry that he needs something bringing to court – do you mind watching Rose while I go?'

'No, of course not, love,' she says, not even turning to look at me, her focus solely on her granddaughter while she makes silly faces, Rose attempting to mimic them back to her.

'It's just easier on my own –'

'It's absolutely fine. Don't worry.'

I reach down for my handbag and get up from the sofa, my legs shaking already from nerves. I dart to the kitchen and lean down to kiss Rose in her high chair. 'I love you, baby girl,' I whisper into her soft cheek.

'Thanks, Mum.' I press a kiss on to the side of Mum's head. As I navigate the traffic on my way to Hampstead, my thoughts are racing the entire drive – what am I going to say? How is he going to react? Am I putting myself in danger?

But I need to speak to him. I need to end this, once and for all.

I drive down Wheeldon Avenue and turn into an adjacent street, pulling into a space quickly, my hands shaking. I need to calm down – he won't be home yet. It will have taken a little while for him to be processed in the cells and released into the great wide world. And then he'll have to make his way back. I have time.

I clamber out of my car, my eyes fixed on his house across the way, and lock the car, not even looking, my focus like a laser. Dashing across and straight through his gate, up the steps and to the front door, I enter the code and retrieve the key, unlocking the door before carefully placing the key back in the hatch.

I step inside, closing the door behind me. And for a moment, I stand still, just inside the entrance, unable to move. The last time I was here it felt as though I was doing something wrong, as though the house was watching, taking in everything I was doing. But now there is a sinister force lingering in the air, the stain of what I now know tainting everything: Linda was trying to get away. Linda was scared of Frank. She was afraid. She died afraid.

I inhale, deep down into my lungs, resting my hands on my chest, then take the few short steps into Frank's office. I know how to handle him.

I sit down in his chair, my knees bouncing up and down as a rush of energy surges through me.

Now there's just one thing left to do.

Wait.

*

His footsteps are heavy on the path. I watched as he approached down the road, as he crossed, making his way towards his house, his walk childlike with anticipation. It takes him a second to open the door. I close my eyes, imagining him scrambling with the keys, his body going through a disorientating level of emotions as he lets himself into his home. The home he hasn't been to in almost a year. The home where he murdered his wife.

I shiver. Linda is gone.

But I'm here.

Is he going to come into the office? Or will he go upstairs?

There is a thud – he must be dropping his bag. But his footsteps don't come towards me; instead they echo as he strides down the hallway, passing the various doorways until he reaches the back of the house. He's heading to the kitchen.

I wonder if it's like he never left. As though time froze, his home waiting for his return before being brought suddenly back to life. His noises recede – he must have reached the back room. I stand and creep out into the hallway, each step careful as I approach his turned back. He is standing completely still, only his head moving slightly as he scans the room. Knowing Frank, he's probably noticing the things that are out of place. A lot will be out of place from when the police carried out their search. One of the armchairs is a few feet off its usual position, the barstools no longer

299

evenly spaced out along the kitchen island. And then there will be items which are missing. They'll still be in the police evidence room. His bloody clothes and tea-towel. Linda's medication. The knife block.

I pause just before the double doors.

It'll be fine. I'm not in danger.

'Hi Frank,' I say, stepping into the kitchen.

He reels around, his eyes wide, his arms lifting upwards in front of his chest. 'Jesus! Fucking hell, Piera, you scared the life out of me!'

'Didn't you hear me come in?' I ask innocently. 'I called your name but you didn't answer, so I thought you weren't here yet.'

'No, I didn't hear you.' His arms lower, his body relaxing, but he still looks at me through narrowed eyes. 'What are you doing here?'

'Harry messaged me saying that you were acquitted, and I didn't like the idea of you coming back here and being completely alone, so I thought I'd come over just to see if you needed anything or . . .'

His face softens. 'Oh . . . thanks. Sorry, it's just you scared me –'

'I know. Sorry, I didn't think.'

His eyes flicker up and down my body and my stomach turns. He holds out his arms and I smile and step into them, hugging him tightly. But my hands are curled into fists.

'Are you cold?'

'No,' I say, stepping back and out of his space. 'Why?'

'You're shaking.'

'Maybe it *is* a little cold in here. But I'm fine.'

'Well . . . thank you for being here. It's nice to know that after everything we've been through we have each other's backs.'

I give him a small smile. This is my chance.

'Yeah, we . . . we've protected each other. And I really appreciate that. I just –'

'I mean, you saved my life.'

I shake my head. 'You would have done the same for me–'

'Oh, Piera, take your credit where it's due. Without your help, I'd be in prison for the rest of my life.'

'You've helped me. And now I helped you. So we're even –'

'What the hell is going on?'

Harry?

I swing around, the world plunging into a strange silence. Harry is standing at the threshold of the kitchen, staring at me and Frank, his wide, shocked eyes demanding answers.

Them

23

Him

'What the hell is going on?'

Piera reels around, her mouth falling open in shock, her eyes like saucers. As though I am a ghost from another time, not meant to cross over into this other life. My eyes dart over to Frank who is watching me also, but the look on his face is quite different. Different to Piera and different to any expression I have seen on his face in the month I have known him. Self-satisfied. Smug.

'What's funny, Frank?'

He straightens his spine, his shoulders squaring towards me. 'Why would anything be funny, Harry?'

Anger churns inside my chest, my hands curling into fists at my sides, my arms trembling as I control myself. But I want to punch him clean in the face. Knock that smirk and sarcastic tone right out of him.

'Piera, seriously . . . what's going on?'

She blinks quickly, her lip trembling.

'Say something!' I shout.

She flinches, unused to me raising my voice. I'm not a man who loses his temper. In all our disagreements,

I remain calm, discuss things rationally, make sure that she knows that even if I'm angry, I still love her. But this is different. What the actual fuck is going on?

'What are you doing here?' she whispers.

I reach inside my jacket and grip Frank's prayer beads. 'I was returning these.' I toss them towards him, hard, but he catches them with a smile, pushing them inside his jacket pocket.

'Why are *you* here, Piera?' I say in a low voice. 'How do you know Frank?'

Frank crosses his arms. 'Well, actually –'

'I wasn't talking to you, Francis.' I turn my glare away from him and return to Piera, trying to soften. 'Just tell me,' I whisper. 'Please . . . I knew you'd been lying to me, I just didn't know why. But this . . . ? I never expected this.'

She steps towards me and I step backwards, my body reacting automatically.

'We knew each other at university. We were friends in our first year.'

'We were more than friends, Piera.'

'Frank, please just stay out of this!'

'Your husband is asking you for the truth,' Frank says, gesticulating towards me. 'So give him the truth. There's no point in lying any more.'

Piera steps forward again and I remain fixed to the spot as she reaches for my hand. I don't pull away but my fingers lie limp in her palm.

'Okay, Frank and I had a relationship during our first

year at university. At the end of the year, Frank and I broke up and he got together with Linda. We stopped being friends. And then we left and I never saw him again. Until recently.'

'So when you've been lying to me saying that you're going to Rachel's or out for drinks, you've been doing . . . what? Visiting him?'

'I only went to see him once. Just once, I promise.'

'He's been calling you . . . You've been speaking to him in prison.'

'Yes.'

I take in a juddering breath, my mind unable to comprehend what is happening. 'You said that you helped him. He said that without you he'd be in prison. What did he mean?'

Piera's eyes fly to Frank and they look at each other, a knowing glance.

'One of you tell me right now —'

'Okay, I will,' he says, crossing his arms.

'Frank, stop. Please,' Piera cries.

'When Linda killed herself, I called your wife,' Frank says. I stare at him blankly. This goes as far back as Linda's death? Piera knew the entire time? 'I called her and told her what had happened,' he continues, his eyes sparkling. 'I was terrified. I thought that I would never be believed. So I asked her for an alibi, but she wouldn't give me one.'

The tightness in my chest releases slightly and I glance across at her, her face pleading. She could have given him an alibi. But she chose not to.

'But she did tell me everything I needed to do to make sure it was as clear as possible that Linda committed suicide.'

The hand gripping my chest squeezes again, so little air in my lungs, the room spins.

'You spoke to him while he was at the scene?' I mutter.

'He needed my help,' she whispers, her eyes brimming with tears.

'Was the scene not how it was presented at court? Frank, did you move things?'

'I did what she told me to do.'

'Harry, he asked me for help and I didn't know what else to do!'

'You could have hung up the phone, told him you couldn't help him! Jesus Christ, Piera – you're a prosecutor, you know what could happen to you if anyone ever found out?'

'I know, I didn't want to, but –'

'But what?' I throw my hands up. 'What could possibly have compelled you to actively help someone at the scene of a death? Nothing would ever make me do something like that!'

'But you aren't your wife,' Frank says, his mouth twisting.

'What the hell is that supposed to mean?' I snarl.

'Tell me, Harry . . . Now that you know that she's been lying to you, helping me, hiding secrets from you for months . . . Do you really think that you actually know Piera?'

'Of course I know her. She's my wife. I know her better than anyone.'

'You thought you knew her. But the Piera I know is . . . quite different.'

'Frank,' Piera says, her voice tinged with a warning. 'Don't.'

Frank takes a few steps towards me, and I lift my chin to stare him in the eye. 'You don't scare me, Frank.'

'I'm not trying to scare you. I'm trying to help you.'

I scoff. 'You, help me? How?'

'Your wife isn't who you think she is. She never has been.'

'Stop talking in riddles and give me some specifics.'

'Harry, stop it, please,' Piera cries, tugging on my arm, but I shrug her away.

'Tell me —'

'Our friend Richard.'

I frown, confused by the sudden change in direction. 'The friend from university?'

'Yes.'

'The one who killed himself?'

Piera rushes towards Frank, placing herself between him and me, but just like I did, he pushes her out of the way. 'Frank, don't —'

'He didn't kill himself.'

'Frank! Stop it, please!'

'What do you mean?'

'It wasn't suicide —'

309

I freeze, bracing myself for what I know is coming as I take in both their faces – Frank's readiness and Piera's pale devastation.

'– it was Piera.'

Them

'Piera.'

The voice isn't the one she expected – not Frank's low growl, but Richard's refined drawl. Piera tears her eyes away from the Oxford skyline to look round as he approaches her.

'Hey Richard,' she says as he stops beside her, lowering his face to kiss her on the cheek. 'How are you?'

'I'm good, sweetheart, how are you?'

'Yeah, I'm good. There's drinks in that cooler.' She turns back as Richard grabs a beer, wrapping her arms around herself as a cool wind suddenly blows towards them. 'Why is it cold all of a sudden?'

'Are you cold? Nah, it's a beautiful evening.' He looks up at the sky, a darkening blue tinged with orange, the sun setting quickly. 'I love it up here.'

'Yes, it's really cool. Frank and I come up here a lot.'

She glances around the roof of Frank's building. He's the only one who has access – the perks of the penthouse. The perks of a wealthy father. A couple of months into their relationship, Frank brought her up here and they lay under the stars, a pile of duvets and pillows surrounding them, talking into the early hours. It was freezing, and at first she was scared of being on the roof, but it turned into one of the best nights of her life.

'Definitely don't think we're meant to come up here,' Richard laughs.

'Frank has permission from the landlord.'

'His dad?'

'His dad.' Piera confirms with a grin.

They laugh together, their eyes meeting.

'He just does whatever he wants . . .' Richard's face turns serious. 'Doesn't he?'

Piera frowns. 'I guess . . . Is something wrong?'

He shakes his head, the corners of his mouth turning downwards. 'No, it's nothing.'

'Rich, tell me, please. You clearly have something you want to say.'

He sighs. 'Frankie is my mate and I love him. But . . . he's gonna hurt you, Piera. And you deserve so much more.'

Piera frowns as she tries to take in what Richard has just said. 'What do you mean?'

'He does whatever he wants. Whatever he needs, he just takes it. And the whole thing with Linda –'

'What about Linda?'

'Well, clearly she's in love with him.'

Piera's mouth drops open. 'Wh—'

'Have you really not noticed? You must have. I know you're not blind to it.'

Images flash through Piera's mind, as though on a reel spinning faster and faster, blurring her vision.

Linda hugging Frank a few seconds longer than anyone else. Her long stares at them across the room. Her comments, seemingly innocent. She nods at Richard, her eyes wide, imploring him to go on.

'Frank knows how Linda feels. And he never discourages her. Yes, he adores you but . . . he loves the attention. He always will.'

'But nothing has happened between them, right?'

Richard says nothing, just watches her, his jaw clenched.

'Right?' she repeats, her voice getting higher.

'Well, where are they right now?'

Piera glances at her watch. Frank was meant to be here twenty minutes ago. He wasn't downstairs in the apartment so she came straight up. And he still isn't here. And neither is Linda.

'Do you know something, Rich?' She reaches out to grip his hand and he squeezes it back, his eyes full of kindness and warmth. 'Please, if you do, just tell me.'

'Not for sure,' he says. 'But I think you need to be careful.'

'But why would he do that?' Piera needled, unable to understand. 'If he loves me, why would he do that?'

'Why does Frank do anything he does?' Richard met her gaze, his eyes steely. 'Because he can.'

'He –'

'There's no rhyme or reason to it. He loves you. But if he can have someone else, he will. And he won't feel guilty about it.'

'You're making him sound like a sociopath!'

'He's a narcissist, Piera. It's clear as day. And Frank knows that you love him so much, you would never leave him.'

'I would –'

'You'd do anything for him, Piera. Anything.'

The door behind them slams and they fly apart, Piera pulling her hand away from Richard's as Frank walks towards them, his eyes darting between them, brimming with suspicion. And just behind him, her cheeks flushed, is Linda.

'What's going on here?' Frank jabs his finger at them.

'Nothing, mate,' Richard says, stepping towards him. 'Just chill out, we were waiting for you.'

'I saw you – when we came through the door you were holding hands.'

Piera faces up to Frank and Linda. 'What's going on with you two?'

Frank laughs. 'Don't try to spin this –'

'I'm not spinning anything. Linda – what's going on with you and Frank?'

Linda stares at the three of them. 'I don't even understand what's happening. We're just coming for drinks like we planned. What the fuck is going on?'

'What's going on,' Frank says, his face stretched into a sarcastic jeer, 'is that Richard and Piera were holding hands and looking very cosy, so I want to know what the hell you think you're doing touching my girlfriend.'

'Mate, don't start –'

'No, Frank,' Piera interrupts, 'the real question is what you and Linda were doing. Where were you?'

'I was just out. I ran late, that's all, and I arrived back here at the same time as Linda.'

Piera shakes her head at him, not believing. She shifts her attention to Linda, who is tugging at her blonde hair. 'Is that right, Linda? Did you just arrive together or was Frank at yours?'

'I-I –'

'What are you stuttering for? Were you with Frank?'

'We were just –'

'Nothing is going on with me and Linda,' Frank shouts, cutting across Linda's stammering.

'Then why does she look like she's going to cry?'

Frank turns on Richard. 'What the fuck did you say to her?'

'This has nothing to do with me,' Richard says quietly. 'This is between you three.'

'Between us three? What, when you're here telling my girlfriend lies and holding her hand?'

'I'm just being a good friend –'

'A good friend? We all know you've wanted Piera since you first met her! You hated it when she met me because it meant you lost the one chance you had –'

'Just because you can't imagine ever actually being friends with a girl,' Richard shouts, his temper flaring. 'Everyone knows what's going on with you and Linda behind Piera's back and I was just warning her –'

'You fucking prick!'

Frank's fist flies forwards, pummelling into Richard's cheek. He falls backwards and Frank launches himself at him, the two of them scuffling, their limbs lashing out.

'Stop it!' Piera cries, desperately trying to break them apart.

By now Richard's eyebrow has been split and Frank's lip is bleeding.

'Stop it, please!' Piera looks round for Linda but she is frozen to the spot, tears sliding down her cheeks as she watches, paralysed. 'Linda, help me! Guys, stop it!'

Piera forces herself between them, barging Frank backwards with her shoulders, but a hand flies out towards her, hitting her hard in the mouth.

She tips her head backwards, and the sky spins above her.

The boys fall still, their chests rising and falling as they attempt to catch their breath. They both move towards her, Frank reaching his hands out to her face. 'Let me see –'

'Leave me alone!' Piera cries, clutching her mouth, as blood pools on her tongue.

'Are you okay?' Richard asks, leaning towards her.

'No, I'm not okay! One of you hit me in the fucking mouth!'

'Just get away from her, Richard,' Frank shouts.

'Me, get away from her?' he yells back. 'You've hurt her now and you're going to keep hurting her, Frank!'

316

'I swear to god, if you don't shut your mouth . . .'

They step towards each other again, Piera between them, their eyes glazing with anger.

'Richard, just back away!' she implores. 'Frank, let's go. Please.'

'Piera, you can't be serious –'

'Richard, just leave it.'

'Leave her alone,' Frank growls.

'You're the one who needs to leave her alone. You'll break her heart one day, you know you will –'

Frank lunges towards Richard, readying himself to fight again, the two of them like snarling animals, unable to back down.

'Piera, you're such an idiot. He's going to break your heart and you're going to let him!'

It's as though time slows as they get closer and closer, centimetre by centimetre, with her trapped between them. She lifts both hands, pulling them back towards herself, and then pushing forwards, her hands planting squarely on Richard's chest with all her force.

But in that split second she doesn't realize how close Richard is to the edge of the building. How low the wall is between them, with absolutely nothing but space beyond it. How easily Richard will lose his footing.

How quiet the small, bewildered cry will sound as he plummets to the ground.

24

Her

'– it was Piera.'

The room spins before me, the kitchen island rocking from side to side, a ship on violent waters. The secret that I have been keeping for fifteen years laid bare for everyone to see. I reach out and grip the counter, steadying myself, searching for Harry's face in the swimming space. He comes into focus but the expression on his face is one that I haven't seen before.

Devastation. Betrayal. He is looking at me as though he has no idea who I am. No idea what I am capable of.

'Piera?' he mutters, his voice cracking. 'Is this true?'

My mouth trembles as he looks at me, his eyes tearing up. Frank has spoken the truth and it is out there. I can try to defend myself. Say that I didn't mean to, that I was just trying to defend my boyfriend, to stop a fight that felt as though it was never going to end. But my mouth is already forming the thing that it has become so used to: a lie.

'No, it isn't!' I say, keeping my eyes glued to Harry as I see Frank's face twist into a disbelieving smile in my periphery.

'She's lying again, Harry,' Frank says. 'Don't be blind.'

'No, I'm not!'

'If I didn't know something terrible about her, something that she would do anything to keep hidden, why would she help me when I came to her after all these years? Why would she help me defend myself?'

Harry narrows his eyes at me, his gaze pleading for the truth. 'Piera? Why did you help him?'

'I'm not the one lying to you,' I say, my voice getting higher and higher. 'He is!'

'What reason do I have to lie to your husband, Piera? You're the one who's been sneaking around behind his back, hiding the truth from him your entire relationship.'

'Don't push me, Frank –'

'Oh, what are you going to do, Piera? You have nothing against me.'

'You lied to him the entire trial!'

He shakes his head in disbelief. 'You really are something. You'll do anything to protect yourself.'

'Me?' I spin towards Harry, grabbing his hands. 'Harry, listen to me –'

'Tell me the truth,' he says. 'I can't believe anything you say unless you tell me the truth. I could see it in your face when Frank told me, but I need you to say it . . . Did you push Richard? Are you the reason he's dead?'

My mouth moves, another lie already sprung and ready to fire. But I swallow it. If I love Harry I need to tell him the truth. Frank won't let the lie stay hidden now. It's time.

'Yes,' I whisper.

His face turns white. 'How could . . . how could you do something like that?'

'I didn't mean to kill him! I'm not a murderer. But they were fighting and I just wanted it to stop, so I pushed Richard away and he fell – from the top of the building. Linda and I wanted to go to the police and explain what happened, but Frank convinced us that the best thing to do was lie and say that he jumped. I thought he wanted to protect me because he loved me – I didn't realize that he was going to leave me for Linda and then keep that secret hanging over both our heads for the rest of our lives!'

'I did love you,' Frank says. 'But you're a liar, Piera. You meant to do what you did –'

'Bullshit!' I scream. 'No, I didn't! I was trying to help you! And you didn't love me. You just enjoyed the power you had over me. That's all it ever is with you – who can you control, who can you have within your grasp? And that's why you left me. You cheated on me because you could, because you could have us both, but when you had to choose, you realized that it was Linda who you could control. It was Linda who would listen to everything you said, hang on your every word, even if it meant you draining the life out of her. You chose her because she was weaker –'

'That isn't true –'

'You could have told me all this,' Harry interrupts. 'I would have believed you –'

'I was too scared, Harry. I didn't want to lose you. I didn't want to lose everything we have, the life we've built. You don't know what he's like, I knew he would twist it.'

'What do you mean, he lied to me the entire trial?'

I close my eyes, inhaling deeply through my nose. 'He –'

'Piera,' Frank says, 'I don't know what you're –'

'He murdered Linda.'

Harry's hands tighten around my fingers as the truth lands, a grenade thrown into a dark room.

'What?' he whispers.

'Oh my god, you really are insane,' Frank says, moving closer. 'You really can't do anything except lie, can you?'

'He killed Linda,' I repeat, urging Harry to believe me.

'And you . . .' He snatches his hands away from me, retreating backwards. 'You helped him.'

'I didn't have a choice! And I didn't know at the beginning when I helped him. He told me that she had killed herself and he was just scared that he wouldn't be believed. I would never have helped him if I thought that he had killed her.'

'Then how do you know?'

I glance across at Frank, who is close to us now, almost within arm's reach, his eyes turning empty and cold.

'I have proof.'

'You don't have any proof,' Frank snarls.

But I don't look at him. Instead, I reach into the inside of my jacket and pull out a piece of paper, folded neatly down the middle.

Linda's letter.

I hold it out, brushing the paper against Harry's clenched fingers.

'What's this?' he says, almost flinching away.

'Just look at it, Harry,' I urge. 'Please.'

His eyes scan the words and within seconds, they widen, his face falling as he finally understands. 'This is Linda's final letter.'

'Yes.'

'How do you have this?'

I look over at Frank. His jaw is set, his eyes stony.

'The day that Linda's sister gave evidence, he called me.'

'When you said someone at chambers called you about the party . . .'

'Yes. Frank asked me in not so many words to let myself into his house and search for the letter before the police could get to it. I had no idea what it would reveal. And then I found this and realized that I'd been helping a murderer, but by then it was too late. I didn't know how to give you the letter or get it to the police in any way that could help without ruining our lives.'

'Did he know you'd found this?'

I look back at Frank and he glares at me but stays silent.

'Yes. But I told him I'd destroy it. I kept it . . . I

thought it was the best way to make sure he left us alone. Left me alone.'

'That letter doesn't prove anything,' Frank snarls.

'You don't even know what it says,' I snap back.

Harry turns to him, blinking slowly in disbelief. 'I . . . I believed you. I defended you. And you . . . she was terrified of you!'

'You fucking bitch!'

Frank launches towards me, his face full of rage. I stumble backwards, desperately trying to evade him, and reach into the back of my jeans, beneath my loose jacket, for the one thing I knew I would need to protect me.

His gun.

He comes to a sudden halt as I hold it out – the barrel just inches away from his chest.

'Piera?' Harry says, his voice shaking. 'Wh-what are you doing? Where did you get that?'

'It's Frank's. I knew it was in his safe so I took it. I knew I wouldn't be safe here. He's a dangerous man.'

'So why would you come?'

'I wanted to end things once and for all.'

'You came here . . . you came here planning on killing him –'

'No! I needed to protect myself.'

'Piera, put it down,' Frank says, taking a step towards us, his eyes fixed on the gun and my finger on the trigger.

'Stay the hell back!' I yell. 'Harry, please, just read the

letter again. Think about what it means.' He looks up at me, his eyes full of fear and horror. 'Please,' I whisper, my heart breaking.

He glances back down at the paper, which is trembling in his shaking hands, his eyes taking in the words again, time slowing until it is almost standing still. Until –

'She was trying to get away, wasn't she?' he says, looking up at Frank, his eyes cold. 'Just like the prosecution said. You tried to kill her by an overdose – did you manufacture being out at work?' Slowly, Harry puts it together. 'In reality you were at home to give her the overdose, then you left the house, assuming it would kill her. You claimed afterwards that you called her sister for help, but actually you knew she wouldn't be able to. Then you got the neighbour to go around in the hopes that she would find her dead and you'd be absolved. That way you had your alibi: you were out at work and you'd tried to protect her by having her sister go around or the neighbour check on her, but it was just too late. But that plan didn't work. She woke up, didn't she? She realized something was wrong and made herself sick. Then she started packing her bag. But that's when you came home. God – she even tried to call her sister. She must have been so scared . . . Go on – say something, Frank. Defend yourself if this isn't accurate!'

But Frank does nothing. Instead he simply stares, his eyes dark and terrifying.

'I have to call the police.'

'Harry, no –'

'I'll say I found the letter, I'll say anything I need to, but I need to say something. I have to –'

A roar bellows towards us and before I can react Frank is on me, grappling for the gun. He shoves me on to the floor and I grip the gun with both hands, screaming and lashing out. Harry grabs Frank by the shoulders, attempting to throw him backwards, but he doesn't let go. His face is red, his eyes wild and vicious. My hand is slipping, I can't hold on any longer –

Frank tumbles back, losing balance, and the gun skitters across the tiles. He kicks away from me, pushing himself to standing, reaching for it –

A gunshot blasts through the room. My hands fly up to my ears. A body crumples to the floor.

'Harry!' I cry out.

I sit up, scrambling forward. But it isn't Harry collapsed in the middle of the kitchen, blood pooling from his temple.

It is Frank.

Frank is dead.

My heart plunges as a picture of how he once was flashes in my mind – his eyes staring across at me the first time we saw each other, that cheeky smirk stretching across his face. The way my stomach turned. Butterflies.

He is gone.

He died in the same place as Linda. My friend. The woman I made my enemy in my mind. Both of them lost in their beautiful home, in the remnants of what should have been their beautiful life. Murdered.

A strange kind of sorrow washes over me, but there is something else there, something stronger. Relief.

He is gone.

Harry is standing over him, the gun hanging loosely from his fingers, his face deathly pale.

I stand, my breaths shallow and quick. 'Harry?'

'H-he was going to hurt us. I didn't know what he was going to do to you –'

I rush towards him, wrapping my arms around him, my head buried into his chest. 'We need to go.'

He swallows, unable to process what I am saying. 'What?'

'We need to leave. Soon.'

'We can't just leave him, we need to call the police.'

'And tell them what? How are you going to explain all this? You shot a man in the head. You killed him.'

'I was defending us –'

'And what if they don't believe you?' I grip his face with both hands, forcing him to look me in the eye. 'We'll both be arrested, we'll go to trial, our lives will be over. What will happen to Rose? What will happen to us? Frank is a monster, nobody will miss him. Not a single person. But us? Rose needs us.'

He shakes his head, the gun falling from his grip and clattering to the floor.

'Harry, we need to leave –'

'I can't do this.'

'Just . . . just wait there.'

I run out of the room, sprinting down the hallway and into Frank's office. I peer carefully out of the front window. Did anyone hear the gun? Is anyone coming?

But the street outside is quiet, the houses all detached, at a distance from each other. And the kitchen is at the back of the house, surrounded by a large garden. There is no one. Nobody heard.

I rush back to the kitchen and scan it quickly. I grab a tea-towel from the stove and pick up the gun, avoiding the blood on the floor, and wipe it thoroughly. Gripping it still with the towel, I bend down close to Frank's body.

'Harry, I need you to pick up Frank's left hand.'

'What?'

'Come here and pick up his hand. I've wiped it of prints but his prints need to be on it.'

'Why can't you do it?'

'If there's any way that the police can identify your prints, that won't matter. You're his barrister, you'll have shaken his hand a thousand times.'

'Why his left hand?'

'Harry, think. You've shot him in the left temple. So it needs to be his left hand. He couldn't kill himself with his right. Just grab it and get his prints on the gun. Be careful not to step in the blood.'

He stares at me, horrified, but still he listens. He kneels down beside me and grips Frank's left wrist, pushing the fingertips all over the barrel and the grip.

'Okay, you can back away now.'

He stands up quickly, tripping over his own feet as he retreats, sniffing quietly.

'Have you touched anywhere else?' he whispers.

'No,' I say, scanning the room.

'Let's leave the letter.'

'What?'

'The letter. We can leave it here with him. The police will find it and at least they might realize that he was guilty.'

'We can't leave the letter,' I say slowly. Carefully. As though I'm speaking to a small child. 'Our fingerprints are all over it. And it doesn't prove anything. It won't help anyone. Frank is dead. He can't face justice for it any more. Linda is dead. All you'll be doing by leaving the letter here is hurting us. Hurting Rose. Think of everything we stand to lose.'

I snatch it from his fingers and shove it back inside my jacket. 'When someone eventually comes looking for him –'

'Who's going to come looking for him?' Harry whispers. 'It might be days before someone finds him.'

'That's even better for us.'

'I . . .'

'What?'

A tear falls from his eye, pooling near his lip and he smears it away. 'I don't know who you are.'

'I'm your wife,' I say, looking up at him pleadingly, my mouth quivering. 'I'm Piera. The Piera that you've

329

always known. And I'm trying to protect you. You might think this is horrifying, but we have to do this. Right . . . we need to go.'

I start towards the hallway but he stares after me, his face furrowed with confusion.

'Harry, come on,' I plead, reaching for his hand, but he pulls it away. 'We need to go.'

'We can't go out the front.'

I sigh, my patience beginning to run thin with his shock. He's a KC, a crime barrister, he's defended countless criminals. And yet he can't think how to defend himself.

'No matter which way we leave, we have to pass other houses and get to our cars,' I say, forcing myself to remain calm. 'We'll be caught by cameras somewhere. If police are suspicious of this and they check cameras, they'll see that we were here. But you had a reason for being here. And people know that you were coming here, don't they? You were returning his prayer beads. He's got them in his pocket. I told Mum that I was bringing you something you needed. So we say that I met you in Hampstead, we gave Frank his beads and left. And after we left, he was so overcome with the grief of being back in his home after losing his wife, that he killed himself.'

I wait for him to say something but he just keeps looking at me with that empty, terrified gaze. Prey staring at a predator.

'Harry, message your instructing solicitors right now,

saying you've returned his prayer beads, you spoke to him, and you're thrilled with the outcome of the case. Thank them for the work. And this will all be over. If the police don't look any further into his suicide we don't have to worry. But if they investigate and see us in the area, we have our story.'

I reach out towards him and hold his hand, gripping it tightly.

'Come on.'

He follows me carefully and we leave the kitchen, his head turning to look back at Frank. I lead him down the corridor and open the front door, fixing my face with a smile. 'Act normally, Harry,' I say through gritted teeth.

'It was nice to meet you,' I shout back into the house.

I nudge him sideways in the ribs.

'B-bye Frank,' he says.

I close the door behind us.

We walk down the path and out the gate, his fingers loose in my tight grip. We cross the road, heading towards the street where I parked my car. We reach it, and I turn towards him, smiling widely. I tilt my chin up and meet him with a fixed gaze. He kisses me quickly and backs away.

'See you at home,' I call out.

I get in the car and drive out towards him, pausing beside his car as he climbs inside and does up his seat belt. As he drives away, heading for home, I follow him closely.

I don't think he would do anything stupid. But you never know.

He needs to know that I'm watching him.

He needs to understand that keeping this secret protects us all.

That's all I'm trying to do.

Protect us.

25

Him

The doorbell rings and I lift my head from the bed in the spare room, my heartbeat pounding in my temples.

'Harry . . .'

Piera's voice floats over from our bedroom. We've been sleeping separately for the last two nights. She keeps asking when I'm coming back, but I can't. I can't be near her. It's as though there's a stranger creeping around my house, looking after my daughter. Lying down in the bed that we used to share.

'Who is it?'

She appears at the door, tying her dressing gown closed, her eyes narrowed. 'The police are here.'

I sit up, throwing myself out of bed, panic pounding through me.

'Shit – what do we do?'

'We stay calm and answer the door. We have our story. We know what happened.'

'What happened . . .'

'We went to Frank's house to give him his prayer beads and collected our daughter. You haven't heard from him since.'

She turns calmly and runs down the stairs. I pick up the trousers that I discarded next to the bed and pull them on over my boxers, then rush to the stairs, speeding up as Piera reaches the door and tugs it open.

'Hello?' she says, her voice innocent.

'Good evening. Is Harry Mason-Hall here?'

'Yes, he –'

'Hi,' I say, reaching the door, standing just behind Piera. 'I'm Harry.'

'Good evening, Mr Mason-Hall. I'm Detective Sergeant Jones, and this is Detective Constable Pearson. We wondered if we could quickly ask you some questions about a recent death that we're investigating?'

'A death?' I say. 'Yes, of course, please come in.'

I step back and Piera manoeuvres to the side, letting them in. They pass us, moving into the hall, and she catches my eye, her gaze hardening for just a moment before softening again.

'Would you like a drink?' she asks. 'You can come and sit down in the living room?'

'No, thank you,' Jones says, waving his hand. 'This should only take a few minutes.'

The ball of anxiety in my chest loosens slightly. Just a few minutes can't be anything too bad. They can't suspect us if it'll only take a few minutes.

'Mr Mason-Hall –'

'Please call me Harry.'

'Harry, you represented a Mr Francis Joseph in his recent murder trial. Is that correct?'

'Yes, I did.' I focus on my features, mimicking confusion. 'Has something happened to Frank?'

'I'm sorry if this is hard to hear, but he was found dead in his house earlier today.'

I allow my mouth to fall open slightly but don't want to over-react. How would I have reacted if I had no idea? Would I have been emotional? Calm? Shocked? 'Really?' I say, opting for mild shock. 'What happened?'

'The death is being treated as non-suspicious. It appears that Mr Joseph used a gun licensed under his name to commit suicide.'

I keep my eyes on Jones's face but Piera is there in the background, her focus locked on to me like a laser.

'Oh wow . . .' I mutter, rubbing my forehead. 'Jesus, I . . . I wouldn't have thought he was going to do that. Not from how he was the last time I saw him.'

'That's why we're here,' Pearson says. 'We discovered from his solicitors in the case that you were probably the last person to see him alive. And we just wanted to confirm that with you.'

'Well . . . when did he die?'

'From the condition of the body it would appear he died on the day he was acquitted. So three days ago.'

'God . . . then yes. It would have been me. I mean – us. My wife was with me too.'

They both turn towards her, and she looks at them with her wide puppy-dog eyes. How many times have I been fooled by that expression?

'Yes, I was there,' she said. 'Harry had asked me to

335

bring something to court for him but I was too late so I met him in Hampstead instead. He told me that he was going there to take something to his client.'

They turn back towards me. 'I had gone to his house to give him his prayer beads. They were his late wife's and he was very attached to them. He used to have them in prison and had them every day with him at the trial. He left them in the dock, but I couldn't get hold of his solicitors to deliver them to him so I thought it was easier to just take them myself.'

'And when you saw Mr Joseph, how was he?'

I clear my throat. 'He seemed okay . . . I mean, he seemed shaken, disorientated. That's to be expected, though – he was back in the home where his wife died after almost a year in prison. But if I'd ever thought that he might harm himself . . . I never would have left him alone.'

'You can't blame yourself,' Jones says. 'People who commit suicide hide it from others. You weren't to know.'

I nod, lowering my eyes to the floor.

'Well, thank you, that's all we needed,' Pearson says. 'A sad ending after you got him acquitted.'

'Yes,' I mutter, my insides churning. 'Quite.'

They walk back towards the front door and relief washes over me. 'Can I just ask something?'

They both glance back at me. And so does Piera, her hands clenched behind her back.

'Can I ask who found him?'

Jones sighs. 'His wife's sister.'

'Eve Thompson?'

'Yes, exactly,' Jones nods. 'Did you meet her?'

'She . . . she gave evidence in the trial.'

'Yes, she told us that,' Pearson says. 'She said she was told that he'd been acquitted, and even though she'd given evidence, after a few days she felt as though she should check in on him because she hadn't heard anything. She let herself in and found him there. In the kitchen.'

'Quite sad, really,' Jones says, nodding. 'She said that she'd convinced herself that he'd killed her sister, but she realized she must have been wrong because a guilty man wouldn't kill himself after being acquitted. She was devastated. Anyway . . . we'll let you get on with your evening.'

'Thank you,' I say as guilt swallows me whole, my eyes glazing over as they turn back towards the door.

'Goodnight,' Piera says, smiling sweetly.

'Yes, goodnight, officers.'

They step out into the night and we watch for a few seconds as they walk down the path, then close the door.

Piera's face changes, her smile falling away, and she drifts over to the living room. I follow her, the guilt swarming inside me. She is sitting on the sofa, in her usual position, feet tucked beneath her. The very picture of innocence.

'That's not how this should have happened,' I mutter. 'People . . .' I sigh, unable to finish my sentence.

'Just say what you're thinking, Harry.'

'People need to know the truth,' I snap.

'We can't tell them the truth about Frank. And it doesn't help anyone. It doesn't change anything.'

I scoff, 'Everything has changed. People should know the truth about you, too.'

'What truth?'

'That you've helped cover up the deaths of two people —'

She shrugs. 'Then I'll tell them the truth about you. It's exactly the same.'

I move closer, my shadow bathing her in darkness. 'No. It isn't.'

'We both killed someone.'

My chest tightens, a strange feeling burning in the centre, red-hot but somehow turning my entire body cold. It isn't the same . . . what I did to Frank. It isn't. It can't be. He was a monster. He deceived us all. He should have been behind bars for the rest of his life. If he had just faced up to what he had done, he would still be alive.

My face flushes. Do I really believe that? I've never believed that before. Vigilantism isn't justice. It isn't for people to take the law into their own hands.

But maybe Frank deserved it.

'I was protecting you,' I say, shaking my head. 'Frank was going to hurt you.'

'And that night all those years ago, I was doing the same. I thought I was protecting Frank when I pushed

Richard. In fact, when I pushed him, I didn't know that it would kill him. But when you shoot a gun at someone's head at close range, you know what the outcome is going to be. If we had gone to the police, you would be on remand right now. I'm protecting you because I love you. I love our family.'

'No! No . . . You've lied to me. Hidden secrets for years. You don't love me –'

'Of course I do,' she says, and she stands, moving towards me. I step backwards but the coffee table hits the backs of my legs. She stops just in front of me, looking up at me through her eyelashes.

'I have no idea who you are,' I mutter. 'But ever since I found you in his house, you have made my blood run cold.'

'No,' she whispers, reaching up to my face, tracing my mouth with her thumb. 'You do know me. You have known me all these years. The only part you didn't know was a dark secret that Frank made me feel I could never tell. You saw what he was like. He made Linda and me keep it a secret, he made us feel like we would be blamed. You know what that did to Linda, keeping that locked up inside all those years. And then he killed her. He's the monster! Not me. I love you. And you've always said I'm the best thing that ever happened to you. Remember?'

'That's what I believed before. Before I saw . . . this side of you. But you really think that I can stay with you now? You think I can stay here?'

'Yes, because you love me,' she says, tilting her head. 'And I love you. I did all of this to protect what we have built. To protect us. That *is* love.'

'Piera –'

'Look me in the eye and tell me you don't love me.'

She steps closer, her hands pressing against my chest, her eyes gazing up at me insistently.

My eyes lock on to hers, and for that split second it is as though our entire relationship is played before my mind's eye, a time-lapse at high speed. The day I first saw her during pupillage, our first date in Camden, that first kiss by the river, our wedding, finding out she was pregnant, and day after day, followed by night after night after night of having her beside me, close to me, my eternal fragment of light, even in our darkest days.

I lean down quickly and kiss her, wrapping my arms tightly around her waist, pulling her closer into my body, her hands lifting from my chest to grip the back of my neck and my hair. I lift her off the ground, and carry her out of the living room and up the stairs, her mouth on my neck. Stepping into our bedroom, we fall on to the bed, both of us fervently undressing. It's as though I am seeing her again for the first time. Touching her for the first time. She guides me towards her and I am inside her, our bodies moving together. Both comforting and exhilarating. Familiar but somehow so different.

We fall apart, our chests rising and falling rapidly as we try to catch our breath. She turns on her side towards me and I mirror her, our foreheads touching. I shift even closer, burying my face in her freshly washed hair, breathing her in, like I have done for years.

'I love you,' she whispers.

Maybe she isn't the same. Maybe she is different.

But maybe it doesn't matter.

Because she's mine.

'I love you too.'

My wife. My Piera. The woman who I have loved with everything I have. The woman who would do anything to protect me, to protect us. We're here now. Both the same. Both with secrets we'll keep between us forever. For us. For our daughter. For better or worse.

Maybe she is right.

Maybe that *is* love.

26

Her

Harry is asleep next to me, his breathing finally steady. It took a while for him to drift off. He kept asking questions which I answered however I could, and we went around in circles, but always returning to remaining steadfastly together. No matter what. This is just something else that binds us. I can't lose Harry. I won't.

I inch myself out of bed, careful not to wake him, and walk over to the wardrobe. I push my hand under a thick pile of jumpers and feel around until the tips of my fingers brush against it. The USB stick.

The gun wasn't the only thing I retrieved from the safe. In the side there was a hidden panel. It's some kind of miracle that the police didn't find it. But the police didn't know Frank like I did. The first time I opened the safe it seemed eerily empty. Just the gun and nothing more. It took some careful feeling, just the right amount of pressure, but eventually it opened. Inside was just one secret – the USB stick. And I knew, without a doubt, what it was.

The video. The footage of that night.

The night I pushed Richard.

I pick up my laptop from the bedside table and tiptoe

out of the room, checking that Harry is not stirring as I pull the door closed behind me. Quickly descending the stairs to the kitchen, I sit down at the dining table and push the USB into the port. The icon appears and I double-click, my heart racing.

I haven't been able to watch until now. But I need to. I need to see it. And then I need to destroy it.

The rooftop appears. Frank must have mounted a camera on to the wall next to the door. How did I never notice it?

And there we all are. Frank. Me. Linda. Richard. The four of us suspended in time.

The fight begins. Richard and Frank squaring up to each other. Me pushing my way in between them. Our faces animated, our mouths moving, but no sound. And then the moment I have replayed over and over in my mind, the moment I have rewritten, from another perspective, everything the same, except for one small detail.

Richard turned away.

He turned his back.

I have told the story to myself in another way for so long. The fight was escalating, I wanted to separate them, I pushed my hands into his chest not knowing how close to the edge we were.

But that isn't what happened. And that isn't what the footage shows.

He was walking away. And as he turned:

'Piera, you're such an idiot. He's going to break your heart and you're going to let him!'

344

Then a blinding white light as rage consumed me. My hands reached out. I pushed as hard as I could. I knew how close he was to the ledge. And I didn't care.

But nobody needs to know.

The only people who did know are dead. I'm the only one of us left.

I pull the USB out of my laptop and walk to the kitchen. I place it in a clear plastic bag and then grab a knife from the block in front of me before walking swiftly out of the back door and into the garden.

I kneel down and place it on the patio in front of me. I glance up at the house. The bedrooms are at the front. Harry won't be able to hear. I inhale, then quickly, with full force, I bring the heavy handle of the knife down on to the USB stick. Once, twice, three times.

It shatters.

I stand, burying it in the bottom of the bin down the side of the house before heading inside. The house is still silent.

I return to the bedroom, where Harry is still lying on his back, his soft breaths fluttering in and out, his chest rising and falling.

A pang of guilt vibrates in my chest but I push it firmly away.

I did this for us. For Rose. For our family. This secret doesn't need to destroy us. I won't let it.

So I did what I had to.

That is love.

Acknowledgements

Book number four! This one has been a long journey but I am so proud that it's finally making its way into readers' hands.

I would like to thank my brilliant agent, Kate Burke, to whom this book is dedicated. Over the past five years she has given me guidance, patience, advice, honesty and more belly-laughs than I can count. My time as an author so far would not have been the same without her. And huge thanks to everyone else at Blake Friedmann for their amazing work on getting my books to various countries around the world.

Thank you secondly to everyone at Penguin Michael Joseph. To Clio, who has been my editor since the beginning, for her brilliant editorial work, and to Grace for taking over the reins. Both of your minds have made such a difference to this book, and I appreciate everything you have done so much. Thanks also to Nalisha, Yasmin, Lily, Rebecca, Nick and Sarah. Your dedication and patience working on this book with me has meant the world.

And finally, thank you to my friends, family and partner Sean, for their unwavering support of my storytelling. I love you all very much.

On a station platform, with nothing to read,
and a four-hour train journey stretching ahead of him...

That's where the story began for Penguin founder Allen Lane.
With only 'shabby reprints of shoddy novels' on offer,
he resolved to make better books for readers everywhere.

By the time his train pulled into London, the idea was formed.
He would bring the best writing, in stylish and affordable
formats, to everyone. His books would be sold in bookstores,
stationers and tobacconists, for no more than the price
of a ten-pack of cigarettes.

And on every book would be a Penguin, a bird with a certain
'dignified flippancy', and a friendly invitation to anyone who
wished to spend their time reading.

In 1935, the first ten Penguin paperbacks were published.
Just a year later, three million Penguins had made their
way onto our shelves.

Reading was changed forever.

—

A lot has changed since 1935, including Penguin, but in the
most important ways we're still the same. We still believe that
books and reading are for everyone. And we still believe that
whether you're seeking an afternoon's escape, a vigorous debate
or a soothing bedtime story, all possibilities open with a book.

Whoever you are, whatever you're looking for,
you can find it with Penguin.